The Darkness Within

Robbie Blackburn

Dedication

[Details need to be provided]

Acknowledgment

[Details need to be provided]

Contents

Page Blank Intentionally

Chapter 1

The Funeral

"I stand before you not as a man of God today, but as a person who is grieving right along with you all. Cheyenne was one of my own. When I heard of her untimely and tragic demise, I was in shock. Of course God wouldn't take someone in the prime of his or her life. He wouldn't strike down someone who was a good mother, good wife and above everything else, a good person. I got right down on my knees in my bedroom at the rectory and prayed. I prayed for the strength to understand why He would take her? I prayed for guidance and understanding. I admit, good people here today to remember a young, lively, lovely person, Cheyenne Bennett, that I was angry with Him..."

Father Michaelson was going on, and on, it felt like to Allen. When he asked him what kind of memorial service he wanted for Cheyenne, Allen deferred to the expert. "You do what you think is best." Allen was still numb at this time; he couldn't focus on anything or anyone for more than a few seconds at a time. The priest was rambling now, really getting into the groove. Talking about how Cheyenne was such a great person and all the things you're supposed to say at a funeral. You don't stamp on someone's grave. That was a cardinal rule of life and, more importantly, death. When they are alive, you can say whatever you want, but as soon as they die, they are off limits.

Allen looked around him, most of the people here he didn't even know their names. He wondered how many people showed up because he was a "celebrity". He had sold a lot of books in his career, enough to call it a career anyway, writing books. He never was a best selling author, but he had a good fan base. He had enough fans to make a good living, anyway. Now Father Michaelson was talking about her achievements, all the things she did to help people. Ways she wasted his money on the poor. If these poor sons-a-bitches only knew the truth. The bitch was cheating on him. She was coming home from her boyfriend's house. He knew this because he read emails she and the bastard had sent. He had a hard time grieving for her right now, because he had felt so betrayed. He couldn't tell anyone at all, though, because everyone thought Cheyenne was perfect. She had been in his eyes, too, until a week ago. He found it peculiar that she went to her friend Anne's when Anne called and asked if she was there. Allen got suspicious and opened the laptop. Something they always promised they would never do, snoop on each other. Well, he had a reason after what he found.

Allen tried to pull his mind back from the memories of that night. He didn't want people to think that he was heartless. If he looked disinterested, then people might think that. He wondered if the lover would make an appearance or not. He somehow doubted that he would. Michaelson was starting to wrap things up now. The procession of mourners was about to start. He hated all these people around him. They were sad that she was gone, and in some ways, he was too. He would miss his wife, but he had to let the anger go first.

"If everyone would like to now say their final goodbyes here before we head to Memorial Park, we will have a few words there. On behalf of Mr. Bennett and family I would like to thank everyone for their support in this tragic time of need. If we could start at the back of the room, please come forward one row at a time," said Father Michaelson.

Everyone got up and started their walk toward Cheyenne in her casket. They would not see her, she had been messed up quite a bit, but to Allen, she looked completely the same as he always remembered. She was achingly pretty. She was what he thought of as perfect. Blonde hair, blue eyes, and a perfect body. She even had a perfect body after having their son. Not that anyone saw her, it was a closed casket. Allen witnessed the body, and that was all. She was messed up enough that he didn't want anyone to remember that way. Within a month she was back to the same. Everyone always said she was too much for him. She was about ten years younger than him. She had known him before he had sold a book though. So he always felt she was there for love. He had met her while working at a bookstore, she was an avid reader, and she asked him what the hottest new book was out, and he jokingly said his was the best. He was painfully shy most of the time. But she had been coming into the bookstore for years. He would guess since she could drive. He had always seen her and thought her beautiful. He wondered what her boyfriends thought about how much she read, but he never really got an impression she cared much for guys. He couldn't tell much from her choices of books about her personality because she seemed to have such an eclectic taste. She would read murder mysteries and love stories. Kids' books were fine with her, too. She loved the teen drama books about sparkly vampires and obsessed puppy dogs. She would read horror and even nonfiction. She loved biographies and history. She seemed far more in love with books than she could ever be in love with a person.

To Allen she seemed to be Belle, from "Beauty and the Beast" come to life. They had had conversations in the past about books, but it was always superficial. Have you read anything good? What's the hottest new book? When she asked that, and he said his, he was surprised at himself. He had never even told her he was an aspiring author. She laughed and said she would read it, but he had to buy her dinner first. From that time, they had nearly been inseparable. She read every page as it was written, and she was his editor at first. They were in love. Allen never really thought he would ever feel love. He didn't feel particularly good about how he looked. He was scrawny, wore glasses and had a gap in his front teeth. He hadn't had very many girls throughout his life, and he was nearing thirty when they met. He'd always wanted to be a writer and was still trying to get that first book published. He thought she had been joking about that dinner, and when he said sure, meet him outside the mall at 10, he was in complete shock when he walked out the doors and saw her standing there with a huge smile on her face.

Allen watched them, tears rolling down their faces as he remembered his wife on that first date. He never was completely comfortable with her when they dated. He always waited for the hammer to fall and her to tell him everything was a big joke, that she never liked him, let alone loved him like she claimed. He was far too nervous to propose although they had talked about it several times, so one day she asked him to dinner and proposed to him. "This is the only way I can prove that I truly love you," as she handed him a wedding band and slipped it on his finger. He was in shock; they didn't have much money, so they had a small wedding. He finally felt at ease. The confidence she gave him by marrying him was more than enough to get him to fight to publish his novels, and he did, too. He made that his career. She made him her life.

Allen watched a group of her friends standing at the casket. He didn't know all their names, but didn't care. They were crying and hugging each other. He hated as they came and hung all over him. He didn't want these people around him. He wanted to be angry. He wanted to feel hate. He couldn't do that because of the outpouring of love these people were showing to his deceased wife.

He looked behind him and noticed there were only a couple rows of people left. He bore all their hugs and tears. Feeling them fall against his face. He wanted to scream. These people were too close to him. Their tears meant nothing to him. He wanted to be alone with his wife.

Finally, her mom and dad got up and hugged Allen, and went to say goodbye to Cheyenne. He felt sorry for them, regardless of the circumstances, he thought the worst thing in life would be losing a child. Luckily, his was still with him. He couldn't face this day today. He wanted to be at home and cope in his own way. No one had asked Allen either, everyone seemed to inherently understand that Austin needed some alone time. Cheyenne's mom was completely supported by her husband as she tried to open and remove Cheyenne from the casket. She was screaming, "I just need to hold my baby one more time! She's my baby; I can't let go! Let me have my baby!" She was trying to climb on the casket now screaming, "God, please take me instead! Let me be called home to you!" A bunch of people were approaching the older couple now, Allen knew some, others he didn't. He still couldn't make himself care at this point. Finally, they were able to get Cheyenne's parents out of the room, and the funeral home director approached Allen, "Would you like a few minutes alone with your wife, Mr. Bennett?"

Allen looked up at him, actually with tears in his eyes for the first time today and found he couldn't speak. He merely nodded, and the director walked away. At first, Allen just sat there. He looked at his wife's casket, only seeing the casket. He couldn't see anything else but knew she was wearing the blue dress she had bought for their fifteenth wedding anniversary, which was to be in a few weeks. When they asked him to provide something to wear for her, that was the only thing he thought of because she loved that dress. He finally got up and approached her. He had only been next to her once since she had died; he had so far been able to avoid it by making meaningless conversation with all the well wishers. He looked down at her. She had died from the accident when she veered off the road and struck a tree. She had been wearing her seatbelt, of course, but the airbag had failed, and the resultant whiplash effect had broken her neck and killed her instantly. At least that's what the coroner's report had said; Allen had not read this yet of course. But everyone was quick to get the information somewhere. "Cheyenne babe, we live in a morbid fucking society." He looked at her. He wanted to open the casket and raise her eyelids. He wanted to see her eyes. Those heart melting light blue eyes. The eyes that watered when she laughed too hard. He wondered if "he" had ever made them water for her.

"Why didn't you just ask for a divorce? If you wanted someone else, all you had to do was say it. I always told you I was never good enough for you, and if you wanted out, just say so. I wouldn't fight. I wouldn't do anything. I'd give you all you wanted.

I told you that I felt I was gifted more from you than I ever could give back in a million lifetimes." Allen was crying now, he was finally letting go. "I can't think how I'm going to keep the truth from everyone, but I will. No one needs to know what you were doing and where you were. I'll take that to my grave, my love."

The funeral director was returning now. "Mr. Bennett, I'm sorry sir, but I have to get Mrs. Bennett ready for...well, you know. If you could wait outside, we will be done in just a few moments."

Allen walked through the double doors. There were people there, but most were already lining up in their cars. He was going to be riding in the limo with her parents. His parents were long dead. He walked out and, got straight in the car and sat opposite her parents. Her mom didn't seem to be any better, but her dad was as stoic as ever. He just sat there and looked out the window. He never even acknowledged that Allen had gotten in the car.

The gravesite was a little better, maybe people were just cried out by then, or the chill in the air had taken their energy away. Father Michaelson was giving the typical "Ashes to ashes, dust to dust" spiel. Everyone seemed pleased with his words. Allen was happy; he was tired and couldn't stand, so he was afforded one of the few chairs set up at the graveside. Father Michaelson had done a good job. He wrapped it up early. He remembered to announce the snacks and refreshments that would be served back at the church in the meeting hall. "Please everyone, if you can come. Come join us. Share your stories. Eat our food, and let us keep the memory of Cheyenne Bennett alive within each of us."

Allen hated these fucking things. Everyone stood around, stuffing their faces, telling stories that made the deceased person look like a saint. He always felt that there was too much laughter at these dinners. He guessed you called them dinners, they were stupid regardless. You always had people coming up to you and hugging you and telling you meaningless shit. Allen was standing next to the buffet table of food and saw the dipshit that had just come up to him. He knew him to see him but again never knew his name. "If you need anything, anything at all you call me. Understand? I don't care if it's 3am, I'll answer the phone." He had said. Allen's initial thought was, "I'm going to call you and say my grass needs mowing right now, and it can't wait until morning. Get over here and get to work, you fat fuck." Allen had heard that phrase more in the last week than he could stand. "If you need me." A week from now, ninety percent of these people will most likely have forgotten who Cheyenne Bennett even was, let alone the ridiculous promise they made to her grieving husband.

"Allen I'm so sorry, when I heard the news. I just said to myself 'it can't be. I refuse to believe it'. Chey dead. She was such a great driver. I never thought she would have died in a car accident. Just goes to show you never know, right? We never know! We have to just live it up and make the most out of our lives. If you need anything buddy, I'm just a few feet away. You can call, email, or hell, just yell out the damn window if you want, and I'll come running!" That was their neighbor. Allen could remember more spats about the trees between their properties than civilized conversations. Everyone was saying basically the same bullshit lines to him all day. He was glad when people started to leave. He snuck out the back. He doubted he would be missed anyway.

Chapter 2

The Return Home

Allen's hopes of getting away from the church undetected failed almost immediately. He got about three steps from the door when he heard a voice. "Sneaking away?"

Allen turned and saw Shane, Cheyenne's cousin. She often called him her favorite cousin. He was in fact, the second person he called when he got the news after Cheyenne's dad. He took the news stoically, that sort of demeanor was how the men of Cheyenne's family lived. Now, he was standing here, smoking his cancer sticks one after another. Allen couldn't remember a time in the last few days when he didn't see Shane without a cigarette in his mouth. Under other circumstances, Allen would have made a joke about how they were going to kill him, but he didn't have any laughter in him at the moment. "She looked good," Shane said between puffs. He said this as a joke, as the casket had been closed. Neither of them laughed.

Allen thought he was going to scream. This was another phrase about death that he despised. When a person is in their coffin, and some idiot says they look good. It's not possible to look anything but dead when you are dead. Fucking idiots.

Allen contented himself to say, "Yeah, they did a nice job

with her." Allen played along; he had no idea why and hated himself for doing so. And before he even said it, Allen knew Shane's next words, "It was nice service, too. Old preach did a good job, I think Chey would have been pleased." This was something else Allen hated. He hated when people said, "It was a nice service." Why did people feel the need to make comments on everything? It was like they were justifying their own survival or something. It was a funeral. There is a dead person in the room. Most people don't like to be around dead people. Oh, and by the way, see that wet shit coming from everyone's eyes? Those are tears. You think all that shit wrapped up and tied together with hollow words spoken by people that barely knew the body in the casket makes it nice? God, people were so fucking stupid about things.

"Yeah Father Michaelson and Chey have known each other a long time. I didn't think she would want anyone else to do it. He actually declined at first, wasn't sure he would be able to get up and talk. You heard what he said, seemed to me like he was pretty pissed off at his God. When the clergy are pissed off at God, what are us lesser mortals supposed to do?"

"I guess we smoke another cigarette and wonder when will be our time. I'll make your excuses for you. If you need anything. You call me. I don't care what time it is, day or night. I'll be there for you. I always considered Chey more than a cousin, more like a sister, and you're my brother." He moved to hug Allen, and Allen just stood there. He was thinking about stuff he needed to do around the house. He thought about Shane in an apron cooking him and Austin dinner because Allen sucked at cooking. He wondered what Shane would say if he asked him to become his cook.

"Thanks buddy, Cheyenne always talked about you in the best of light, and you were always her favorite." He decided to say instead.

Allen walked away as he heard Shane flicking the flint and steel of his lighter to another cigarette, Allen thought he didn't slow down they'd be attending his funeral next. He got to the car and almost instinctively walked around to the passenger side. Ever since Cheyenne had died, people must have thought he was afraid to drive. They were always saying they would drive him everywhere. He corrected his course and walked around the driver's side of the car. When he got in, he wondered if anything would ever be the same. Right now, he sat in his car and stared at the rain specks on the windshield and thought about his dead wife's last drive. Not where she was coming from, but what had been going through her mind as she drove. He wondered if she thought about him and if she should tell him. He sat there and wondered if he'd ever be able to get into a car to drive again without thinking about her last drive. In a way, he hoped not, because that's not how he wanted to remember her. In another way, at least for right now, he did because he still wanted to be angry with her. He started it up and started to pull away. This was literally the first time in a week that he had driven. He had gotten tired of being chauffeured around all the time. He enjoyed driving and wouldn't let her accident deter him at all. As he got on to the highway and began to drive, Allen checked his speedometer and noticed he was pegged at 40 miles per hour. Maybe he was scared after all.

He finally made it home and saw that there were a few cars in his driveway. This disappointed him because that meant when all the idiots got done at the church, a few of them were coming back here. He wished he would have listened to Cheyenne's nagging and cleaned the garage out because he could then pull into it and his car couldn't be seen unless someone entered the house. Which they wouldn't because he would be locked away somewhere, and he figured Austin would be too. He finally got out of the car and decided to go in through the garage. Have a look around. See if he couldn't shift a few things and make the room he needed. As he unlocked the door and shut it he realized that the last argument he and his wife had was started because of this garage. Not the mess in it but about the light being blown out. Cheyenne was going to do it herself because, as she put it, "my husband can't get his fingers far enough from the keyboard to be bothered with anything else." It was a jab, a playful one, but he wasn't in a good mood, and he fired back that, "if I didn't write, we wouldn't have all that shit you have in the fucking garage in the first place!"

"All I want you to do is get up for five damn minutes and change the fluorescent bulbs so I can do it myself. I know you're too busy with your newest creation. You always disappear when you write, and you're too damn cheap to let me hire someone to do the repairs around the house claiming it's 'my house I'll do them'. Well do them! You can't sit and write all day, every day, Allen. You have a family here that wants to spend time with you!"

"I spend time with you all the time, we always go out to eat and to movies."

"Oh yeah? When is the last time we went to a movie and got anything that wasn't fast food?"

"I don't know, couple weeks ago probably. I've been in a good groove. You know how well I write when I'm in that groove."

"Almost three months Allen, you've been holed up in your office for three months writing your book. You haven't noticed at all. You just live in that world until it dries up, and you return to this one. Well right now, I'm in this one, and I need the damn bulbs changed!"

"Fine, I'll do it. Do we even have any bulbs?"

He watched as Cheyenne went into the closet where they kept all the spare bulbs and odds and ends. He heard her rustling around in there, he eventually snuck over to the door and peered in, and she was moving everything around. Grunting and groaning like she always did when she got frustrated.

"Find anything you're looking for?"

"No!" She shrieked back.

"I know. That's why I hadn't replaced them; I knew we didn't have any."

She sat down on the step stool. She was sweating, and her hair was sticking to her face, hiding one of her eyes. He walked into the closet and pulled the door shut.

"Light in here seems to be fine," he mused, a sly coquettish smile on his face. "Maybe we can see what we see in here?" He was pulling her to get feet as she tried to hide her face. He kissed her across her sweaty hair and down her lips. He pulled her close to him, and his body immediately responded. His pulse seemed to double. He felt like he fell in love with her all over again every time he kissed her. He brushed her hair out of her face. "Do we really want to clean the garage today?" he asked as he kissed her again. She was now getting into it. She was usually the more sexually aggressive one in their relationship, and he liked it that way because he was so insecure. She started to slowly undress him and went to her knees.

Allen snapped back, he was staring at the burned out fluorescent bulbs. That had also been the last time he and his wife had made love too. It was too painful right now to let that memory continue. He looked around, the feeble light from the kitchen shining in the garage illuminating the boxes and piles of stuff that belonged to his late wife. A few of the boxes were his. Most of his were books he used to own or had written himself. He kept a copy of everything he'd ever written. When he got to where he could afford to do it, after every writing session, he printed out the day's work and presented it to his wife for approval. She rarely ever told him anything sucked, but she was a good critic. She was his female voice. Any time he struggled with writing a female lead, he turned to her for help. She was the perfect sounding board. Never too soft, never too harsh. She got him. She knew what he wanted to say before he knew he wanted to say it a lot of times. He had of late started to transfer a lot of his books into a digital format on his Kindle, but he just couldn't get rid of the paper editions yet. He knew he would eventually, but right now he couldn't because he couldn't quite decide if he liked reading from Kindle or not. He gave it up as impossible. He was just going to have to deal with people when they showed up.

He closed the door and walked through the house. There were no signs that Austin had ever come out of his room. When he asked him if he was going to the funeral this morning, he simply said, "No." There was no yelling, no screaming and no argument. Allen didn't argue because he knew exactly how the kid felt. He didn't want to go either. The house was unusually quiet. He guessed Austin was sleeping, which he seemed to do a lot because he barely made any noise anymore. Allen again knew what the kid was thinking; he himself was exhausted. He wanted to get a shower but just didn't have the energy right now. He was going to sleep. He didn't care if friends and relatives beat his door down later. He was going to sleep right now. He turned to go down the hall from the kitchen to where the guest bedroom was located. He had been sleeping in here since he got the news. He just felt weird without Cheyenne in their bed. He hadn't slept without her in more than ten years. The guest bed was a twin; he felt he wouldn't miss her as much if there wasn't as much room. It didn't work. He missed having her next to him at night. He felt he'd forgive her for the affair just to have her sleeping next to him right now if he could. He knew he was being stupid. He knew he was going to have to sleep in his own bed once again. So, despite feeling no desire to get up, he dragged himself up the stairs to the room they shared. There was no sound from Austin's room. Allen assumed the kid was in there, but didn't check. He walked down the hall, pulling off his tie and shirt. He opened the door and looked at the bed. It looked the same as it did when he was awoken by the phone a week ago. He hadn't been in it since. He thought that his complete exhaustion was going to outweigh any overwhelming fear of loneliness he might have. Allen was falling toward the bed; not quite sure he had finished that thought before he was asleep as his body settled into the bed.

Chapter 3

The Phone Calls

Allen was heavily asleep. This may have been the best sleep he had since he was a kid. Of course, the phone ringing ruined it. He tried to bury himself deeper into his dreams, but the intruding sound of a ringing phone just wouldn't let him. It chased him through his dreams. He fumbled around in the dark, searching for his cell phone and couldn't find it. He then woke up a little more and realized that it was his landline phone. This was odd because almost no one called that line except for telemarketers and politicians. It didn't seem to matter whether or not you registered your numbers under the national "do not call" registry; those bastards seemed to find it. He looked at the clock as he reached for the phone. It was 2:22am. For the first time since he heard the phone ring, he realized his wife wasn't in bed next to him. He looked around quickly for evidence that she had been home and just wasn't in bed, there was none. He felt a heavy lump build in his stomach. He glanced at the clock again; yes, it was definitely the middle of the night.

"Hel-Hello?"

"Hello sir, am I speaking with Mr. Allen Bennett of 5476 Union Court?" said the authoritative voice on the phone.

"Yes, that's me. What's going on? Has something happened?"

"Is your wife Cheyenne Bennett?"

"Yeah, why? What's going on?" Allen's voice became a little hysterical.

"Sir, there has been an accident. Your wife was involved in a single motor vehicle crash. She struck a tree and it appears that the airbag on her vehicle malfunctioned. I regret to inform you of this sir, but your wife did not survive the crash."

"What do you mean? 'Did not survive the crash?' "Allen's mind was in overdrive at this point. He immediately flashed back to his earlier call from Anne. She had been looking for Cheyenne, had this accident happened while on her way there? Could he have started to snoop without good cause? He thought not after what he'd found. Several emails with a guy named "Roger". He didn't read the emails. All he saw was the subject line "surprise for my baby!" He knew he didn't want to know the details. He just wished his wife was dead for betraying him like that, and now here he was on the phone with some asshole telling him that his wife was dead. It had to be a sick joke. The man was talking, giving him details that he couldn't follow and honestly didn't want to know.

"Sir, do you need someone to come pick you up? Even though she had identification, we need someone to identify the body." The officer sounded concerned that Allen hadn't spoken in what seemed to be an eternity to him. "I could have an officer drive you to the hospital if you want?"

"Yeah, yeah that'd be fine." Allen could hear another phone ringing, wondering what in the hell was going on, and he looked around for another phone and realized it was the phone in his hand that was ringing.

"Hel-hello?" He was confused as hell at this point.

"Allen, hey, did I catch you at a bad time man? Well, I know every second is a bad time right now, but you sound confused man. What's going on? You ok? Or as ok as you can be at this point?"

Allen had no idea what was happening. In order to simplify things, he hung up the phone and, unplugged the cord from the base and went back to bed.

It seemed to be hours later, he woke up to the phone ringing again. This time, it was his cell phone, he knew it because of the music ring tone he had on it. He looked at the landline phone and just stared. He couldn't remember everything about his dream, but he knew he'd dreamed about the phone call he got when the cop told him his wife was dead. He looked around casually for his cell phone;

if he found it, he would answer it. If not, he didn't really care all that much. He glanced to the dresser, and there it was, ringing and lighting up a little. It was face down, so he didn't get the benefit of the screen lighting up. His initial thought that it was hours later was wrong, he looked at the clock as he answered and saw it was only about two hours after he had gotten home.

"Hello?" Allen said groggily.

"Hey Allen, it's Shane. You sound out of it a little bit man. I just wanted you to know that I persuaded everyone to give you some time. We are all just going to pick up our cars and head out for the night. You know, go drink an adult beverage or fifty to Chey's memory. She didn't really drink but we will more than drink her share tonight! You want to come? I know you don't, but I think we should invite you."

"No, that's ok Shane, I am wiped out. Was just sleeping when you called. Think I'll just head back to bed. Try to sort everything out in my head a little bit tomorrow. Thanks for keeping the vultures away. I know people mean well and all, but sometimes it just feels like they want to pick at me. Too many fucking questions, if you know what I mean." Said Allen, he was so overwhelmed with gratitude for Shane right now he felt his eyes begin to leak again.

"I know exactly what you mean. I'll swing by tomorrow. If you need anything tonight, you call. Don't hesitate. No matter how fucked up I am, I'll find a way to your house." And with that, he hung up. That was Shane, he never really said bye. He'd say his piece and be gone.

Allen turned and looked at the other phone in the room. He saw that it had been unplugged, so that part had been real. He plugged the phone back in. He couldn't figure out his dream. He noticed the little flashing light that indicated he had a message waiting. He picked it up and dialed the requisite numbers, and heard the recording. Punched in the password. And felt a pang in his stomach. It was their anniversary. The cool recorded mechanical female voice indicated that the message was left at 4:38 pm, today. He looked again at the clock. It seemed no matter how many times he looked at the damn thing, the time just wouldn't register in his mind. He stared at it for a couple seconds. It was 4:59 pm. This made it about twenty minutes ago. He finally pressed 1 to listen to his message.

"Hey Allen, it's me, Bob Cooke. I'm not sure what happened. I called a minute ago, and it sounded like you answered and I started to talk, and the line went dead. I just wanted to call and see how you were doing? I know you're not doing well at all right now. Cheyenne was a tremendous woman, and to lose her at such a young age is just tragic. Makes you question a lot of things, I tell ya. Anyway, I called your house instead of your cell because I wasn't sure if you'd still be at the funeral or not and didn't want to interrupt or anything. I'm sorry as hell I couldn't make it up there for the funeral. I know you got a lot of good people around and all."

Again, Allen knew what was next before he even said it, the phrase was growing so tired, "If you need anything you just let me know, and I'll get it done." His agent hung up. He was another that didn't like the word bye; Allen seemed to know a bunch of them. Anything he needs, huh? Allen thought, "I'll need someone to clean the house," that's something else that I suck at doing. He pictured his fat, sweaty agent in a little French maid's outfit with a big old feather duster waddling around the house. For the first time in a long time, he laughed out loud to himself. He would probably just hire someone to clean his house, and of course, bill the services back to Allen. Allen wouldn't care because money wasn't an issue.

Speaking of money, he needed to find the insurance policies that Cheyenne had insisted on them having. She was always the prudent one. She seemed to plan for everything. She wanted to make sure that if something happened to him, she would be taken care of because, as she liked to say, "I don't have a talent for a job." So she had placed a couple policies that'd pay millions to her if something happened to Allen. He was ok with this; he didn't think his wife was going to bump him off like one of the characters in one of his books might. She had seemed genuinely madly in love with him. Had seemed to be anyways. He still couldn't wrap his mind around an affair for her, but he had the evidence if he wanted to read through it. He had thought about just erasing the hard drive on the computer so he'd never be tempted. It would suffice to keep him from reading the emails because he sure didn't know her password. Hell, half of the time, he couldn't remember his own password. Allen was having trouble concentrating, his mind kept returning to that like the way your tongue likes to find a sore in your mouth and just irritate it. He knew where she kept the important papers but had no idea what he was looking for in them. He knew their lawyer would have copies of all this stuff, but this felt like a venture he needed to complete on his own.

He was standing in her office. She called it her office, but she never used it. There wasn't much in the room. A couch, a desk, a paper shredder and a safe. On the desk was an old desktop computer that she referred to as her "slot machine". She loved to play video slots on it, would never put the programs on her laptop and contaminate that. Also, she would never go to a real casino more than once or twice a year. She didn't want "to waste real money on that nonsense when I can use all the fake millions I have on here." Allen, who enjoyed slots quite a bit, along with Texas Hold Em poker, felt his heart break. In that moment, he saw that twinkle in her eyes, the casual way she could look over her shoulder at you. In that moment, he forgot that she was dead. He forgot that she was having an affair. He forgot everything that was going on around him.

In that moment, in his mind's eye, he fell in love with his wife all over again.

He was brought back to reality by the phone, again. He couldn't think who would be calling. His agent wouldn't call back, and Shane had said he would keep the vultures off his back. He went into the bedroom and picked up the phone. For the first time, he actually looked at the caller ID. It was his editor.

"Hello."

"Hey Allen, it's Eugene, Eugene Martin."

"Hey Gene," his editor always seemed so unsure of himself on the phone. He was a great editor. Always had great insights into what Allen was trying to say and tips to make the dialogue clearer and more to the point. Get him on the phone though, and his confidence seemed to drain away for some reason. He seemed to Allen to be a rare person that couldn't tell you over the phone your book or ideas sucked, but had no issue telling you face to face. It was an odd quality in a person.

"First of all, I just want to say how sorry I am about Cheyenne. She was a great, great woman and human being. It doesn't make sense the way God chooses to take people so soon." To Allen this had a very practiced sound to it, almost as if he'd written it down in advance. "She was a great wife and mother, and I don't understand it at all."

"I know, thanks Gene."

"I hate to talk business at a time like this, but I know you were working on a project." That was something else he did, never called it working on a book. It was always a project. Allen had asked once why, and he said, "Books are those things on the shelves over there. Until it can sit up on a shelf on its own. It's a project."

Allen brought himself back into the conversation, "I know when I talked to you a couple weeks ago, you had told me that it would be done on time and ready for print in the summer as usual. Well, I don't have to be the one to tell you, you're the boss after all, but there is no hurry whatsoever for it. You take your time, you heal up, and we will get everything squared away. No problem."

"Thanks, Gene, it's almost done, though. I think I have maybe another couple chapters to do, and it'll be finished. I'll just get that done in the next couple weeks and then see where things stand at that point." Allen said.

"If that's what you think is best, like

I said you're the boss." He hesitated, then said, "I'm sure you've heard this a million times, but if you need anything, you just let me know right away. I'll get someone to do it for you."

"Thanks, Gene, bye now." Allen actually chuckled a little bit.

Allen went back and sat on the bed. He had decided he didn't give a shit about the insurance papers right now. He was thinking he had gotten three phone calls; he looked at the clock and was surprised to see it was 6:14, in the last hour and a half. Everyone had said if he needed anything. Why was he the needy one? No one had asked about Austin one time. He felt bad that people were forgetting the poor kid; he had just lost his mother after all.

Chapter 4

The Confrontation

Allen decided he would just go back to bed. He would try to figure out what to do with Austin later. For right now the kid seemed to just want some alone time. He had been like this ever since he had told him the news. It was the worst thing he had experienced in the world. Telling his fourteen-year-old son that his mom was dead. Allen knew that he had a better relationship with his mom; he was a lot more like his mom than he was him. He was tall, good-looking, smart, charismatic and just different from Allen in almost every way. He loved sports. Allen was far too clumsy to ever play them so he never had interest. Austin was a great baseball player, and Allen never missed a game. Anyone else in attendance, though, would have seen that there were about a thousand places he'd rather have been than at the game on his face. Allen knew the boy was going to need some help. He just didn't know how to approach him. If he were a character in one of his novels, then he would be able to write about it. That was the trouble with Allen; he sometimes couldn't bring himself out of that fantasy world for very long to deal with things in the real world. He loved to write, he would say it was a very, very close second to loving his family, and he would never admit it to anyone, but on some occasions, it actually surpassed his family. When he was really in a groove, he would completely forget that he even had a family. He'd spend hours in his study just pounding away on his keyboard. Putting down on paper what he saw in his mind. He loved the stories. Even the bad ones. To him it was the fun of telling himself the story. He would sit for hours even after he was done writing and make up side stories for each character, really getting to know them. He wanted to know everything he could about each person. He'd ask himself questions, and yes, answer those questions. Sometimes out loud. Allen never thought that maybe he should get to know his own son in this way by asking many of the same questions he asked of himself about his characters.

He sat there on the bed, thinking about when he got the call from the officer; he couldn't even remember his name now. His first thought after hanging up was that he should have asked if Austin was in the car, he hadn't seen him since Cheyenne had left, but that didn't always mean much. Austin loved to play on his computer, and he was good at it too. Cheyenne had told him that he wanted to be a computer programmer when he was older. The kid didn't want technology either. If he wanted it, he got it. Not that he was overly spoiled. He just got what he wanted, which wasn't much more than any other kid. At that point, Allen's mind was in total disarray. He couldn't concentrate. His brain just wandered down any path it could so it wouldn't have to try to process the news he just received. He knew he needed to tell Austin right away; his first instinct was to ask Cheyenne to do it. Allen laughed out loud at this thought. He thought, "Honey, will you go down the hall and tell our son you're are dead?"

He supposed he was in shock, he had never been before, but he guessed this is how it felt. Slowly, he got up and walked down the hall, he heard music playing. This made his heart skip a beat. It meant that Austin was alive and in his bed. Asleep, safe and sound. Allen stood outside his door. Even though he heard the music, he was still scared. He knew he had zoned out a little bit while the officer was talking. He hoped he hadn't missed anything that was vitally important, and it seemed now that whether or not his son was in the car was vitally important. He raised his hand and knocked, a little too softly. There was no answer. It felt like his heart had stopped in his chest. It was a weird time to have this thought, but Allen welcomed it. After what he had learned earlier and the distance between him and Austin, he thought to himself, "God, do I still love my family so much." This thought driving him; he knocked louder this time and said "Austin" at the same time. This time, his heart started again because he heard movement behind the door. His son was really here, was really alive. He opened the door and the two looked at each other, and Allen threw himself onto his son and was weeping. It seemed that seeing his son brought the truth home in a way none of the words the officer had spoken could. "Austin," he said, running his hands up and down the kid's back and head, "there's been an accident, your mom was killed. She's dead Austin.

She died tonight!"

Austin pushed him away, "What do you mean she's dead? She can't be dead. She promised to take me to a football game next week. She just ordered the tickets. Stop joking dad. It's not funny!" His voice was becoming progressively higher with each word. His shock was starting to settle in on him.

"She's gone; I just got off the phone with the police. They found her car. They said the airbag malfunctioned." Allen was trying to make Austin understand.

"This isn't funny! She's not dead. Why would you say that if it's not true?" Austin was screaming at his dad how. Allen didn't know what hurt him more at that moment. Knowing his wife was dead or that his son was broken hearted.

He lay back down on the bed. His head was hurting, and his heart was aching. He never thought this would be the way it would happen. He always thought his marriage would end in divorce, not death. He wished he could just ask Cheyenne why she felt she needed to sneak around. He loved her, he wanted her to be happy, and if it wasn't him that made her happy, he would let her go, no matter how much it crushed him to do so.

He heard a door close, he thought that Austin might finally be up and moving around. He wanted to go talk to him, but didn't know how. He knew Austin wouldn't come to him, he couldn't remember a time when the kid actually sought him out to ask him a question. Never anything about puberty, or girls, or sports or school. Cheyenne always answered those questions. Allen always felt like a ghost when Austin was around. Cheyenne always loved Austin more than Allen, and in a way, Allen understood from the moment they found out she was pregnant that Austin was going to be her priority. He always felt that's how mothers are with their children. Some men got that, others didn't. The ones that didn't always seem to end up with other issues, whether it be drinking, drugs or deciding that the woman needed a slap now and then to remind her who was in charge.

Allen got up; he had decided that he needed to talk to Austin; just to make sure the kid was doing okay. He saw his bedroom door was still slightly open, which meant that he wasn't in his room. He looked around and heard movement in the bathroom. He knocked on the door. "Austin? When you're done, can we talk?"

No answer, just the flying open of the door. A nasty glare from the kid, and then he swept past him into his room. Allen had known Austin was in pain, anyone that knew Cheyenne was in pain, but the kid had looked more than heart broken. He had looked defeated.

Allen opened the door that Austin had left cracked open. He stood in the doorway. "Can I come in?" he asked.

Austin looked at him and shrugged, then turned and looked out the window. Allen looked around the room, it was the antithesis of what he thought a teenager's room should look like, and it was spotless. Bed made, no papers lying around, no cups or snacks or anything. The bed looked as though it had not been touched in a week. Allen wondered if Austin had slept at all lately. Maybe what he had thought of as a defeated look was actually a look of total and utter exhaustion.

"Austin, I know what you are feeling. I miss your mom so much," Allen began with no preamble. Austin didn't turn or respond. "It was a tragedy; everyone loved her more than they may have even known." Allen didn't want to let Austin know he knew about the affair. He wanted to make it seem like she was coming back from her friend Anne's house, let that dirty secret die with him. He could take it, hold it and keep it for eternity. Telling people wouldn't bring Cheyenne back; the only purpose it would serve would be to tarnish what people thought about her. Austin still said nothing, "I want you to know that now that your mother is gone, I am going to be here for you. I know I haven't been the greatest dad in the world, but that will change. I want to get to know you better. I feel like we have grown apart the last few years. I want to be able to show you that I can be there for you, I know I can never replace the bond that you had with your mom, but maybe we can build one between us that may be just as strong and build a nice strong friendship."

Austin finally turned from the window; he looked at Allen as though he had never seen him before. He looked like he had something to say, something that was horrible and difficult to get out. He opened his mouth, and closed it. Seemed to try to gather himself and finally said, "You want to be here for me? Where have you been all week? You've been out with friends, family, and business partners. Whoever." Austin was shaking, Allen didn't know if it was nerves or anger or a combination. He had thought Austin would be feeling a lot of things, but anger at him had never crossed his mind. "You, who never paid attention to me, always paid more attention to the characters in your books. You think we are going to be close? You think that I want to be your 'friend'?" Austin was breathing hard; he had fully turned now and was facing Allen. "You think I want to be around you? When you're the reason my mom is dead? You think I want to be your 'friend' when it's you who drove her away. I knew she had a boyfriend. I knew she was planning to ask for a divorce. You never paid any attention to us; it was always your damn books. We aren't your family. Those people on those pages in that room downstairs. Those people are your true family. They are the ones you care about the most. They are the ones you are going to be close with, not me. You'll lose yourself in those shitty stories you like to tell. You won't pay any attention to me anymore now than you did before!"

Allen, who was standing in the door way, raised his hands to his chest as his son approached. He didn't know what to expect now. He didn't know if Austin was going to attack him or something else. He tried to stand firm, but Austin raised his hands and placed them on his dad's crossed arms and shoved him back out of his room and slammed the door in his face. Allen just stood outside his door. He felt much the way he did the night he came to this door to knock and tell the occupant of the room inside that his mom was dead. He wanted to knock, but was scared to find what was behind the door. He was afraid of his son. What he had said had hurt him. Was it his fault that his mom was now buried in the ground? Had he been so inattentive lately that she had left seeking comfort, love and attention from someone else? He thought he had been earning them a living. That his hard work would pay off, and he would have books in storage, and he could take years off writing and just send in some of the stuff he had already written. This had always been his plan. Over the past five years he had written nearly ten rough drafts of books. He was storing them the way a squirrel stores nuts. He was saving them for when he wanted a break from it all. He was striking while the iron was hot, and his creative juices were flowing like a raging river. He hadn't been ignoring anyone. He had been working. Making their lives easy. He was getting them their nest egg. He was making sure everyone could live comfortably. It wasn't his fault, was it? If Allen had asked the young man behind the door in front of which he now stood, he had a feeling that the answer would be a resounding and emphatic "Yes!" As he walked away from his angry son's door, he thought to himself, "I planned to make it up to them."

Chapter 5

The Neighbor

Allen struggled over the next few days. He was hurt by what his son had said. He questioned himself constantly. He wondered what his motivations actually were the past few years. He knew he loved his wife and son. Did he fail in showing them? He had always thought that the way to show love as a husband and father was to provide. Provide a roof, food, clothes and transportation. He had done that. His writing had done that. He couldn't grasp the idea of Cheyenne questioning his motivations. Thinking he didn't love her or Austin while he was pounding out his stories and selling books. He never went anywhere without them. His books were always released in the late spring, and he did tours during the summer when Austin was on summer break. He had never thought about having an affair, not that he didn't have his chances. He'd gotten suggestive fan mail with pictures included. He just tossed them away. He even has been approached in public. Not that he was worldly known and immediately recognized, but people came up to him. Women came up to him. They knew he was an accomplished writer and had money. It wasn't anything more than that. He just brushed them all off. The letters went unanswered, and the face-to-face offers were turned down easily enough with a flash of the left hand and the wedding band that resided there.

He still provided, even feebly, as some may say. He was an awful cook. He ordered delivery every night after the funeral. It seemed that the people who were concerned about him and Austin disappeared much the same as Cheyenne's coffin disappeared into the dirt. Fewer and fewer people called as the days passed. Allen had only gone out on a few occasions. Had answered the phone fewer and fewer times. He was tired of hearing the same drivel over and over again. "I'm sorry for your loss. If there's anything I can do. I'm always here if you need me." It was always the same things over and over again. He was tired of it. His editor had called and been very cryptic in asking whether or not he had started to write again. He seemed to be backing off his statement that he didn't need to worry about writing right now. Allen could have told him he had books saved back, but for some reason, he always wanted to send in the latest that he'd written. He didn't want to send in his stored nuts just yet. He couldn't explain just why, though. It just didn't feel right to him.

Allen had only left the house twice in the days that followed the funeral. Once to sign papers at the lawyer's office. Luckily, his prudent wife had sent all the forms for insurance to him. He had prepared everything and just needed Allen's signature. Cheyenne didn't have a will. Allen's lawyer assured him that this would not cause a problem because he, as next of kin, was now responsible for everything in her estate. The other time he left he had gone to the local dollar store and bought a TV dinner tray table. He had so far knocked on Austin's door and been given the silent treatment for the first two meals of the day. Allen felt he and Austin both could handle breakfast and lunch if it involved lunchmeat or something microwaveable. Anything more complex and it was out of their league. He knew he'd have to eventually hire a cook and someone to clean the house, but for now, delivery was good enough. He wanted the tray table so he could leave food outside Austin's door. He knew the kid wasn't going to speak to him any time soon. Even with that, he felt that he needed to show him he could eat in his room and come out and talk to him when he wanted to. Allen hadn't seen Austin since the previous night. When he returned home, he set the tray table outside Austin's door and put the food he'd picked up from what he knew was Austin's favorite restaurant. He knocked a few times, received no response as he expected and simply said, "I know you're in there. You can eat in your room for as long as you want. I bought a table here for you to use. I'm down the hall if you need me."

Allen walked away, fully expecting to hear movement in the room and was disappointed when he didn't hear anything. He went to his own room, pulled his table tray to him and began to eat, even though he had no taste for food. His body just craved it. He didn't enjoy it at all.

Still lacking sleep, Allen fell into an exhaustive sleep

immediately after he finished eating. He slept through the night. His sleep was dreamless and uneventful. He woke up the next morning, fully expecting to find that Austin had eaten his dinner and returned the dishes either to the tray or even taken them to the kitchen himself. He was completely unprepared for what he saw; the plate had not been touched at all. He wondered if Austin was on a hunger strike or if he was just too upset to eat. The kid wasn't that big. He couldn't afford to miss too many meals.

Allen would make something small, or order something over the next few days for both he and Austin. He would set Austin's food on the tray, knock to let him know that it was there and retire to his own room where he ate. Lately, only a few rooms of their big house were being used, he and Cheyenne's, well he guessed just his bedroom now. Austin's bedroom. The bathroom and the kitchen. He hadn't been in the living room since before the funeral and had no intention of going there. Also, he hadn't stepped foot in his office either, he was taking his editor at his word on not worrying about work. He thought about working. He wondered if he had a normal job and if he'd been able to return to it by now. He thought not, he couldn't understand how companies could get away with only giving people three days off work when a loved one died. It seemed ludicrous. As if you could be functional again so soon. He knew if he worked a regular job, he'd have been fucked because he was barely able to take care of his and his son's basic needs at this point, let alone returning to the grind of a job. He was blessed that he did what he did for a living.

Between meals, Allen seemed to escape into sleep. He napped; he was beginning to think his life was regressing. He would eat and immediately need a nap like a baby. When he woke up, it was usually time for the next meal. He would call or heat something up and he noticed Austin would never touch it. He was beginning to be concerned about him. He had seen him that morning. He had been coming from the bathroom when Allen was going down the stairs. He tried to ask him what he wanted for breakfast, but the kid just kept walking. Allen thought about having a counselor come to the house to talk to Austin but dismissed the idea, but told himself if things didn't turn around over the next few days, he would look into it, if for no other reason to make sure the kid was eating.

The fourth day after the funeral, Allen decided he needed to get some air. He hadn't been out for a couple days, and he needed exercise. He wasn't a fitness freak like Cheyenne was, but he tried to stay in shape for no other reason than to keep up with her. He was now in his late forties, he didn't look it, but he was, and there were days when he actually felt it too. As soon as he turned at the end of his driveway, just beyond the row of trees that had always been a source of bitter feelings between him and their neighbor, he wished he hadn't decided to do this, because standing there was Robert Meadows. The damn neighbor he didn't want to see. He hoped he hadn't seen him so he could just sidle back up to the house, but no such luck because as soon as Allen took half a step toward the house, Robert had raised his hand in a wave.

"Hey Allen, how are you doing?" Allen wanted to tell him how he was really doing, but we rarely, if ever, fully express ourselves. Even to those we love the most. And to assholes like this, we always lie and tell them what they want to hear.

"I'm doing well, you know. All things considered."

"Good good. Everything settling down then? I remember after my wife passed, everything was chaos for about a week, and everything began to get back to a routine. It's definitely different not having them around. They are our rocks. Regardless of what we think and say about them when they are alive and how often we think we can be better without them, deep down we know we wouldn't be very good without them." Allen didn't understand why this man was talking to him, he only ever talked to him before to tell him to cut and trim his damn trees. Now he stood here giving him advice on how he should handle adjusting to being a widow. Allen didn't think the situations were at all comparable. His wife died in a car accident, his neighbors had cancer. She had a slow, torturous death of this Allen was sure, but at least Robert, never Rob or Bob always Robert, got to say goodbye to her. He knew what was coming.

Robert was talking again, "...fine woman. Fine, fine woman.

When my Martha passed, she was there for me. She helped me so much. She was very supportive for me. You were busy of course; she talked about how you seemed to disappear into your own world when you were writing. She understood it, and she accepted it. Sometimes, she said though that she felt lonely. Austin helped, of course, but sometimes she just wanted to have you. Have you back from whatever world you were creating in your mind."

Allen couldn't believe what he was hearing. It seemed like his wife had talked to this guy, whom she knew he did not care for, about some of the issues they had in their marriage. Not that he knew they had these issues. Cheyenne had always been supportive about his writing. Had always read every page as he printed them out. Always critiqued his writing. She was his best critique. If she could tell him something he was writing wasn't very good, why couldn't she have said that what he was writing took too much time up and he needed to be there for his family?

Without realizing he meant to say anything until it came out of his mouth, Allen heard himself say, "I'm having a lot of trouble with Austin. I don't know how I am going to get acceptance with him. There's just so much anger and blame right now." Allen stopped himself; he didn't want to empty everything he was feeling onto this guy he almost loathed.

Robert looked a little uncomfortable. He and his wife

didn't have any children, so he didn't have any experience to draw upon. He tried to say something, stopped, licked his lips and said, "Well Allen, these things take time. You can get acceptance for anything within a few days. As for blame and anger, blame God, be angry with God. He has broad shoulders. He can take it all, and when you're ready, He will be there for you with waiting and open arms."

"Yeah, time. That's what everyone says. Time heals all wounds. I just don't know how this wound will heal." Allen started to walk away, turned back toward Robert when that man had said his name; Allen knew it was coming again. He'd heard it less and less in the past couple days, "If you need anything, I'm here for you. I know things haven't always been the greatest with us, but I cared a lot about Cheyenne and Austin. Just let me know if you need anything, and I'll do it. I noticed your grass is getting high; I'll send my guy over and take care of that for you. I know Cheyenne usually did it for you guys, not even sure you know how to run a mower!" Robert chuckled to show this was a joke, and when Allen didn't respond in kind, he immediately stopped. "Anyway, I'll take care of it, and it's on me. It's the least I can do."

Allen just nodded and mumbled a "Thanks" that was barely audible. He had decided he didn't want to walk now anyway. He was getting a headache again. He felt like he needed another nap. He turned away again, and then came back up to Robert, who was standing in the same place, watching him. He raised his hand to shake with his neighbor, this time speaking "Thanks" to where it could be heard. His mom always taught him that when someone does a good deed in your favor, you shake with them and give them a good hearty "Thank You". With that done, he went back up to the house to lie down. This headache seemed like it may be the worst yet.

Chapter 6

The House Hunting

When Allen got back into the house, he realized two things. The first was that he still didn't like his neighbor. No matter how many kind words he said. And the second was, he didn't want to live here anymore. There was too much of Cheyenne in this house. She had always been the one to decorate and make the house a home. Without her here, everything just felt empty. All the decorations, they just felt like they didn't have the same appeal. He loved the way she set up the house. She had her own styles, he could never explain them, but they somehow worked.

He went into his room, picked up his phone, used one of the applications to find a realtor, and tapped call. He waited for the ring, he didn't know what kind of house he wanted or where. He just knew he had to get out of this one as soon as possible.

"Century 21, this is Audrey. How can I help you today?"

"Hi, yes, I was just thinking I'd like to move. I recently lost my wife, and there are too many memories in this house. So what I am thinking is that I'd like to get out of here as soon as possible."

"No problem sir, if I can just get some information from you, I would be happy to come show you some homes we have for sale. Can we start off with your name?"

"Allen Bennett."

"The Allen Bennett? The author?" she seemed to be unable to hold her professional tone. It was okay, Allen was used to that when he gave people his name.

"Yep, that's me."

"I'm so sorry to hear about your wife. I read about it in the paper. That's such a tragedy, and at her age and all."

"Thank you very much." Allen felt tired. He was growing weary of everyone's well-intentioned words of sympathy. He didn't know why, but suddenly, they were bothering him. He felt a stab of pain every time someone said they were "sorry" about his loss. All he wanted now was to get off the phone. He needed, and should have passed this idea by Austin first. He wasn't impulsive by nature, but this had been impulsive. He had just grabbed the phone; looked up the number, and dialed. He seemed to be on autopilot with Audrey, she was asking him basic information. She wanted to know his price range and all that. He didn't care. He just wanted to be done with this. He answered her few remaining questions. His headache got worse than ever now. He vaguely remembered them setting up a meeting for a few days from today. She would bring some printouts of houses she thought would be appropriate. If he had questions, call her. She gave her personal cell number. He wrote it down without really thinking. He hung up, gratefully.

He went to Austin's room and knocked. He couldn't hear anything from the kid's room. He knocked again, louder this time, and when he didn't hear anything again, he opened the door. He noticed that, yet again he hadn't touched the food he'd set outside his door for him. He hoped he was eating. He knew they had a huge stockpile of food. They had three refrigerators in the house and three freezers. If the kid was hungry, he could find something to eat. Plus, they had set up an account for him, he didn't get an allowance per se, but a certain amount of money was automatically deposited into the account. Cheyenne had felt when he turned fourteen he deserved some privacy as to what he spent his money on. He wouldn't have to ask permission to buy anything; he just knew what his limits were. If he needed something big, then he asked his parents. He rarely did though; he usually was really good with his money and very rarely spent it on anything. He was a parent's dream for the most part. So, if he wanted to order his own food, he had his own money. Allen wouldn't be none the wiser. Allen wondered if this refusal to eat the food he bought or made for him was ever going to end. They needed to talk. He felt that each of them had about enough time to settle down, and now it was time to start healing together.

He looked around the room and didn't see Austin in there, and then he noticed that Austin was sitting on the floor between the TV stand and his desk, just looking at the floor.

"Austin, I wanted to talk to you about something. I have been thinking today, that we don't see much of each other right now. I think part of it is that we don't want to go out into the house. We go anywhere; we are going to see things that remind us of your mother. It's just too painful. There are too many reminders here. I think we need a fresh start. I called a real estate agent, and they are coming over later this week to show us some houses. I wanted to get your input on where we move. We both know I can work from anywhere. It's more important that you are comfortable. That you like where we live." Allen was talking, but he wasn't sure Austin was listening. He had his head down still. "Son, are you listening?"

"Yeah. I was hoping you'd feel this way. It, it's just too hard to be here. I can't go anywhere without something reminding me of her. It's too painful, like you said. I don't care where we go. Just as long as it is not here anymore. I think I'd like to move away. Not real far. Close enough to see the people I know here but maybe a few towns away or something." Austin said this in an almost dead tone, he didn't make eye contact. He just hugged his knees and stared at the floor.

"Ok son, we will find what we are looking for. What do you want in a new house? Pool? Jacuzzi? Bigger? Smaller? Big yard? Small yard? Fenced in? We could get a dog if you wanted if we got a fenced in yard." At this, Austin's face lit up. It was the first positive emotion Allen had seen on Austin's face in a very long time. He'd always wanted a dog. Every kid wants a dog, but Cheyenne had been severely allergic, so it was never a possibility. Allen thought to himself, "Maybe some good can come of this. Even if it's just something so small as a dog. Maybe something good can happen." To Austin, he said, "Yes, we will definitely get a fenced in yard. Maybe a pool, too. Dogs love pools. I'll get to looking for houses, and you get to looking for dogs."

"Yeah, okay!" Allen turned to leave, "Dad, I'm sorry about what I said. I know it wasn't your fault."

"Water under the bridge, son. You were hurting, and you lashed out at the only person around, me. It's perfectly fine. Everything will be just fine now." He walked through the door wondering if he'd just made a statement that he could never back up.

A few days later, Audrey arrived right on the minute when she said she would be there. He saw her coming and greeted her at the door. He didn't know whether or not this was just the guy in him or if this meant that he was starting to heal, but the first thing he noticed about her was what a stunning body she had. She wore a two-piece business skirt suit. It was tight in all the right places and Allen felt a part of him move that he actually thought might have died right along with Cheyenne. It appeared it did not.

"Hey! I see you found the place just fine." He greeted her more warmly than even he had anticipated he would.

"Yeah, it wasn't too bad. I sold a house down the street last year. I knew the neighborhood pretty well." Audrey replied, raising her hand to shake Allen's outstretched hand, smiling.

"Good, good. Would you like something to drink?" He asked.

"No thanks." She said, but Allen thought he could see a glint in her eye that said she would love more than a drink.

She surveyed the house.

"I know you want to move Mr. Bennett—"

"Allen, please call me Allen."

"Okay, Allen. I assume you want to sell this home at the same time?"

"Yeah. I mean, selling this house isn't contingent on buying another. If it has to sit here for a while or whatever, that's fine."

"Good, that makes it easier. Now, what is the time frame you are looking to move in?"

"As soon as humanly possible. I would love to be blown away by something you show me today, and I'll write out a check immediately. I'm ready to go."

"What are you looking for in your new home?

"Well, we would like to have a fenced in yard and a pool. See, we want to get a dog. My wife was severely allergic to them, and now that she's passed, we thought we could get one. Maybe it would help with the healing."

At the word, Audrey looked around the room and up the stairs, not seeing evidence there was another person in the house. Allen noticed her looking around, "My son, he's not here right now. He said he was going out for a while. I think it's the first time he left the house since Cheyenne died. He wouldn't even go to the funeral. Poor kid, he's having such a rough time with everything right now."

"Oh, I see. Well, I have a number of properties here for you to look at. I plugged in the information that you gave me the other day. I didn't know fenced in yard and pool were priorities, or I would have made sure I got more like that." She pulled a folder out of her briefcase and started to lay the printouts on the coffee table. Allen, who was sitting in the chair next to the couch now changed to sitting next to her. He hadn't been this close to a woman since Cheyenne had died. He knew it was only a couple weeks ago, but a part of him was awakened to her. Her body, the way her skirt rode up her leg, the curve of her knee. The smell of her perfume. He tried to focus and couldn't. She turned. He hadn't noticed just how beautiful her eyes were. They were dark, he wasn't sure of the color. Hazel maybe. All he knew was that he couldn't think about houses right now when all he needed was a bedroom.

"Mr. Bennett? I asked you would be willing to buy a house

with just a fenced in pool where you could fence in the yard after purchasing the home?"

She had returned to calling him mister. He thought he had been busted checking her out. He was ashamed of himself for two reasons. First, she was probably only in her mid-twenties, if that. Secondly, he felt he should not be having these lustful thoughts so soon after Cheyenne had died. "Yes, yes. That's fine. The pool is more important than the fence. Yes. Yes, that'd be fine." He was stammering like a high school freshman being asked by the senior cheerleader captain if she could borrow a pencil.

She showed him a few houses, and he looked at them. Then, one of them on the page just called to him. It was smaller than this house by a lot. This was good because it was just him and Austin and he had no plans on bringing in a third person. It had a pool. It also had all hardwood floors, which he loved. One of the few changes he suggested when they bought this house. It had three bedrooms and a converted bed into an office. It was in a different town, about twenty miles away. Allen thought it was perfect. It would fit what Austin wanted, and that was what was most important to him at this time. He felt he could be reasonably happy anywhere. It was Austin he needed to cheer up the most.

With Allen settled on seeing one house, she went into a little more detail. She said it had a new furnace, air conditioning unit, and hot water heater. All the appliances were also included. It was a "turn-key" house. That all you had to do was turn the key, move in your personal belongings, and start living. She said that the only downfall of the property was that the house didn't sit in the middle of the property; it sat almost at one edge. This meant that the neighbor was only about seventy-five feet from the house. Allen said that wouldn't be a problem. It was still three times the distance between him and his neighbor now.

Audrey wanted to look around. She said she wasn't sure if Allen had wanted to sell this house or not but she had done research anyway in order to be prepared. Allen told her to go ahead. He'd be ready to sign any papers as soon as she was done.

When she finished. She had him sign the papers to commit to selling his house. He was eager to go tour the other house. He already felt like it was the place. He knew he'd walk in and love it. He wouldn't even haggle over the price.

She said she could meet him there in about two hours. Allen said that was perfect. They shook hands, and Allen asked if the homeowners could be present during the tour. Audrey said that was unconventional, but would see if they would allow it.

Allen really felt that this was the house. He went upstairs, got a shower, and started to get ready. He thought about calling Austin and seeing if he wanted to go with him. He thought he should have a look at the house too but decided that he would surprise him. Upon leaving earlier Austin had told him that he trusted his judgment. That had made Allen feel better than anything else in the world. He felt that maybe his son was forgiving him and that they could become a lot closer. This could be another positive from this tragedy.

Allen was in high spirits as he dressed. He had a plan, and it would work, he thought. He got in the car. He still had over an hour to get to the house, and it was only half an hour away. He tapped the address into the GPS and drove off. He stopped at the bank because he needed some cash.

The bank took a little longer than he had anticipated, and he arrived a few minutes later than he wanted to. When he pulled into the driveway, he fell in love. The house was much more magnificent in person than on a printed page. It was perfect. He didn't even need a tour. He reached back into the car and grabbed his briefcase.

"Hi, Mr. Bennett, I talked to Mr. and Mrs. Brown, and they agreed to be here while you toured the home."

They went inside, and he greeted the Browns with a hearty smile and a strong handshake.

"This is a lovely, lovely house," he said to them. And without much of a preamble, he put his briefcase on the table and said, "I'll take it!" He opened the case, and there was one hundred seventy-five thousand dollars in cash.

Everyone in the room just gasped.

"Mr. Bennett, I'm sorry. It's a little more complicated than that. We have to sign papers and everything. I don't have anything prepared for a sale. You'll have to keep your money for a few days. Always assuming Mr. and Mrs. Brown accept your offer."

"Why wouldn't they accept it? It's five thousand more than they are asking for the house!"

Mrs. Brown chimed in, "We accept. Get the papers ready, Audrey. We are ready to move. We can be out by the end of next week!"

With that the couple and Allen shook hands. Allen had unofficially just become a new homeowner.

Chapter 7

The Move

As it turned out, Mrs. Brown's proclamation to be out by the end of the next week was a little bit hasty, Allen found out as he listened to Audrey explain, "I'm sorry for the delay. I know you wanted to move right away, but we have to give the current owners time to find a new place. They didn't expect someone to show up with a briefcase full of cash, they expected a long, arduous process with banks and inspections. They agreed to be out by the end of the month, if not sooner. They have a couple properties that they are interested in and are going to view those properties today." Audrey explained. It wasn't that bad, Allen thought, because the end of the month was next week. He just thought he would be done with this whole process by now. He never really thought about it in terms of what other people have to go through with banks and loans and inspections.

Allen was excited when he arrived back home after seeing and offering the money for the house. He was feeling another slight headache coming on; he attributed it to being out in the sun for such a prolonged period after being shut away in his room for most of the past week or so. When he arrived home, he was somewhat disappointed because he didn't see any sign that Austin had come home yet, he went into his room and looked around, but didn't see him. He called around the house. Austin had told him that he would be back by this time. He decided to look in his room, and when he did, Austin was sitting on the bed, looking over at the wedding photo of Allen and Cheyenne.

"Hey kid! There you are. Guess what?! We are going to be moving soon. Hopefully, in the next few days! I found a great house. It's about twenty minutes from here. It has a pool like you requested. No fence, but I already talked to a contractor, and as soon as we sign the papers, we will have him put one up, and then we can go dog hunting! Have you decided what kind of dog you wanted?"

"No, not really. Dad, did you love mom?"

Allen, who had expected a little more enthusiasm from Austin about the house, was taken aback by this question. It was as though he didn't hear anything except the end about the dog. He hesitated, not because he had to think about whether he loved Cheyenne or not, but because the question seemed so random to him.

"I love your mother, still with all my heart. There has never been anyone more important in my life than her and you. Why?"

"How come you never really paid attention to us? You say you love us and are the most important people in your life. It seemed the characters in your books are far more important to you than us. You know this is," he held up the wedding picture, "the only professional picture I've ever seen of you two?"

"I wrote a lot son, so we could be comfortable. I never ever thought the people I made up were more important than you two." Allen dropped to his knees in front of Austin. He didn't try to hug him; it just didn't feel right at this time. "Please understand that. Please! I have lost her. I don't want to lose you!"

Austin seemed to not be paying much attention to what his dad was saying, "If you love her so much, why are you running away from the memory of her? Why do you want to leave this house where we made so many memories? I'm sure there were happy times here."

"I thought you wanted a fresh start? We wanted to be able to heal together. I thought you understood that I don't need a house to remember your mom. She will always be in my heart, and she will always be the finished piece of my soul." Allen was sobbing. He had come here to break the good news to Austin, and now he was crying as hard, if not harder, than he had at any point since Cheyenne died.

"Son, please. I want to remember your mom. This house won't help with that. I need a fresh start. There are too many memories here. Yes, there are good. Very good, in fact. But there are also bad. Every time I look at that phone, I see myself standing there listening to the officer tell me about the accident. I see myself as my world shatters. I see everything collapsing around me."

"Please, let's talk about the new house and what kind of dog we are getting. I don't want to argue with you anymore. I don't want the pain that's eating at us both to tear away the relationship that we have. I know it hasn't been great. Like I said before. I want to work on it and become as close as you and your mom were."

At this point, Allen almost uttered the words he had been pondering the last couple days. Ever since the accusation by Austin that Cheyenne was having an affair because of his own negligence. That she had strayed because he was more in love with his characters and stories than he ever was with her. He had almost told Austin he would quit writing. That he'd retire. He would tell him about the books that are done already. He would just submit those every year for the next few years, and then he'd just tell everyone. "Oops. Sorry. The well ran dry. You know how it goes. Strike while it's hot. So on and so forth. Thanks for the ride. Oh, and he's my forwarding address. Keep sending those checks. They won't be enough to bring back my dead wife, but maybe they'll help me keep my son around." He couldn't do it. He loved his son, but at the same time, he loved himself too. He felt that he needed to do something that would keep him happy for a little while. He was starting to feel the itch again anyway. He found himself thinking of story lines. He found himself thinking of new plots. He had an idea, and he wrote it down. He hoped he could build on it soon. He thought when they moved, he would begin to write again.

He wanted to change the subject. Both in conversation and

in his own mind, "What do you say we go online and look at some breeders around here; see if we can find a dog that we want. Maybe we can get it before we move."

"When are we moving?"

"I'm not sure. I already offered and paid for the house I looked at today. I'm telling you. You're going to love it. The pool has a diving board, slide, and a roof. You will be able to swim anytime you want. The yard is big and flat. It's nestled against a copse of trees. The only problem is that the neighbor's house is nestled against that same copse of trees. But they are kind of thick, so we won't be able to see them much. The houses are a good 50-60 feet apart through the trees. I guess the reason they are so close is that the neighbor's house used to be the guesthouse for this one. When the owners sold it they planted the trees between them to give more privacy."

"Dad, you can go pick out a dog. I'll be happy with anything. I have just always wanted a dog. Just do me a favor and make it a rescue dog. No breeders." He walked past his dad, and halfway down the hall, he turned and said, "Everyone deserves a chance to live."

Audrey had told him not to go home and start packing just yet. She didn't want them to live out of boxes for what could be a month. So instead Allen had decided to start going through things he didn't need. He had only meant to go through his things. He had decided to leave all the furniture except for his office furniture and all the things in Austin's room.

He had at no point even thought about what he was going to do with Cheyenne's things. Some part of his mind just told him she would take care of it. He still hadn't fully grasped the concept that she was dead. It was like a bad dream that you sometimes stumbled upon remembering throughout the day. It was like when he was brushing his teeth, he thought, "Well, at least Cheyenne won't have to worry about this anymore; she always hated doing it anyway." It was small, stupid things like that; these are what reminded him that she was gone. He would do something and tell himself, "At least Cheyenne won't have to worry about that anymore." He didn't know why that was what made her death more real to him than actually seeing her body or even her death certificate. Somehow it did, though.

When he walked into the second closet in the master bedroom, it hit him hard once again. She wasn't here and she wasn't going to go through all these things. She had a lot of stuff. He didn't know what to do with it. He supposed he could call a charity group and donate everything. He'd be their hero because Cheyenne had at least a different outfit for every day of the year. It seemed to him that she never wore the same outfit twice in a short period of time when she went out. When she lounged around the house she would wear the same clothes often. But when she went out with him or her friends, she never ever wore the same thing. Something jarred in his memory. He suddenly remembered the last two times she went out with Anne, she had on the exact same clothes. He wouldn't normally notice this kind of thing, but for some reason, he noticed that night. He thought maybe he was imagining things, but now that he really cast his mind back to that night, it was true. Coincidence, most likely, but he thought it was not.

He pulled himself from that night, the memories were still too fresh, and the wounds were still open. He would have to deal with that eventually, but for now, he needed to decide what to do with all this stuff. He just sat in the closet crying instead. He couldn't deal with this right now, he was going to have to take everything with them, and eventually he may feel like he could get rid of it. For now, though he will just move everything there. Maybe not set it up with everything in his room, but in another bedroom. Make it her room. A place where he could go and feel a piece of her whenever he got too lonely to carry on anymore. He hoped he wouldn't make it into a shrine, but he thought that could happen. He knew it wouldn't be healthy if he did that but sometimes what we know is good for us and what we do are not in agreement.

When he got the call from Audrey, it was a bittersweet day. He knew the day was coming, he knew it when he delivered the blue dress to the funeral home. The day she called and told him he could pick up the keys was the day of his and Cheyenne's fifteenth anniversary. When he didn't sound too excited, Audrey asked, "Everything ok? You were all fired up about moving two weeks ago, and now you seem ho hum about it."

"Yeah, we are excited. In fact, I just watched the movers' driver pull away. They were here boxing everything up that needed to be boxed up and decided how they wanted to do everything. I hadn't expected the call today, but I am happy. It's just tough because today was to be my fifteenth anniversary."

"Oh, I'm so sorry. I didn't know, of course. That's me though, always sticking my foot in my mouth!" Allen could feel the heat from her face because of her embarrassment through the phone.

"It's fine. How would you know? So anyway, on to happy thoughts. When can I get the keys from you?"

"Well, I need you to come sign some papers and everything. You know all the legal documents. The deed and that. And then I hand you the keys. The Browns are completely out of the house. It's ready for you to move in right away."

"Sounds good. I can come in this afternoon and sign away."

"Good. I will have everything ready at 2. Maybe you can bring your son with you; I'd love to meet him."

"Yeah, maybe, I'll see what he's up to. He hasn't wanted to

be around many people since the accident. When the movers came today. They came in the front door he was sneaking out the back. He is just having a hard time adjusting right now. But if he's home before I leave, I'll see if he wants to come or not."

The signing of the papers was easy. Austin hadn't been home yet when Allen left. When Allen got the keys, he had a feeling that everything was going to change. He just hoped it was for the better and not the worse.

He called the movers on his way back and said he'd pay them double if they came back and moved everything today. They agreed. He was starting to feel another one of those nagging headaches he's had recently coming on. He might have to see a doctor. He assumed they were stress, but you were never sure. He was in his mid-40s now. He didn't want to take a chance.

When he got home, he looked around and saw Austin sitting in his room. He had boxes all around him.

"We are moving today!" He dangled the keys and shook them.

"That's great. Dad, can you pick me up at the park after the movers come and move everything? I don't want to be here for that process."

Allen was a little crestfallen, but recovered quickly. He

understood that moving from this house was going to be hard on Austin. He didn't want to be here when it happened.

"Yeah. Sure, no problem."

Chapter 8

The Promise

Allen was a little perplexed, but thought he understood, about why Austin didn't want to be around when the movers were there. He might feel they were leaving his mom behind. He didn't want to ask because he did not want another argument. It was a big day, after all. They had a lot of stuff, a lot. He had decided to take everything except for some pieces of furniture, which included all Cheyenne's things. He knew he was being stupid about it, but he couldn't help it. Having her stuff was almost as good as having her, in some ways at least. He could look at her makeup case and her jewelry box and picture firmly in his mind the way she looked in those things. He could picture her putting on her makeup. The casual way she put it on, not to hide her face, as so many women tend to do, but to enhance the beautifulness of it.

Allen was trying to think about his situation with Austin. He couldn't remember since the funeral whether or not the kid had ever been in his presence when someone else was at the house. He seemed to sense when people were coming over, even if Allen hadn't told him. Earlier in the week, Allen had invited Cheyenne's parents over for dinner. Well, his version of dinner. Where everyone got into a car and drove to a fancy restaurant. He was planning to tell them about the purchase of the new house and the upcoming move. He was about to go tell Austin when the kid was walking out the door, saying he was going to his friend's house.

The dinner went well. Allen was surprised to see that they took it well when he told them about the move. They didn't balk, argue, cry, or raise any kind of question as to Allen's motives. They just said that yes, they understood. It was a relief to Allen because he had been worried about their opinion. Since he had lost his parents at such a young age, he always valued Cheyenne's parent's opinion. If not, their approval. He always felt like they liked him. At first, though he thought they were suspicious of something. Because here he was much older than their daughter and she was head over heels in love with him almost from day one. They seemed to accept that their daughter loved this man. It was even later, he had learned, at her father's urging, that she be the one to propose to him. They were engaged six months from the day they went out that first night and married in another six months. Allen was caught in a whirlwind and loved every minute of it, if this was a dream, he hoped he'd never wake up. But he was awoken with the ringing of the phone. He still cringed every time the phone rang.

At dinner, Cheyenne's parents never mentioned Austin. They seemed to understand the kid better than he did. They understood that he needed time alone. They didn't question it. No one seemed to question it.

Allen picked Austin up at the park just as twilight was approaching. The park would be closing soon. He wondered where Austin would have gone when it closed. He had just left the movers at his house. He told them to set up the bedrooms tonight; the rest could wait. They were going to be able to stay in the new house tonight. He thought that Austin would be excited, it would be the first time he sees the house. The bed sounded the best to Allen, though. As he was driving to the park, he was racked with another excruciating headache. These things were becoming a huge nuisance. It was hard to think when you could feel your heart pulsating in your head.

He saw Austin sitting on a lone stationary swing in the very back of the park. He walked up to him, and the kid seemed to be in his own world. He didn't look up until Allen was within a couple feet of him.

"You ready to see the new house now? I just talked to the movers, and they are going to set up our rooms. They said it shouldn't take more than an hour or so. They called in a few extra people. So we will be sleeping there tonight."

"Do you think anything will change? Will I miss her less there? Will my heart start to heal without seeing everything that reminds me of her?"

Allen sat down on the ground in front of his son, looking up into his eyes. For the first time, he noticed just how tired Austin looked. It looked like he hadn't slept in years. They were the eyes of a careworn kid that just had enough. He wondered if his own face mirrored that of his son, were people looking at him and wondering when the last time he had a good night's sleep occurred. He slept, and he slept a lot. But he would call his sleep shitty at best. On the nights he felt he was just getting into that good sleep, he would dream the phone was ringing and snap awake. That would end the good sleep for that night and usually the next night as well.

"I can't really answer any of those questions. Will things stop reminding you of her? I doubt it. I think we will see your mom in the flowers. In the way, people laugh. In everything we do. We will see her face in strangers. It will make us do a double take. We will catch glimpses of her in reflections in water and mirrors. Songs on the radio will make us think of her. In the mall, the muzak will make us remember how much she hated it. It will make us remember how she talked constantly when she was shopping just so she wouldn't have to hear it. Everything we do every day has the potential to remind us of her. As far as will we start to heal. I can't really answer that either. I don't know that we ever truly heal from tragedies such as this. I think we are eternally left with a gaping hole in our hearts that no matter how much we try we can't fill it back in. Will there be a time when the pain stops? Maybe. Maybe not. I don't think so. I think when we think about her, we will have pain. Pain for two reasons. Pain for our loss. And pain for her because of what could have been. Your mother was a great, great person. Nothing I have learned recently will change that fact in my mind. I will love her forever. I promised her that the day we got married. I don't ever plan on breaking that promise." Allen paused, looked around the park, and assessed the approaching darkness, "What do you say we go get some food and eat at our new house? Tomorrow, we get a dog." This actually brought about a small change in Austin's affect. He brightened a little. Allen was already heading toward the car when Austin caught up with him.

"Dad?"

"Yes?"

"Did you ever want me? I have always gotten the feeling that you never particularly liked kids. You never seemed to be as involved as other dads of my friends. The most I've seen you involved in the decision about my life was when mom wanted to take me out of school and home school me. I think that's the most I ever heard you talk about me."

Allen stopped, turned Austin toward him and knelt down. "Listen to me please; I have loved nothing else on earth more than you and your mother. Nothing matters to me more. If I was ever distant with you then I apologize. Your mom was always more the involved one because she had more time. I was a part of every decision. We endlessly discussed what was best for you. The best way to make you grow into a good man. Never think that I haven't always loved you. I'd give everything for you if I were required."

"Thanks. Just ya know, sometimes you were off in another world."

"Yeah, I know. Come on, let's get some pizza!"

"Ok! I want extra cheese!"

That night, Allen sat staring at the pizza box that once was home to the pizza they had devoured. He was stuffed, far more stuffed than he thought he should have been. It felt like he ate the entire pizza himself. He knew he wasn't going to be able to sleep right away. He hadn't had the movers bring his office stuff tonight because he never thought that he'd be in the mood to work, but as he sat there slowly digesting his pizza, he thought he actually had the urge for the first time in weeks. He had his laptop. He carried it with him everywhere he went. When you made a living by writing down words, you always needed your instruments with you. He felt good, really good, for the first time since the accident. His headache was gone for now, although that pesky bastard didn't seem to have a schedule. It just popped up whenever. He pulled his computer out of his traveling case. Opened it up. It was the first time he'd even had it open in almost a month. He hadn't had a case of writer's block. He just didn't have any desire to write. Partially, it was because of the accusation that Austin had laid on him just after the funeral. He almost felt that if he started to write, he would start to move on. He knew there wasn't a time frame for these things, but at the same time, he felt that not even a couple months was enough.

He read through what he'd written. It was a story about a girl who was kidnapped as a child and held for a long time by a group of guys. They used her for whatever they wanted. The girl had escaped and, when she was a teenager, vowed revenge on her captors. He was almost done. He was just about to get to the climax when the girl was finding and tracking down the head of the group of guys. He was a prominent figure in town, and it wasn't easy to get to him. She was in the process of devising her final plan of revenge.

He started to type. The first couple sentences were tough. He struggled just to make his fingers go. They seemed to remember where the keys were but seemed to have lost their dexterity. He was slow and sluggish. He was getting frustrated with the number of mistakes he was making. His headache was starting to come back again. Eventually, though he got into a groove and really started the fly. He had written for about an hour, and he realized he had written nearly 20 pages. It felt good to be working. He thought he might just write all night and finish this book.

"So that's why you wanted to move. You didn't want to write anymore in that house. You wanted to come here where you could forget her and get back to what you did when you ignored us. I knew it was about that. It wasn't about helping me or a fresh start for us. It was all about you and your stories. You felt guilty writing in that house because you knew that when you were there, you used them to kill my mom!" Austin was sobbing hysterically. He was barely able to speak. Even so, Allen heard every word with crystal clear clarity. He never thought about it like that. But now that he sat here writing. He realized that a vice grip had been loosened, and he had felt free. He hadn't felt any guilt about writing. He hadn't even thought about Cheyenne in the past couple hours while he was working. With this realization, he was flooded with guilt again. He knew that some part of his mind had needed this so he could work. He thought maybe he had lied a little to Austin earlier when he told him that he and Cheyenne were the most important things. He knew now that writing was just as important. It was now after she was dead, and it had been before when she was alive.

"Austin please, I just wanted to finish this book. Then, I was going to take a break. I may even not write again. I have finished books already. I can send them in. I promise. This is the last one. I want to show you how important you are. I will do that by giving up something I love to do. I'll be a full time father. Everything else will be secondary. I realize now how wrong I have been toward you guys. It's my fault. I drove you guys away. Please let me finish this. I'll be done tonight. I promise I'm done after this. I promise." Allen looked at his son with pleading eyes, he just hoped he believed him and would give him that chance for which he was asking.

Chapter 9

The Confrontation 2

"I don't know what to think right now. I want to feel sad, but at the same time, I want to be angry. I want to love you, but I want to hate you too. I want to know your side of the story, but you're in the ground right now." Allen was standing in front of Cheyenne's grave. He felt he needed to talk to his wife. "I keep trying to pretend you're still alive. I brought all your stuff when we moved. And the new house? You're probably wondering why we moved. I thought that being somewhere new would start the healing process. All it's done is start more problems. Create more fights between Austin and I."

Allen was standing here in his sleeping clothes and coat. He had left in a hurry.

He had been sitting in the walk-in closet in his new master bedroom. He had lain in bed for hours and try as he might, sleep just wouldn't come. He tossed and turned, fluffed pillows and punched them. He even took something to help him sleep and he just laid there. He had too much on his mind. He wondered if he did the right thing by moving here. He wondered if it made any sense to move and bring all her stuff with them. He was realizing now that it wasn't the walls and rooms and windows that kept reminding him of her. It was her stuff. He would look at the closet and see a dress and remember her wearing it. He would look at her jewelry box and still remember when she wore certain pieces. He realized now it wasn't the house that reminded him of her, it was himself.

He had the mover set everything up pretty much as it had been before. He couldn't bring himself to get rid of anything of Cheyenne's. He was looking through pictures and boxes of all the things Cheyenne kept. He was rubbing his temples, he couldn't focus. He didn't know how to feel. He had been up all night trying to sort through his feelings. He knew some answers were on the laptop he set up in the room he called Cheyenne's office. He could just go down there and power it on and just read the emails. He had gotten as far as the closet in this venture. He didn't want to do it. It was as though some part of his mind was driving him to go check the computer. He wondered what that sick and twisted part of his mind meant for him to see. Were the emails rich with details? He knew there were a couple of attachments that were sent because he remembered seeing the little paper clip on a couple emails. Especially the last two. He wondered, and it had almost become an obsession, as to what kind of picture he had sent her. He was driven to look at it, and hopefully, he would see his face and not just his genitalia. If he could see his face, maybe he could know who it was and get some answers that way. It seemed like a long shot, but it was possible, he thought.

Unfortunately, or fortunately, who is to say for sure, there was another part of him that fought against this. It knew no good could come from finding the identity of the guy. No good could come from a confrontation. He had held out for over a month now, and had changed things in their lives. Had even gotten a dog as a distraction. None of it worked. He still kept thinking about those emails. He tried to compromise with himself, "One email." He said to himself. Just one. I can confirm the affair. I won't look at one that had the pictures attached. I don't want to see some guy's dick that was inside my beautiful wife. No, he thought to himself, that wouldn't do any good at all.

He got up and walked down the hall. He just sat down at her desk and lifted the lid to the laptop. His vision doubled momentarily, and he had a sharp pain shoot through his head. He stopped unexpectedly. He wondered if this was God's way of telling him he shouldn't be doing this, he decided he didn't care what God's wishes were on this matter. He opened it and pushed the power button, but nothing happened. It seemed the month that had gone by had drained the battery of all its juice. He hunted around for the cord, and was just about to look in the closet when he heard a rustle of clothing behind him. He turned. Austin was staring at him.

"What are you doing up? It's the middle of the night." He asked.

"Couldn't sleep, seems a common ailment tonight. What are

you doing?"

"Looking for the cord to the laptop. Your mom had some pictures and stuff I wanted to look through."

He could see in Austin's eyes that the kid hadn't bought one word of his lie.

He tried to remain casual, "Haven't seen it, have you?"

"No. What do you really want from her computer?" Austin looked at him intently.

"I just told you."

"You're lying. I know you're lying. You're trying to snoop on my dead mother. You think you're going to look through her computer and find something. Find something so you can justify how much you neglected us. So you can say to yourself, 'See, it was her, not me'. Well, you won't find it. I knew you'd eventually want to look at the computer. I got rid of the cord."

"Austin, you have no idea what you're talking about. I just wanted to look for pictures. I wanted to make this room into a memorial of sorts. A place we can come to remember her and look at pictures."

"No, you don't. You're looking for a reason to hate her. You don't care about her or us; you want to make yourself feel better. That's why you brought all her stuff with us. You could have sold it or given it away. But no, you brought it here. This house has turned into an old house. You've had it all set up the exact same way. You want everything to appear different to the outside world while inside you, you want to be reminded of what you feel right now. You want to keep her alive in you, not to remember her and love her, but so you can hate her. You think I didn't realize this? You want to hate her. You don't care about her. You drove her away by ignoring her and now you want to blame her because you're such a failure." Austin stopped. He was glaring at his father, almost daring him to argue.

Allen stood there, he tried not to let the anger he felt register on his face. He felt Austin had the right to have his say, even if he was wrong. He brought her stuff because he couldn't get rid of a piece of her, not yet. He'd lost her body and soul, but he could keep her spirit alive in her belongings. He could always remember her through the things she had and used and owned. That's why he kept everything. Not because he wanted to be reminded about the affair. He was trying to get past that in his mind. He wanted to forgive her. He knew if he just held on to any piece of her he could, then he'd always remember her. Not the end, the last night was by far the worst of any night they had, but the days and years before that when they had been truly happy.

Austin was still talking, his voice raising. "Why did you bring all this stuff, huh? You think this will bring her back?" He picked up a ceramic bowl that he had made her in school. He threw it against the wall. It shattered into a thousand pieces. "You think all this stuff in essentially the same place as the old house is going to make her be here? It won't. You're just an idiot who won't let go. She's gone. Move on. Get rid of the stuff, and she will go too. You won't forget her, but holding onto all this stuff won't bring her back. I need you to get rid of it because it's torturing me to see all this stuff laying around. It's like she's here, and she's using it. And I know she's not here and using it. It's a facade. My mother, your wife, is gone. Having this here isn't making her be here."

Allen wanted to scream and rage at his son as he turned away from him. He wanted to pick up the other bowl that was on the desk and bash him in the head with it. He never knew there were ever two bowls. He didn't care about this question right now. Right now, he wanted the kid to feel some of the pain that he had just inflicted on him. The worst part of all this, is that the kid saw through everything and knew exactly why he'd brought the stuff here. Knew exactly why he'd even been in this room. He left the mess that was made. He didn't care if he ever cleaned it up. He walked down the hall, grabbed his coat and left in his pajamas.

"I want to feel anger at you," he said to the headstone. "I want to hate you. It's your fault I'm in this mess. I want to hate you. I want to hate you. That's all I tell myself. I didn't do anything wrong. I can't shoulder the blame. You knew what I was like. That writing was a major part of my life. If you couldn't accept it why did you marry me, hell why did you ask me? I don't understand why you would do this. I have a broken heart. It's broken in two places. The part of me that loved you and lost you is broken. So is the part that I gave you. You shattered it. You didn't care about what it would do to me if I found out. I don't know what to feel right now. I feel betrayed and angry. But I don't know what causes me to feel more. The fact that you died or the fact that you were having an affair. It's too mixed up in my mind. I just want to love you as I did up until I opened your computer and saw all those received emails. If Anne had just never called, I would have never known anything. I think that would have made me so much happier. I wouldn't feel like I was being ripped into two pieces. I wouldn't have to deal with anything but losing your life, and I wouldn't have to deal with losing your love. As it is, though, I don't know which one hurts more. And you aren't here to explain your side of the story. After the fight with Austin earlier, I don't think I can even bring myself to attempt to look at your computer and read the emails. I don't want to lose him by trying to keep you. I think that's exactly what I'm doing, too. If I could have five more minutes with you then I think everything could be resolved. Unfortunately, that's not how death works. The person we love is gone, and all their words die with them. All that we are left with are questions without answers. And if we do find answers, then what we end up getting is a thousand more questions that can't be answered. No matter how hard we try and how many unanswerable questions we find answers for, we will never understand death, will we? So you will just continue to lie in the ground in a box feeling nothing, and I'll be up here living and breathing, feeling way too goddamn much."

Allen walked back to his car; he didn't feel any different than when he first arrived at the graveyard. Like most of our questions and prayers to God, our questions to the dead shall go unanswered.

Chapter 10
The New Neighbor

Allen didn't feel like he accomplished much while he was at the graveyard. He was hoping to at least sort some things out in his own head, but all he seemed to do was make himself angrier at Cheyenne. She got to be dead, and he was stuck with being alive. He had to feel the world crashing in on him while she just lay there and moldered. He was left behind trying to sort through all his feelings while having one-sided conversations all the time. He felt he was going to go crazy if he continued to try to work through everything this way. He wasn't equipped to handle anything this big in his life, or maybe the apropos phrase is he wasn't ready to handle anything this big in his life. Here he was in his mid-forties, and he wasn't completely sure he'd gotten over his parent's deaths yet. They had been much older, his dad in his late forties when Allen was born, his mom in her late thirties. His dad had a heart attack at fifty-five, and his mom had pancreatic cancer ten years later. Allen had been on his own ever since. He thought if he had such a difficult time with their deaths, which some would deem "of natural causes", then a tragic accident of this magnitude would probably take twice as long to get over, if not longer.

One benefit of Allen's trip to visit his dead wife was that it seemed to alleviate the pain in his head. Something few other remedies had been able to accomplish. He was feeling good as he came home. It was full light now; he had spent several hours at the graveyard without even realizing it. He wondered if Austin would want to try to do something. He felt a father/son bonding activity would be good. The problem was that every time Allen asked Austin to go do something, he always had an excuse not to do it. Since Cheyenne died, they had not done anything together outside of the house except for when they talked in the park the day that they moved.

Austin hadn't even wanted to go pick out their dog. Allen went by himself. This may account for why the dog absolutely loved Allen, and seemed to not pay any attention whatsoever to Austin. He was a cute dog. When Allen went to the shelter to get him he looked at several dogs, but none were all that appealing to him. He then saw a puppy that looked a little bit like a pit bull, but was just as playful and friendly as could be. The shelter worker said that he looked just like a dog that had been wrongfully put down, and they even named him after him, his name was Lennox.

"He's been here for a few months. All the other dogs and pups around him have been adopted out. I would bet we've turned over the dogs in the other cages at least twice and, in some cases, three times. No one seems to want him. We are a no-kill shelter so he will stay here as long as needed. It's sad, though; he's sweet as can be. He has never bitten anyone or even shown any aggression.

People are just judging him by how he looked." said Becky, the shelter worker. "We even knocked the price down a bit for him, hoping he'd find a home."

She opened the cage for Allen and Lennox came bounding out and practically jumped into Allen's arms.

"I think he just found a home."

"Good, that's great!" Becky exclaimed excitedly. "Just step this way, we have to fill out some paperwork, and sadly, I have to ask you some questions before I can let you take the animal, regulations, you know. We don't want to send an animal into a bad situation." Becky said, a little sheepishly.

"I understand. Shouldn't be a problem." Replied Allen.

He filled out the application, and handed it over to her. She gasped at his name, "You aren't THE Allen Bennett, are you? The author?" She began to giggle excitedly.

"Yeah, I've had a few, or ten books published." He said with a sarcastic smirk.

"Oh my God! I can't believe you're here! I love your books! Can I get your autograph, please? Oh my god, I can't believe this!" She raced around, looking for something for Allen to sign. Allen still wasn't used to this aspect of his career. He never thought that someday people would recognize him and actually want him to sign things. It was still kind of overwhelming and a little intimidating to know he could be approached at any time. He had become marginally famous. He wasn't sure he liked that, but he loved to write and have people read what he wrote, so he guessed it was the trade off. He signed a few things for Becky and her family. She said her grandma just absolutely loved him. He left with Lennox in a carrier. The puppy was wonderfully behaved. He hadn't even cried once or anything.

Lennox seemed to learn quickly about where he needed to do his business and did a good job of holding himself. Allen had bought a crate, set it up and used it exactly once for Lennox. He put him in there at night once; the poor guy had looked heart broken. Allen assumed it was because he'd spent so much time in a cage at the shelter. The next night, Lennox slept on the floor beside his bed. That's where he usually slept. He was either there or in the master bathroom behind the toilet.

When Allen got home a few nights later,his first instinct was to yell for Austin, which he did and there was no answer. They had a lot of woods behind their house now and Austin had taken to spending most of his time in them. Allen had no idea as to what he did, but it couldn't be too bad because when he did see the kid again he seemed no worse for wear. He was never dirty or disheveled like you'd expect a teenage boy in the woods to be.

He was hoping to catch a nap because he had hardly slept at all in the last couple nights. But as he walked into the house Lennox had come running to the door. He seemed to need to go to the bathroom. Allen couldn't understand why Austin never would take the poor dog out to the bathroom. He wanted the dog, but didn't seem to want to care for him. Allen wondered if it was jealousy because Lennox had immediately taken to him, rather than Austin. Whatever the case was, the pup had to go, and the frantic pee dance he was doing told him he had to go now!

Allen got his leash and hooked him up. He really hated to do this; he had been contemplating the shock fence collar, but couldn't get over the fact that it seemed kind of cruel. He hadn't gotten around to having the people install the fence yet; he had been struck with a case of laziness in that. He wanted the fence, but at the same time, he loved the open feel of the front yard. The gentle slope down to the road. So he hooked up the leash with the extendable string. He wanted that because he thought it would be awkward for him if someone were five feet away while he was trying to take a dump. He didn't want his dog to have the issue.

Lennox usually liked to go over into the copse of trees next to the house and do his business. Today, however, he was pulling Allen toward the road. There was a lot of commotion as there were a couple moving trucks parked in the driveway across the street. Allen had noticed the house was for sale when he moved in. He wouldn't have liked it because it was kind of small with very little yard. He had by far the biggest land piece around. He guessed, and had it confirmed, that his house was once the only house around, but over the last seventy-five years or so, the family that owned it, the Browns and Mr. Brown's parents, had sold it piece by piece until there was just what Allen had purchased which was more than enough for him and Austin.

He let Lennox pull him close to the road. He noticed they weren't using a moving crew that they had driven their own uHauls to move. So far as he could tell, there were three of them, mom, dad and what looked to be a late teens daughter.

Lennox, always the people person, was barking crazily at them. Allen, who was just curious, was hoping not to be noticed, but of course, he was. They waved, and he waved back. He felt obligated to go over and introduce himself. He crossed the street, shortening the leash as he went.

"Hi there, I'm Allen Bennett. I just moved in myself a short time ago." Allen wanted to say how long, but for the life of him at that moment, he couldn't remember how long he'd been here.

"Hi," said the man, "I'm Wes Steele, this is my wife Emma and that over there is our daughter Tara. Tara, come over here and say hello to Mr. Bennett. She turned around, and Allen was stunned, he knew she had been late teens just judging by her height from across the street, she had her back turned to him then. Now, as he looked her in the face, he felt he was looking at perfection. Her hair was a dark blonde, almost brown color, and she had the lightest blue eyes he had ever seen. She was stunning looking. Allen was momentarily speechless as she approached. He couldn't see her body because she had on a heavy coat because of the cold, Allen had a feeling he was very fortunate he couldn't see her fully at that time.

"Hi, Mr. Bennett." She stuck out her hand and shook Allen's. He felt something when she touched him, but maybe it was his imagination. Or maybe it was the old pervert that they say is in every man, but he was instantly attracted to her, and he wanted her. At that moment, he had forgotten his wife was dead, his son was distant or even that he had a son. All he knew was he wanted her, but he knew he couldn't have her. "That's a really cute dog!" She leaned down to pet Lennox, showing no fear that people had labeled these kinds of dogs as dangerous. "What's his name?" She asked, looking up at Allen.

"L-Lennox." Allen stammered a little bit as he replied.

They made small talk, and Allen was somewhat relieved to learn that they hadn't heard about him or his wife dying. Allen excused himself and wished them well with their move. He wondered if Tara had felt anything when they touched. He didn't think she did because she didn't change her expression or anything.

He had to be imagining it, he was tired, and his mind was playing tricks on him. That had to be the case, no girl that age and that beautiful would ever want him. He needed a nap. That's what he needed. He and Lennox got back to the house, and he got a cold drink, he didn't plan on driving, and who cares if it was 10 am, he got a whiskey and coke. He downed in a couple swallows. He didn't know why he was feeling this way, but this girl affected him in a way no one ever had. Not even his wife. He had loved Cheyenne and still did. He had never in his life been overcome with lust the way he just was, he needed to calm down before he did something stupid. He wasn't even sure she was eighteen anyway. He was just going to have to avoid them at all costs, be a friendly neighbor and wave and be polite, but no more contact.

Before he even realized it, Allen was getting into the shower, little Al was wide-awake at the moment. He turned the water on full cold and got in. It had the effect he hoped. He then finished his shower and decided to take a nap. Austin still wasn't home yet, and he was bone tired. He went to lie down, and he was asleep before his head touched the pillow.

It seemed like he'd been asleep for ten minutes when he heard the doorbell. He felt heavy and disoriented as he tried to climb his way out of sleep. The doorbell rang again. He wondered what could be so important. He stumbled to the front door and opened it. Standing there was Tara, "My parents went to the store, and I'm supposed to be unpacking, let's make this quick." She was wearing a full-length coat; she most definitely didn't have one earlier. She opened it and let it fall to the floor as she shut the door behind her, pushed Allen against the wall behind him and started to kiss him passionately. Allen was right to be glad he couldn't see her body, it was, if nothing else, more gorgeous than her face. He felt himself get hard immediately. He was always shy when it came to sex with Cheyenne; she almost always had to initiate it because of his lack of self-confidence. Here however, he took control. He pushed her backward against the other wall and kissed her and feeling her body, little Al was becoming bigger Al; she was fumbling with his pants, trying to free him. She pulled it out through the zipper, and Allen moaned into her mouth as she stroked it gently a few times. They never broke the kiss. Allen was feeling the pleasure of her caress in his stomach. He tried to pull away, tried to keep it from happening when it happened. He arched his body back and let out a scream that was a mixture of pleasure and guilt as he came against her stomach. She laughed and said "We will do better the next time," kissed him and walked back out the door. Allen stumbled back to the couch and seemed to fall back asleep immediately.

The phone was ringing. It seemed far off; he came out of his sleep. Stumbling over himself. He was in his bed again. He didn't remember walking back here after Tara had left. He barely remembered anything. The phone was still ringing. He stood up and looked down. He was wearing athletic shorts. Nothing with a zipper. Allen now wondered if he had dreamed the entire thing. He had no idea as he went to answer the phone.

Chapter 11

The Publisher

Allen stumbled around the room; he hadn't yet had a landline put in, although he knew he'd need one eventually for faxes, if nothing else. He was looking for his cell phone, and couldn't find it. He knew it was about to change over to voicemail. He had no idea how many times it had rung before he woke up. He was a notoriously light sleeper. Cheyenne used to complain all the time because she said he woke up every time she farted in her sleep. He finally found it, but it had stopped ringing. He waited for the voicemail to show up so he could listen to it. He checked the missed calls and saw that it was his publisher, Jessie Anderson, who had called. He had no idea what he would have wanted; he only called to give dates for publication. It took a long time for the icon to show up, which means he must have left a hell of a long voicemail. He saw the icon pop up and say voicemail. He tapped it and listened.

"Hi, uh, Allen, shit, I'm never good at these things, that's why it took so long for me to call. Umm. I'm sorry to hear about what happened. It's a damn tragedy. No one knows better than you. I, uh, don't want to seem, uh, insensitive or anything. But uh, I was wondering when we were, uh, going to get that next best seller? You know we are a small outfit here. We don't have anyone bigger than you. And without you, I'm not sure we even exist. I don't want to push you back when and if you're not ready. But you know we count on you. I talked to Gene and Bob recently, and they were both convinced that you were almost finished with your newest book. Even was almost done when the accident happened. If you could get that finished or do what you need to do, we will take care of the rest as usual. So whenever you get this, give me a call back. Again, I'm sorry about what happened. Life's a bitch sometimes." He ended the voicemail without saying bye or anything. To Allen, he seemed almost relieved to have gotten voicemail rather than actually talking to Allen, but had seemed unsure what to say when Allen didn't answer the phone.

Allen sat down with his cell phone. He sat on the bed and looked around for the pants he had on earlier. He saw them tossed on the floor beside the bed, he was very neat. He had to have just tossed them aside when he was half asleep and changed. He thought he'd figured that much out. Now, to figure out if Tara had actually come over or not. He didn't think there was any way he could do that. He pulled down his shorts and underwear, everything looked normal down there. Nothing to give him evidence one-way or the other. He knew he couldn't simply ask her. He figured if it had really happened, she would be bold enough to make another move. She had to have known he was half out of it when she came over. He hoped his dream was real. What man, no matter what age, wouldn't want a young woman like that attracted to him? Of course, and this happened many times before, she might be more attracted to his fame and fortune more so than him, but he was smart and could handle dealing with that. Out loud to himself, he said, "Never know though. She might actually like me." Which he thought was entirely possible because she didn't give much of an inkling that she had heard of him before today.

Allen pulled his mind back, with great difficulty. He needed to decide what to do with the message he'd just listened to. He had told Austin he wasn't going to write anymore, but he thought he could finish the current book he was working on and then be done. Call it quits. He'd sit Austin down and tell him he had books stored up that he'd send in over the next few years. Then, when those were done, he would be done. He'd miss writing, of course, other than Cheyenne, it was his greatest love. He would never, and it would never do anyone any good to admit he felt he actually loved writing more than Austin. He had had a good career. He has written 10 books over the last fifteen years that were published. Seven of them had been big sellers. He hated the term best sellers; he just called them big sellers. He thought best implied they were the best books around, he knew his books were good, and he had a good fan base, but they weren't going to exactly change the world. He had at least half that amount saved on his computer and also sent it to four different email addresses as a backup in case he was ever hacked or had something happen to his hard drive. He would have to do minimal work on the books he'd completed, he thought. Just some rewrite work, some editing and so on. He thought Austin would accept this because this kind of work only took him a couple hours a day, not the 10-12 hour days he sometimes put into his writing.

He went to Austin's room to explain his plan to him. He hoped he'd be here for once. He was rarely here. Allen was beginning to wonder if the kid wasn't missing the old place and biking the fifteen or so miles back there. He hadn't put it up for sale yet. He didn't know why he hadn't. He just felt like if he did, he was selling off memories. He couldn't do that just yet. He knew Austin had a key still to the other place, he felt that as long as he was safe, he was ok with him transitioning slowly to the new house.

Before Allen could even walk toward Austin's room, the phone started to ring again. He hesitated to go pick it up. He hated the phone. It seemed like there were very few good things to come out of it. He almost wished he had lived a couple hundred years ago when bad news traveled slowly. He looked at the caller ID again, and again saw that it was Jessie Anderson calling.

"Hello." Allen said after he slid the answer bar to the right.

"Allen! Hey, I was hoping to catch you this time." Allen wasn't sure if that was true or not. He didn't have time to decipher it much as he heard another phone ringing in the bedroom. He had no idea whose phone it was and why it would be ringing. He only had one cell phone, and it was in his hand. He didn't give the mystery a lot of thought because Jessie was still talking.

"Voicemail before. I didn't want to come across as being an asshole or anything. I just have people here with jobs that are counting on you. You're our big ticket. Any way. I wanted to apologize in person for sounding as if I'm pushing you back when I know you need to take time to heal. These things take awhile, I'm sure."

"Yeah, Jess, look, I have almost finished with something. I just have to put on some finishing touches, and then I'll send it to you. Then I have..." He wanted to say he had to talk to Austin about the rest of the books, but couldn't mention him for some reason. He didn't want his son dragged into his work. At least, that's what he thought then. "Then I think I need to take a break. I'm sorry. It may or may not be a permanent break. I do have a couple things almost finished. Maybe in a year or two, I'll feel like getting back to it, but for now, I just need a break."

"That's understandable, Allen, after such a heartbreaking and tragic situation, anyone would need a break." Jess said, but it sounded like he wanted to argue with Allen. He sounded disappointed.

"Thanks for understanding Jess. Bye now." Allen hung up. He didn't think much had been accomplished with that brief conversation, but he didn't care. Jessie seemed to be appeased. The more important mystery to him right now was the other phone in the room.

He had thought he'd heard it on a couple other occasions but couldn't be completely sure. It was a very soft ring, as though the ring volume was turned all the way down. He was looking everywhere. The drawers, the desk. Under the bed even. He was about to give up when he saw a phone on the floor behind the nightstand. He reached around and grabbed it. He knew immediately that it was Cheyenne's. He looked at it and saw there were more than twenty missed calls. He also saw the little battery icon flashing at the top. Which meant the battery was about to die. He wondered who'd called Cheyenne in the last few days so many times. He had gotten the phone from the police a few days before. They wanted to see if she had been texting or on the phone while she was driving, Allen, who knew his wife never did either, said it was fine. They told him when they returned the phone that she hadn't made or received a call within two hours of the accident. The last text message was actually to him, asking to pick up some take out because she wasn't going to have time to cook before she left.

He opened it up; it was an old flip phone. Cheyenne wasn't the technology junkie he was. They guessed Austin got that from him, one of the few things he seemed to get from his dad. He pressed the button marked menu; he'd forgotten just how archaic it felt to use a cell phone like this. He was not all that surprised to see that all the missed calls were from "Roger". He didn't leave any voicemails, though. Allen screamed. He thought he was finally in the process of putting this part of the tragedy behind him a little bit, but here it was on his dead wife's cell phone. She had given this guy her number, and he'd called ten plus times in a few days. The cops hadn't said anything about missed calls. Allen was overcome with a fit of rage and bent the phone back, snapping it in two. He then threw the two pieces across the room.

Immediately after he had done that, he regretted it. He should have looked at her contact list and gotten the fuckers number. If he had talked to him maybe he could sort things out. Find out what exactly was going on with them. Allen said to himself, "Are you a fucking retard Allen? She was fucking him. That's all you need to know. You want to know how many times? What positions they fucked in? Locations? Do you really want to know any of the details?" Sadly, Allen thought yes, knowing all the details might actually help. He'd either forgive her and go back to loving her memory or hate her and try to forget her. He knew there was still hope to find out all he wanted to know. It was on a laptop down the hall. He got up and walked toward it. He was just about to walk into the room when he stopped. He wanted to talk to Austin. If he catches him in here, there will most likely be another huge fight. Allen didn't have the strength for that. He looked around. Listened to see if

Austin was here, he couldn't hear anything. and walked down and knocked on the kid's door. No answer. He opened it. He peered inside. Nowhere around. Good. He went back to the room he called his wife's office. He opened the door at the same time the doorbell rang. He inexplicably thought Austin had rigged an alarm on the door. He shut it quickly and just stood there. Austin was smart enough to do it, he knew that. Before he could decide if he wanted to try it again or not, there was a knock on the door. That seemed to decide it for Allen, no alarm. Just a coincidence that both happened at the exact same time.

He went to the door; it was getting close to dark. He had no idea who would be here at this time. He opened the door.

"Hi! I didn't wake you, did I?" Tara was standing there looking at him in a waist length coat. It could not have been more different than the one he had dreamed about. He was almost convinced it had been a dream now.

"No, I was awake. Just upstairs looking through some stuff."

"Oh good, I was worried that I did. I just wanted to bring this little guy back," she tugged a leash, and Lennox came into view, "he was over our house sitting on the porch barking like crazy. He must have scented our dogs and wanted to play."

Allen couldn't help but look at her; he wished the dream was real. He felt he needed a woman's touch even if she was barely a woman. Although underneath those clothes, she had been more than enough woman for him to be able to handle.

"He's a good dog." Allen heard himself say. He wasn't this close when he was awake and talked to Tara. He was absolutely mesmerized by her beauty. Cheyenne was gorgeous beyond words, and this girl was in that same class. In a dream like state, Allen bent down to unhook Lennox, "Bad boy running away from home like that! How'd you even get out?" He then looked up at Tara, "When I laid down for a nap, he was in. I know he was." The confusion must have shown on his face because Tara started.

"He must have gotten out when I was here earlier; don't you remember me coming over? I knew you seemed a little out of it, but I thought for sure you'd at least remember!" Tara sounded hurt; she seemed to think she wasn't worth remembering. "I'm sorry I interrupted your sleep. I'll just go home now."

"No, Tara, wait!" Allen almost shouted in desperation. "Believe me when I say you'd never be forgotten by me. I just didn't know for sure. I haven't been sleeping well lately. I was in a heavy sleep when you came by, and everything happened so fast. I didn't know what to think. Because the next thing I know, I'm back in my bed in different clothes. I felt like it had to be a dream because I didn't think anyone as absolutely stunningly beautiful and as young as you would ever be interested in someone like me!"

"Of course I'm interested! You're soooo sexy!" She leaned forward and kissed him on the lips, brief but firm and confidently. She bent and patted Lennox on the head, "You be a good boy and take care of him."

She turned and walked out the door. Allen watched her go, about halfway across the yard; she turned and waved to him. It was this, not the kiss or the admission about what happened earlier, that confirmed that he was indeed awake before, just as he was now.

Chapter 12
The First Date

Allen closed the door slowly. He felt fourteen again. He was crushing on a girl. The only difference was that the girl seemed crushing on him, too. He wondered briefly what her motivations might be. Is she after his money? Revenge against her parents? Was there some other mundane aspect of her life out of joint? At this point, he wasn't sure he cared. If she wanted money, he had plenty of it, he was just happy to be feeling something besides despair for once. He didn't think she was angling to be a trophy wife. Because, again, she didn't mention his fame. He thought she didn't read much, or at least not his genre. He was actually smiling, and not a small one, either. He'd classify this more as a toothy grin.

He went to the couch and sat down when Lennox jumped up on him. He was just thinking how he was going to talk to Tara when Lennox answered the question for him, because tucked underneath his collar was a small folded scrap of paper. He took it out from under the dog's collar and then hesitated. He wasn't sure what the note could say. He flashed back to his senior year of high school. He had liked a girl named Tonya for years. He had mowed grass for her neighbor and had started talking to her and her sisters when he took breaks. He had always been taken by the middle one; she was a year or two younger, but that was just fine with him. He remembered he wanted to ask her to homecoming his senior year, but he knew she was always dating a loser boyfriend, and he couldn't ever get her away from him. They broke up a few days before homecoming. She had already had a dress and everything. She knew Allen didn't have a date because he never did. So she asked him to take her. He gladly accepted because he thought this was his big chance to show her how happy they could be if just given a chance. He went out and bought all new clothes and reserved an expensive restaurant for them to eat at. He wanted it to be perfect. And it was perfect. The girl, she was perfect. She looked amazing in her dress. The meal was fantastic. The dance was great, too, until the ex-boyfriend showed up and said he'd seen the error of his ways. They then spent the rest of the night dancing and having fun while Allen sat at a table and watched with his heart somewhere near his shoes. She came up to him at the end of the dance and asked if he would take her home because if her mom had seen her returning with her ex, she would have a fight, and she didn't want to have a fight. Allen being the soft-hearted sucker that he was, had agreed with her. He even thanked her for a lovely time.

He wasn't able to drive all the way home because he couldn't see through the shield of tears that had developed over his eyes. He pulled over about a quarter mile from their house and cried as hard as any time he had in his life up until that time or since. The next day, they had school, and she handed him a note in the hall. His heart started racing. He hurried to his next class, but couldn't pay any attention because he didn't want to read the note in class. He was sure it would say that she had been wrong and that she was ready to give him a chance. It did say she was sorry, but he was not to be given a chance. She was just sorry about how she acted. It seemed the ex was to be given his chance. Allen was glad he had waited until he got to his car to read the note, because the tears flooded down again. To this day, it was a heartbreak he had never completely healed from, but how many of us ever truly healed from our first real love and that first real heartbreak?

Ever since that happened, whenever Allen was handed a note, he couldn't help but think when he expected it to be good that it would turn out to be excruciatingly humiliating and painful. He took a deep breath and unfolded the note. It was short and was a number. He didn't suspect anything that had a number included could be bad. He read the note. "Here's my number. 202-555-7575. Text me so I have yours. P.S. I'm not as young as I look. I'm 24!" The low self-esteem monster poked his ugly head up at this point and told Allen it was most likely not her real number, and that it was just an elaborate joke.

Allen was glad that he opened the note anyway. He immediately went and grabbed his phone. He didn't know the etiquette these days, but he didn't care. He was going to make contact right away. He tapped in her number, wondering again if it was her real number. "Only one way to find out." He said out loud to himself. He typed out a brief message. He hit send. Again, he felt like a teenage boy. He was so nervous his hands had turned cold. He didn't have to wait long to find out about the number. It was a matter of seconds. Allen could picture her sitting in her room across the road, all her stuff spread around her, most of it still in boxes, just waiting for him to find her number and message her.

They texted for a while then Tara said she needed to get stuff done before her dad blew the roof off. Allen did have enough time, and courage to ask about the age difference. He knew a lot of people would question it, not that he cared about most people. Who he did care about was her dad. Even though he was older by a few years, he didn't want to disrespect anyone with his actions. Tara had assured him her happiness was the most important thing to her dad and that she had dated older men before, and he had no issues. This relieved Allen more than he would have admitted. Although he still planned to talk to him before anything could go any further. They planned to go to dinner the next evening. She said Allen could show her around town.

Allen was nervous. Much more nervous than he had been when he took Cheyenne out for the first time. He didn't have time to get nervous then because he hadn't expected her to be waiting for him after his shift. She had been, and as they say, the rest is history. He was nervous because he hadn't been on a date in a long time, and besides that, he hadn't been on many dates in his life. He wasn't exactly a pro at it.

He was also nervous because he wasn't sure if or when he should tell Austin. Maybe he should wait and see if anything develops between him and Tara. Right now, they were just going out for dinner. They weren't even going to go to a movie.

Another reason he was nervous was because he wondered what other people would think, not about Tara's age. He didn't care about anyone but her parents' opinions on that matter. But he wondered what people would think about him dating so soon after Cheyenne's death, namely his and Cheyenne's family. If he told them the secret that he had, they might be a little softer on him, but then again, maybe not. Ultimately, it didn't matter if they didn't hit it off. If they didn't, then no harm, no foul. If they did, he'd just have to say he needed to move on at some point.

He heard movement from behind him and saw Austin walking into the living room. The kid looked relatively happy for the first time since the accident.

"What's up, where have you been?" Allen asked.

"Oh, just walking in the woods. I enjoy it out there. It's quiet." he replied.

"You look to be in a better mood. I don't think I've seen you smile in a few months."

"Yeah, it's been a good day. Say, Dad, you want to go out there with me tomorrow? I can show you where I go. It's so peaceful. It's beautiful. I think mom would have loved it there."

"Yeah, I can do that. No problem. Listen Austin, I wanted to talk to you about something." Allen could feel another brain-busting headache coming on. Seemed to be this time of day it happened. "I know you don't want me writing anymore, but I'm almost done with the book I was writing when the accident happened. Would you mind if I finished it? I could probably do it in a couple hours and then send it off to have them look it over. Then, after that, I want you to know I've written several other complete books that I'll just send in when they need something from me. Then, when all of that is done, I'll just be done. This way, they are getting what they want, which is more Allen Bennett specials, and you and I have all the free time we need to walk into the woods and have fun together. So what do you think? Is that a deal?" Allen looked at his son and realized he couldn't predict his answer. He didn't know his son at all anymore.

"Yeah, as long as you don't write anything new except the one you're going to finish." Austin answered after a few seconds of thinking about it.

"Good. It's a deal then. Hey, I'm gonna go lay down. I have

a killer headache. We will talk about everything after I wake up and finish the other book." Allen said, hoping to keep the relief out of his voice.

"Okay, Dad. Dad?"

"Yeah, Austin?"

"I love you."

"Love you too, son."

Allen went to lie down; he didn't fall immediately into sleep, though. He was wondering if he should have told Austin about Tara. A part of him said yes, and a bigger part said he shouldn't. He didn't like to keep things from Austin now, especially since he had made a promise about not writing and he talked to him about finishing his book. It almost seemed like he had just gained his trust a little and was immediately going to abuse that trust.

The next day, Allen sent off in an email the finished product of his latest book to his agent, editor, and publisher. He told them in the email he was stepping back from the revising process. He trusted them all with it; afterward, he and Austin took a walk into the woods. They walked for a long time; it seemed at least an hour. They didn't talk much while they were walking. They both seemed to have a lot on their minds. Allen found thinking difficult as he had woken up with another headache; they were starting to concern him.

Allen though was just about to say something, because he felt like Austin was lost or something when the screen of trees opened up on a clearing. There was a babbling brook in the middle of it, and on the far side, which could be accessed by what had to be cleverly placed stepping stones, was an enormous flat rock. It was toward this rock that Austin now headed. It was in the sun right now and Allen had an idea that if someone were to sit on it as the sun faded away, it would still hold the heat for hours after. This explained to Allen why Austin could stay out here for hours; even after the sun had started to set. They approached the rock; Allen placed his hand on it and was not surprised to feel the immediate warmth. Austin climbed up on it and sat down. Allen followed. Allen thought the kid was right. This area was beautiful and peaceful. The brook calmed you down. The arrangement of the trees made you feel protected. And the openness made you feel free. Austin broke the long silence, "This is where I go. Nice, huh?"

"Yeah, it's phenomenal!" Allen exclaimed.

They sat there in companionable silence for a long while. They both seemed content with their lives. They didn't need to discuss accidents, moms, books, or new girlfriends. They were at peace with life and each other in the time they sat atop that rock.

They sat there for a couple hours. Few words of consequence passed between them. Allen laid back and relaxed. The warmth from the rock relaxed his body, and he dozed. Deeper and deeper until it became deep sleep. He slept that way for a couple hours. When he awoke, both Austin and his headache were gone. He was happy about one, disappointed about the other. He vaguely remembered a dream that Austin woke him up and told him he was heading back to the house to get something to eat. Allen had acknowledged him and then went back to sleep. Allen wasn't concerned about Austin, he just wondered if he could find his way home.

It turned out that he had no issues and walked straight to the house without issue. It was getting close to time to pick up Tara. He had time to take a shower and get ready. He felt really good. Austin's secret place had been extremely refreshing.

When Allen knocked on the door to Steele's house a little more than an hour later, it was Wes who had answered the door. Tara had left him a text while he was gone that her dad wanted to talk before they went out.

"Come in, Allen, sit down." Wes said.

"Thank you," Allen replied

"First off, Tara told me that you two are going out tonight; now, I don't have a problem with that. She has said many times over the last couple days that she thought you were a handsome man. I just wanted to say to you that please be careful with her. She's coming out of something bad, as are you, with your wife passing.

She's a good girl. Just be careful with her, please." Allen wondered how this man knew, he didn't think that he had mentioned anything about Cheyenne to Tara.

The sincerity in the man's voice and eyes caught Allen off guard. He had been expecting, and maybe this was his lack of self-confidence speaking, to be reprimanded for taking out a girl half his age on a dinner date. However, the man was simply telling Allen don't break my daughter's heart. Allen had no intention of doing so; he hoped Tara had the same feelings.

They ate at one of the nicer restaurants in the area. Allen was extremely nervous again now. He didn't know what to expect out of this evening. With her coming over with just a long coat on and then giving him a hand job, he wondered if she was going to make good on her promise "we will do better next time" tonight. Allen really hoped not. He was not that kind of guy; yesterday, she had caught him off guard and half asleep, or he wouldn't have let that happen (at least that's what he told himself here and now, with her fully clothed with a table between them). He knew she would have to make the first move. He was extremely sexually shy. Not that he'd ever tell anyone, hell he'd never even told Cheyenne; she was his first and only partner. Cheyenne had always been the one to almost always initiate sex. On the rare occasion that he did, he always felt ridiculous and that she was definitely going to reject him, which she never did. However, he hoped if she did make the first move, he'd be able to let her gently. He liked her, he knew that. He hoped his loins would keep their peace tonight. They made small talk, nothing deep or interesting. They both seemed to want to stay away from the hurtful areas of past relationships.

Everything was good that night. When they left the restaurant and went home, she didn't object when he pulled into her driveway rather than into his. He walked her to the door. Again, he felt absurdly like a teenager. He hugged her and said goodnight. He wanted to do more. His lust for her was becoming overwhelming. He didn't give in, though. He walked away, and got in his car and drove across the road to his house.

Once he was inside, it was nearing eleven. He went to his room. He was happy. He had a good time and, at the very least, felt that he had made a new friend. He hoped it would go to more than that. He had time to get it there. Right now though, he was battling something internal. It wasn't the lust anymore, which had been quelled by the coolness of the night air as he walked into the house from the car. No, he was battling with himself. He was trying to figure out what was more important. His happiness or a promise made to his son.

Chapter 13

The New Book

Allen went to bed happy. He thought his date had gone well. This was confirmed by the fact that he received a text message from Tara about forty-five minutes after he got home. It was simple, but sweet. "Thanks 4 a gr8 time 2nite. Hope 2 do it again soon! XOXOXO<3." Allen knew enough about texting shorthand to decipher what it said. He was most happy about the idea of doing it again soon. He did get a little pang of guilt, though, as though Cheyenne was trying to remind him that he was married. He wasn't, though. He was a widow. His wife was dead, and aside from that big fact, she had been unfaithful to him.

Allen was struggling more so with the other idea he had as he came home. He wanted to write. He was happy when he wrote. He thought that maybe it was unfair of Austin to accept his promise not to write anymore. He hadn't really thought it through all that much, had promised rashly. Now, he could pay for that rashness with his happiness if he decided to abide by the promise. He thought that he could be a little sneaky with it, though. He could just write at night, or when he knew Austin was out in the woods. That'd make it easy for him. The kid was gone a lot of the day, so he'd have plenty of time to write. He thought he had a good idea for a book, too, and didn't want to let it go. His idea was sort of similar to his situation.

A guy loses his wife in some way. He hadn't decided how she died. Maybe just use his entire situation. She dies in an accident, and then he finds out she was cheating on him, and not just with one guy. She was cheating with many guys. He basically finds out his wife is a prostitute. As he discovers the identity of each of the guys she screwed around him with, he kills them. He thought that five or six guys would be sufficient for the grieving husband to kill. He hadn't quite worked out all the details after that. About where the story was going to go. How the guy would get caught, and what would happen? He thought about giving the guy a kid, but decided against it. He just wanted to make it a little simpler. Right now, though, he needed to get some sleep. He'd work out the details later. They would come to him; they always did.

He fell asleep feeling the best he had for months. However, he started awake, sitting bolt upright in bed. He had come home, thought about everything with his new book, and even a little, at least at first, about his date. He hadn't even thought about Austin. He didn't know if the kid was home or not. He didn't check to see if he left a note, or sent him a text or anything. He had gone off into his own world like he did all the time when Cheyenne was alive. He told himself he was going to have to do better. He could spend a little time a day in that world, but he could not, absolutely could not spend all day inside his own head. He needed to be there for Austin. He had to be responsible. He knew it was going to be tough to balance everything. He thought it would take him a long time to write this book, because he was going to have to be a little more subdued about writing it than he ever had before. There was no Cheyenne around to keep an eye on the kid. He didn't feel comfortable asking Tara to hang around and keep an eye on him. He'd just have to figure out how he could do everything himself.

He tried to get some sleep, he laid there and tossed and turned for what seemed like hours. He kept looking at the clock, and began to wonder if it was broken. It seemed to move at a snail's pace. He couldn't get his mind to shut off, which wasn't a new situation for him because he hadn't been able to shut his mind off for months now. This was different, though, because he was thinking about positive things. A new girl and a new book. His son seemed secondary in his mind. He realized how bad of a father that made him, but he just couldn't change overnight.

Finally, he gave up and went down the hall to his office and got his laptop. He opened it up and brought up the document-making program and tapped the keys to make a good working title, "The Prostitutes Unknowing Husband." He didn't think that it'd be the ultimate title, but it gave it a feel of the truth and kept him online and focused on what the story was about. He worked a couple hours into the night. He thought that he loved being a writer for so many reasons he couldn't ever properly explain them all, but the two biggest were he could work on his time, and he got to do something he absolutely loved.

He wrote about ten pages or so that night. He always worked slowly at the beginning as he was working out some minor details, such as character names, descriptions, and occupations. He always wanted to know a lot about his own characters, so he would work out family trees and a lot more details than he'd ever need in his book. He had a very detailed analysis of his books. He thought it was something good to do, if only for himself, because he thought that he was prepared to write sequels if the desire ever occurred to him. So far he hadn't reused any characters in any of his books. He didn't think any of his ideas went deep enough to write a series of books. He was good for about three to four hundred pages per story, and that was about it.

When he finally rested his head on the pillow. He did so with a satisfied mind. The finishing of the book he was working on when his wife died hadn't given him the satisfaction that this was giving him. Writing was his therapy. Austin had that big, flat, warm rock. Allen had a keyboard, a blank screen, and his imagination. The guilt he felt earlier about betraying his promise to Austin just melted away as the story flowed from him. He loved to write and tell a story. But he loved to hear the story just as much. He always has been that way. He would make up scenarios for just about everything in his life. Times when he would be a hero or get that high-paying job. He would make everything work out perfectly, and everyone was happy. This brought a chuckle to him because the actual books he decided to write down were nothing like this. They were usually full of hatred, murder, mystery, and few people ever ended up happy.

He slept in for the first time in a very long time. Probably would have slept longer except for, once again, the phone ringing and waking him up. He would have to say he was sick of this happening. That was his initial thought, but then he woke up a little more as the ring continued, and he thought that it was probably Tara calling him. Although she hadn't yet, like they always say, there's a first time for everything. He fumbled for the phone and saw that it wasn't Tara. It was an unknown number. As a general rule, he never answered these. Today however, he felt that it was going to be ok because he was still feeling the euphoria of his date and the fact he started a new book. So he picked up the phone and slid the button to answer it.

"Hello." He said

"You fucking touch her, old man, I'll fucking kill you. Do you fucking understand me? That's my fucking wife you're fucking around with. I saw you two last night. I followed your every movement. I'll kill you if you touch her again or if I ever see you with her again, you mother fucker. You're fucking old. What the fuck are you doing with someone half your fucking age?" At this point in the monologue Allen was baffled. He was so thoroughly shocked by the verbal assault this man was laying on him that he couldn't even respond or hang up. It was as though he had been waiting for something like this to happen. The beautiful young woman was coming to him and showing interest in him. There was no way she couldn't have had a bunch of baggage. Allen didn't think this would preclude him from going out with her again but it did dampen his spirits a little bit. She had never mentioned being married, though. They had stayed away from the subject of previous relationships and families, but Allen assumed she stayed away because he had just lost his wife, not because she had secrets to hide. "You don't know what you're getting yourself into, old man. You know she's just after your money, you stupid old piece of shit. She's a gold digger, and she's mine. If you touch her again, I'll fucking kill you." And then he was gone.

Allen looked at the phone in his hand, trying to decide if that had just really happened or if he'd just had a very vivid dream brought on by his guilt of writing and of going out with someone nearly half his age. He felt dazed, like he wasn't fully awake yet. He checked the calls list, and there it was, "unknown". Nothing else was listed. He tried to start 69, the number, but it didn't bring up anything as he figured that it wouldn't. He didn't even know if that feature worked with cell phones or not, probably didn't.

He sat down on the bed and tried to decide what to do now that he was thoroughly awakened. He looked at his text messages, hoping that he had one he hadn't seen. There were none there. He went to the window and looked across the road to Steele's house and didn't see the vehicle that Tara drives there. A pang of jealousy rolled through his stomach. He didn't know why it was there, hell they'd only gone out once. He didn't expect her to be madly in love with him or anything. He again checked his phone and reread the messages they exchanged the night before. He was looking for some clue that she said she would be going somewhere today. He knew that she said she wasn't going to do anything today because he'd directly asked her because he was already thinking about a second date at this point. He hadn't quite had the courage to go ahead and ask her right there though.

He decided to text her a good morning message and see what she was up to today. Then maybe he'd ask her about tonight. He sent her the message and then waited. As it always seems, when we are anticipating someone calling or texting us, we think the phone has broken for that time period alone. He waited about twenty minutes. She had never taken this long to text him before. He decided to open up the text message box and send himself a message. Just to check to make sure the network was still working. Almost instantaneous with tapping send, he got a message. His first thought was, "See, it was broken, and I fixed it by sending a text message to myself!" However, when he opened it, it was just a message from himself. He was heartily disappointed. He thought that it had to be the network.

He even used the land line phone he finally installed and called his phone after waiting for another half an hour. He knew the phone worked. That fucked up guy had called him. Allen thought about that call. It didn't worry him much at all; he'd gotten strange calls at all hours of the night and day with people pissed off about him killing off their favorite character in a book or killing a child or something else equally stupid. He had decided that, as a fundamental rule, people were just fucking stupid. If the guy did kill him, that was, but so what? Because he was not afraid of death anyway. He could handle it. He thought Austin would most likely be better off because he knew that Cheyenne's parents would take him and raise him. They'd been successful with Cheyenne, so he was certain they would be again. They had even called and hinted at this with cryptic messages in their phone calls, such as "If you need any help with anything, let us know" or "Are you sure you can handle this on your own?"

Allen took that last one as being directed toward his parenting skills. They seemed to be implying that he couldn't raise Austin without Cheyenne around. Maybe they were right but he didn't think he was going to give in to them on this. He loved Cheyenne's parents. He never had a problem with them. Didn't really have a problem with them now. They just seemed to be a little clingy lately. They seemed to accept without asking that Austin wasn't around. They wondered out loud why Allen had basically set up the new house the exact same way he did the old house. They thought the dog was a great idea because Allen needed some companionship. This was before he had even known Tara Steele existed. He thought he could do this, thanked them for their help and concern, and they left.

Right now, his concern was that Tara still hadn't answered him. It was now almost nighttime. He had refrained from sending another message or even calling. He didn't want to be "That guy." He kept himself busy around the house. He had hired a housekeeper, but she only came once or twice a week. Today wasn't one of her days so he tidied up around the house. Not that there was a lot to do. He barely did anything. Slept or lay on the couch staring at the TV. He was content with his life at this point, but he still glanced at his phone every few minutes to see if he missed anything. He even got it into his head that it wasn't working because he was right next to it. So he went into the other room to make a cold sandwich. As soon as he was done, he practically sprinted back to the living room, certain he'd heard it ding his message alert. As he picked it up and looked through it, he saw nothing. Just his homepage screen. No missed calls or text messages.

Again, he was more disappointed than he wanted to let himself believe. The words the caller had said to him. He had never raised his voice. It was as though they were having a conversation. He was just talking. His words, though, were menacing. Allen wondered if he should ask Tara about it or just let it go and see what happens. He was slightly scared for Austin, though. He didn't want his relationship to affect him in any kind of negative way.

Chapter 14

The Second date

Allen was still perplexed by the lack of response from Tara the next day. He wondered if maybe he had done something wrong, or maybe she talked to her dad and maybe he had put his foot down about her and his age difference. Allen knew twenty-plus years was a big difference. He also knew he didn't really look to be in his mid-forties. He was in good shape, had all his hair, and it was still the dark auburn it had been since he was a kid. He didn't have any wrinkles or anything else that makes a person look old. He hoped this wasn't the case because he really liked Tara and thought they had a great conversation. Plus, the conversation had flowed so easily. He never was good at talking to women. He even had trouble at times talking to his wife, even up until the time of her death.

The other thought that Allen had, which he attempted to bury quickly, had to do with the phone call that he had received the day before. He hoped he was wrong and that he had potentially only dreamt the entire thing, which he couldn't entirely dismiss. If that wasn't the case, then he hoped it was just a bluff from a jealous ex or something like that. All of that considered, he hoped that the guy who was on the other end of the line claiming to be Tara's husband was not the type to act on his threats. He assumed, which he always knew was a bad idea, that if he had called him then he almost assuredly called Tara as well. And if he had spewed profanity laden threats at him, then he'd have done the same with Tara. He hoped that if that's the case it hadn't gone beyond threats, that the guy hadn't done anything to Tara.

Allen sent another text, and just said that he was worried. He assured her that if she didn't want to go out with him again, there would be no hard feelings, and he hoped they could remain friends. He asked her to message him back just so he knew she was okay. He had started to get a little more worried as the day went on. He still hadn't seen her car in the driveway, he even went as far as walking Lennox down to the edge of his yard, hoping to see someone in Tara's family. However, it looked as though no one was home, so he returned to his own and pondered what all of this could mean.

He decided to just let it go, for now; he couldn't control it anyways. She either liked him and wanted to go out again or she didn't like him and didn't want to talk to him again. He just hoped she was safe. Besides, he was having trouble concentrating again as his headache was returning. He kept wanting to make an appointment to see the doctor when he had one, but the times when he didn't have a headache, he felt so good he seemed to completely forget all about having the headaches. He laid down on the couch to take a nap and seemed to feel his late night catching up with him immediately as he dozed right away.

He woke up what seemed to be hours later, but in reality was only about fifteen minutes. He felt like he had many dreams during his sleep, but now they were becoming confused and jumbled. What had awoken him was that he heard Austin walking around. The kid never seemed to want to be quiet when Allen took a nap. Other times, you hardly knew he was even around.

"Hey Dad," Austin said.

Allen's headache seemed to have intensified while he was asleep rather than abating. "Hey Austin. How are you today?"

"Oh. I'm, you know. Doing okay. Can I ask you something?"

"Sure son, what is it?" Allen replied, looking at his son.

"Do you miss her?" He asked after just a moment's hesitation.

"Of course, every day with all my heart." Allen didn't even hesitate to give the answer. It was as though he knew it was coming.

"Me too." Austin seemed to be more down today.

"Hey, what do you think about me making us an appointment to see a grief counselor? I think we both could use someone to talk to. Just someone to get all these bad feelings out in the open. Maybe if we let them go, they'll go forever. Not that we won't love your mom, but maybe we can let go of the pain a little more and be able to feel better on a daily basis."

"Nah, I don't really think talking to someone is going to help me. I haven't talked to anyone but you since it happened. I don't even know where my phone is anymore. I dropped it somewhere and didn't bother to look for it. I don't want to talk to my friends. I think they understand I can't talk right anymore." Said Austin, tears starting to overspill his eyes.

"Well, if you want to go or change your mind. Let me know. I'll get us an appointment." said Allen. "Hey, do you want to go back to the old town and go to your favorite restaurant? We haven't been out to eat together since...we moved. We've been living on takeout and microwaveable foods."

"No, I'll just throw a TV dinner in the microwave. That new housekeeper does a good job of getting the foods I like. It's like she knows me, and we've never even talked!" Austin laughed, it might have been the first laugh Allen had heard from him in weeks.

"Okay, son. I think I'm going to lie back down because I have a really bad headache."

"Okay, Dad, feel better. I'll be up in my room."

When Allen woke up, he felt like he'd slept about twenty minutes, but he looked at the clock and saw that several hours had passed. It was creeping toward evening now. He couldn't believe he'd slept so long. He checked his phone and saw that there still weren't any messages from Tara, or anyone else for that matter. He was really worried now. He got up and dressed and decided to walk across the road and knock and see if anyone was home. As he walked down the driveway, he already knew this was a wasted trip because there were no lights on at all in the Steele household. He decided he wouldn't knock, but just walked up the road a little way to see if he could see any evidence that anyone was home. He found none.

Allen was disheartened by the time he returned back to his own house. Regardless of how much he told himself and sent messages to Tara saying that it wasn't a big deal, he felt rejected, and no one likes to feel rejected.

Over the next few weeks, Allen saw Tara's parents over at their house but never her. He never approached them to ask about Tara. He assumed, again that word, that if something had happened to her, they would have informed him about it. At least, he hoped that was the case. He and her parents seemed to have hit it off well the few times they had spoken. Allen thought maybe she was married, and although the guy had been completely hostile toward him, maybe it was just him being protective of his wife and she had decided to go back to him and thought saying nothing to Allen was for the best. Allen had sent one more text message and only tried to call once which went immediately to voicemail. He didn't leave a message. He thought that maybe she just didn't want to hear his voice and had hit ignore.

He was shocked when he was just about to go to bed when his phone rang with a text message. He had just been texting Shane, who said he was going to bed because he was too drunk to stay up and text anymore. His grammar and spelling seemed to back this claim. Allen almost ignored it, because he was tired himself. He decided to roll over and look at it and saw just a number with "Hey!" as the message. He thought it was probably a wrong number or something, and again almost ignored it. He couldn't do it, though. Something said to answer it.

He asked, "Who is this?" within a minute, he got the reply.

"It's Tara. I'm sooooo very sorry that I haven't been around lately. Can we go to dinner tomorrow, and I'll explain everything?"

Allen, who had been hurt by her absence again, wanted to ignore this the way he felt that she was doing to him. He decided to just give a "Sure." He wanted her to know he was interested, though, so he added, "Sounds great."

"I'll pick you up at 6, and we will go. I'll pay and drive."

Allen agreed and said he was going to go to bed. Now though, the excitement had taken over him, and he decided he wanted to write in his new book. He'd written about fifty pages in the month or so since he started. He wasn't writing this one as fast as he had written the other books. Of course, he was only writing at night when he was sure that Austin was sound asleep. This limited his time greatly. He was ok with this, though, it made it feel that much more satisfactory whenever he finished a chapter.

After writing for about an hour, Allen felt that he had written well tonight. He had finally gotten to the point where his main character had killed his first victim. The guy was the last guy his wife had slept with for money. Allen did not know how to feel about writing a character's death now. He never had an issue before with it, but since Cheyenne died, he was having trouble with it. He knew he would have to do it, though, because that was the basis of a lot of his books. When he writes about a character's death now, even if it was a minor character, he feels almost too godlike, as if he didn't have a right to delve out death according to his own whims. He felt a little guilty now for some reason.

Allen put his guilt aside and got into bed under his covers. He felt good. He wrote again, and he had a second date, at least he hoped it was a date, with Tara. Life seemed to be turning back around.

The next day, when Tara picked him up, Allen was nervous. She knocked on the door, and he opened it up and she immediately jumped toward him and gave him a big kiss on the lips.

"I'm so sorry I've been so flaky the last month. Let's go."

Allen, who was already ready to go, followed her out the door and got in her car. She drove into town to a nice restaurant.

She walked up to the maitre d' and, gave her name and was taken to a seat. Allen followed, marveling at her confidence. This was shattered slightly a few minutes later when they were seated.

"You look in awe of my powers of persuasion. Believe me, I have none. I made the reservation a week ago. I was sure you'd accept. And you did. So here we are."

"You were sure I'd accept? Why is that?" Allen was a little miffed by her presumption that he could be so easily led around by the leash in his pants.

"I think curiosity mostly. I told you I had a great time. That I couldn't wait to do it again and then didn't talk to you for a month. I thought even if you didn't really want to be out with me, you'd at least come to find out why."

"So, why did you not talk to me for over a month?" He asked.

"Well, that's a little complicated and won't make much sense; at least, I don't think it will anyways. First, I wanted to thank you for not pressing the issue. I received just a couple texts and one call from you. Most people would take that as you weren't interested at all. I took it as the opposite. That you were comfortable with how everything went and that I had to take care of something else. That you were waiting for me to come back to you."

Allen nodded, "Yeah, it was something like that. I didn't

want to be 'that guy' and go crazy with calls and texts. I'm not a teenager, so I can't act like one."

Tara reached across the table, put a hand over Allen's, and gave it a gentle caress. "Thank you. I needed a little space. That was all. It comes down to that. When I first saw you the day we moved here, I was in shock. Then, when I came over to see you later that day. I felt like I was a groupie after a concert. I thought I'd shock you. I knew your wife had recently died and that you were probably lonely. I wanted you badly. But then you—"

"I had a touchy trigger." Allen said.

"Well yeah, but that's okay. I was just being a slut and wanted to say I had done you. But then you texted me, and we chatted, and I decided that it wasn't just a groupie thing that I really liked you. Then we went out on a date. The first date I had been on in a really long time. When you dropped me off and didn't try anything or even invite me over to your house, at first I was offended, but then I thought, 'That is how a gentleman acts'. And with that, it scared the hell out of me. I'd never had a guy who didn't want to fuck me after the first date, and sadly I'll admit that I gave in on more than a few of those occasions. I feel horrible about it now. But you scared me. Because at first, I had an agenda, just to be able to say I had sex with you, and then I tabled that. Then I thought for sure you had an agenda, to be able to say you had sex with someone close to half your age. Then when you did nothing. I was confused. I didn't know what you wanted. If you wanted anything at all. So I got scared. I went away to my friend's house and stayed there. I didn't know what to think of you. I honestly think I have already fallen in love with you. I know that sounds stupid and crazy, but it's true." Tears were running down her face as she spoke. The waiter seemed to realize they were involved in an in-depth conversation because he stayed away. Allen was glad. She needed to get this out. She had bottled it up for a while now. She needed to get it out so he could tell her he liked her as she was and wanted to be slow with everything if need be. She looked at Allen, searching his face for answers. She must have liked what she saw there because she smiled weakly.

"I won't say I love you already. I think with everything that's happened my heart isn't ready for love just yet. But I want to be with you. I know this now. I wasn't sure about this at this time yesterday, but sitting here, across from you, watching the tears run down your cheek, I can very easily see myself falling in love with you, too." Allen said softly, barely audible.

"Thank you. I feel so much better you don't even understand." She whispered back hoarsely.

They talked; the conversation had lightened considerably since the confession of early love. Dinner was just as good as Allen had eaten recently. He sensed, however, that something else was on her mind. He didn't know what it could be, so he just asked her outright. "What else is on your mind?"

"Your son." she said simply.

"Yes, what about him?" He tried to keep the defensiveness out of his voice, but he felt like he failed miserably because she started at his words.

She composed herself quickly and said, "I know you have one, but you haven't mentioned him one time. Why is that?"

It was Allen's turn to start. He was sure he had at least mentioned Austin once or twice. "I'm not sure. It's just that it's hard dealing with him right now. With everything else that happened all at the same time. There have been so many changes that I don't know how to deal with him right now, too."

"I think I understand. I don't want to press or anything. I just want to be completely honest from the start."

Allen must have given something away in his face or body language, because she asked, "Is there something else you would like to ask me?"

Allen didn't want to but almost felt compelled to tell her. "Well, the morning after our first date, I was awoken by a call on my cell phone. I answered it and was immediately verbally assaulted by what sounded like a younger man. He told me to leave you alone. That you are a gold digger. A slut. That he'd kill me if I touched you. And most interesting of all, that you were his wife." Allen stopped and just looked at her. She seemed speechless.

After what seemed like a very long pause, she finally spoke with great difficulty, "Okay, I had hoped Taylor had only called me. I know he knows people that work at the phone place at the mall, and they will look up people's numbers for him. But I never thought he'd look up yours. Let alone call you."

"Well, he did call me. He didn't yell. He kept everything conversational. He just said what I already told you. I'm guessing you received a call as well. That he was part of your scare."

"Yes," the tears were coming again, "I thought I was done with him. He is why we moved here in the first place. My parents thought I needed to get away from him. He found me so fast it was scary. No, he never came here," reading the thought in Allen's eyes, "but he was able to get my new number and find out where we moved. He knew you were the only person besides a couple friends' numbers he already had that I had been in contact with. He has a lot of connections. He was able to get your name from your number. I'm so sorry. He's not a violent person. He just gets mad and yells a lot. He never hit me, I promise. He's all bluff and bluster. And no, we were never married. We were engaged. I broke it off about two months ago. We were supposed to be married the day after our first date. Maybe he was just more angry that day or something. I don't know. Has he called you anymore?" Allen could read something in her face, but seemed unable to identify it at this time.

"No. I thought maybe you had realized you still loved him, and that's where you went. Back to him and that all the threats and yelling were just territoriality or something. Like when an always docile dog will bark at a strange dog on its lawn, but you and he both know he'd never attack or anything." Said Allen.

"Yeah, that's exactly what he's like. But that's not what happened. I stayed with a couple girlfriends of mine back by where my grandparents live. I changed phone carriers and numbers. He hasn't bothered me either." Tara seemed to grasp onto that metaphor, seizing it the way a drowning man will a floatation device.

"That's good because I really like you. How about we get out of here and go back to my place for a little while?" Allen was shocked at his own boldness.

"I'd love that." Tara replied.

As they walked toward the door, Allen reached for Tara's hand. He was nervous doing so, but his apprehension was baseless because as soon as he touched Tara's hand, she immediately interlocked her fingers into his, and that was how they entered the night outside the restaurant.

Chapter 15

The second Promise

What awoke Allen wasn't Tara moving in the bed beside him, but the sharp pain in his head. He thought this might be the worst headache he'd had yet. It was so bad upon waking up, he wasn't even sure who or where he was, and once he figured that out, he couldn't exactly remember how he had gotten into bed with Tara. He remembered the date, they had made up, and he remembered leaving the restaurant. He had felt a twinge in his head at the time but had ignored it. Now, he was paying for that ignoring. He sat up in bed and tried to get his arm from underneath Tara's body. It was a full moon and it was shining through the window. He could see that she was naked. He had to restrain himself from pulling back the covers. He had seen the top front the day she moved in, but he couldn't remember seeing the rest. Right now, though, he had to focus on not waking her up because he wanted to deal with the headache on his own, even though, at times, it was causing his vision to be blurred. It almost felt like palpitations in his eyes, with each heartbeat, it seemed his vision doubled.

He extracted his arm from under Tara's back, and she rolled toward him, still sound asleep. Allen was in so much pain he couldn't even marvel at her perfection. He had loved Cheyenne with all he had; he thought she was by far the most beautiful woman he had ever seen, clothed or not clothed. However, his assertion was being tested as he looked upon Tara. He had to physically turn his own head away; he reached up and, with both hands, turned away from her exposed breasts. It would have been comical had he not been in so much pain. He tentatively took a step as he stood up, and the room held steady. Something he wasn't sure it would do until he tried.

He walked into the bathroom, flipped on the light and then immediately flipped it back off, the light was certainly not his friend that night. He felt his way to the toilet, put the lid down, and sat on it, putting his head between his knees. Willing the headache to go away. At this point, a wave of nausea hit him, and he was just barely able to scramble off the toilet and vomit into it. Miraculously afterward, he felt a lot better. He crawled to the bathroom door, not trusting his ability to navigate the room in the dark and opened the door.

"You ok, babe?" Tara asked softly.

"Yeah, something I ate must not have agreed with me or something." Allen replied.

"I hope it wasn't me." Tara stated coquettishly.

"No dear, not you for sure. Might be the headache I have. I woke up with it a little while ago. I've had a lot since, well you know, the accident." Allen was still uncomfortable mentioning his dead wife to Tara. Although it wasn't that he was ashamed of what he was doing, it just was still awkward.

"Stress, most likely." Tara remarked back. "You know what I heard is the best medicine for a headache? Women would be screwed if the masses of men knew this, though sex is the best medicine. So why don't you rinse your mouth out and come over baby. I'm awake and ready." She threw back the covers to prove her point. Allen didn't need to be told twice. He grabbed his mouth wash and rinsed thoroughly, and walked to the bed.

"Feel better, baby?"

"Lots babe. Thanks." Allen lied back to Tara. He didn't necessarily feel worse, but he sure didn't feel better. The sex had been great; he lasted much longer this time than he did the first time. And her moans and clutching at him had turned him on more than he imagined that it could. Cheyenne had never been very much into moaning loudly. Luckily, his room was on the other side of the house from Austin's. He didn't think he would be able to hear. It was after he worried about this. He had never actually thought about Austin this entire night until this point. He knew Austin was old enough to look after himself but he probably should have checked that the kid was home. He didn't think he would want to meet Tara yet, if ever. He hadn't even told him about going out with her yet. It would be extremely awkward if she were to meet him after they'd had sex a few times that same night. He thought he'd try to get her out of bed early in the morning and just explain to her that this wasn't how he wanted to have them meet, with it being early in the morning.

Luckily, Austin wasn't an early riser. With him being home-schooled, he did his classes on his own and in his own time. He didn't have any early meetings for his online classes, so he usually wasn't out of bed before ten.

Nonetheless, Allen woke up early the next morning. He hoped that Tara would understand without going into too much detail about why he was feeling that way. The good thing upon waking was that Allen felt no leftover effects from the terrible headache he had awakened with during the night.

He gently nudged Tara, he was somewhat thankful after their second round during the night that she had decided to put on a t-shirt. He wasn't sure if he'd be able to resist her if he had seen any part of her body. She seemed very tired. She was mumbling in her sleep, so he nudged her again, and she rolled toward him and opened her eyes. He almost lost the battle with his lust in that moment when he looked into her eyes. It was an enormous struggle to look away, or he would be leaning into kiss her and then all would be lost. He didn't know why it was such an urgent matter to get her to leave, but he felt that he just didn't want her here in the morning so soon.

"Tara sweetie, you need to wake up."

"Oh Allen, I'm so comfortable. Do I have to?" Even the way she mumbled in her sleep was beyond sexy, damn, he thought I'm falling in love already.

"Yeah. I think it'd be kind of weird if Austin were to see you coming out of the room or something. He might get the wrong idea or something. I don't know. I don't know exactly what I'm trying to say." Allen was feeling very nervous at this point. He didn't know why, but he had a heavy block of dread in his stomach. "It's not that I'm ashamed of you or anything like that. I'd just prefer for Austin not to meet you this way. I want him to meet you properly and in the right setting. Not wearing one of my t-shirts walking out of my room in the morning." He concluded and was almost begging her to understand with his eyes.

"Ok, I understand. I'll do it. I just hope I get to meet him soon. I know that you said he's been a loner since your wife died, but he has to interact with people eventually again." She smiled, seeming to ask with her eyes if there was time.

He ignored the question, "I know. I need to talk to him about that. I really am starting to think I need to take him to someone. He seems to be holding so much in right now."

"You really do, babe. He can't go ignoring everyone and everything in his life forever." Tara said as she was getting dressed.

"He isn't ignoring everything. I'm sure he's doing his homework and stuff for his classes because I haven't gotten any word from his teachers saying his work has been incomplete." Allen looked at her; again, his lust almost defeated him.

"That's good, I guess, at least he's doing that. Although I think you might want to consider sending him to a regular school so he can interact with more kids and stuff."

"I know. I was thinking about that, too. Right now, I think it's too much to put on him. I think that he would rebel completely. We've had so many issues as it is with everything that's gone on."

"Ok babe." She leaned over and kissed him. It was not a sisterly kiss, either. It was long and passionate. Any thoughts that Allen had about her only being after his money were gone. He didn't think anyone could fake that kind of passion.

With more willpower than he thought he ever possessed, he was able to break the kiss. "Babe, we will go out again soon, I promise. But for now, I gotta let you leave."

"I know. I just didn't want you to forget about me."

"I don't think that is possible."

Tara was now dressed; well, she put her pants back on. She told him she was going to keep the shirt as a "memento". He jokingly asked if she wanted him to autograph it or not. She said you can autograph something else on me later tonight or tomorrow. They kissed at the door, and he watched her walk to her car, wondering how in the hell he was able to get another woman like this.

When Allen got back to his room, he saw the bathroom and the toilet, and it triggered that he was sick last night so he decided to finally make an appointment with the doctor.

He was able to get to the doctor that day.

He had been in the waiting room for what seemed like forever when they finally called him back.

"I don't get the headaches every day. I don't get them with the same intensity every time. I don't see any relationship between anything I'm doing and when I get them. They will come for about an hour or two. Then they will be gone. Medication doesn't seem to help at all. Last night was the first time I've experienced nausea with them." Allen tried to explain the way they felt but he couldn't seem to put into words what exactly they felt like. This was frustrating because he made his living with words. But here he was, sitting in this doctor's office, unable to find the words.

"Well, I don't see anything physically that can be causing them." The doctor said. "We will take some blood and see if those tests tell us anything. If I were to guess, they won't tell us anything. I believe it's probably just stress. You've been through a lot of traumatic events in the past few months. This is your body saying how about we slow down. You work hard. Anyone who uses their brain a lot like you do will understand. Others who don't think that sitting at a computer tapping keys is easy wouldn't understand. My advice to you is to go home, and relax. Maybe go somewhere and relax. Get out of the area for awhile. Try to find yourself again. Right now, you're just struggling with that exact thing. If they keep coming and with more intensity, I'll write you a script. As of right now, my doctorly advice is to relax." The doctor said. Allen loved his doctor. Never had any issues, and she was always straight with him.

"Thanks, Doc. I think I may just do that if they continue."

Allen left with the band aid on his arm. He hated to get blood taken, but this time, he was okay with it because he thought it would show if there was something seriously wrong with him or if there wasn't.

There was a pang in his head as he pulled into the driveway. He didn't think it was one of those headaches returning, but he couldn't be sure. Although this one had come on him like a tidal wave and then immediately receded like the ebb and flow of the ocean.

He walked into the house and Austin was standing at the top of the stairs. He didn't look happy at all. Allen was almost afraid to ask what was going on. He didn't think he wanted another fight at this point. So he thought it might be best to just head it off and be completely open with him, at least to a point. He didn't need to tell Austin that he really liked Tara. He didn't want Austin to think he was trying to replace Cheyenne. He was old enough now to understand that adult men and women had needs. Adults had the need for sex. It was healthy for them. Kids thought they needed it, but once they got older, they'd understand the true need for it.

"Hey Austin. Where were you last night? I was looking for you. I had someone I wanted you to meet."

"I was out. Who is she? Is it that bimbo from across the street? I've seen her walking up and down the road, looking over here, trying to see if you're around. I saw you and her the day they moved in. You let her touch you down there." Allen didn't understand where this jealous attitude and seeming regression in his son had come from. He was always comfortable talking about anything.

"Well Austin," Allen seemed pleased he was able to predict that the conversation was going to go his way. At least he was prepared. "Men and women, adult men and women that is, have the need for sexual contact. I know it should always be between a man and a woman that are in love. Sometimes, it just doesn't happen that way. When that happens, you just have to be careful."

"You do realize that people are going to laugh at you right? She could be my sister. She's barely older than I am. Maybe I should be the one that does that stuff with her and not you."

Again, he had that pestilent child tone in his voice. "Austin, you're being ridiculous. She's older than you think. She just looks a little younger. She's almost eleven years older than you." Allen didn't know why he had said almost eleven rather than ten. In that moment it just seemed to sound better to him. He felt stupid standing here explaining this to Austin anyway.

"What?" Austin was speaking and Allen had missed it.

"I said I won't call her mom!" Austin practically screamed at Allen.

"Who said to call her mom? She and I went out a couple times. Just as friends. Nothing is going on between us. That day you saw us was a one time thing. We are friends. I'm allowed to have friends, you know. Maybe you'd feel better if you talked to your friends." Allen regretted this from the moment it had passed beyond his lips.

"Yeah, that's right. Push this back on me. Make me the one who is the bad guy. I'm just a stupid loner kid who has a dad that doesn't give a shit about him. You're out trying to find a new wife while you forget that you have a son you talk to about once a week. You're never around."

"You're never around!" Allen actually was getting mad for

the first time in a long time at Austin. "I've tried to talk to you. I look for you, and you're always out in the woods or sleeping or just nowhere to be found!"

"You're just trying not to find me! You're probably going to marry her and forget about me like you're already trying to do. You're trying to forget me and mom ever existed!" There were tears streaming down his face.

"There is nothing serious between me and Tara. I promise. It's just hanging out. Like you used to hang out with your friends, that's all we do." Allen tried to keep the anger out of his voice. He thought that so far, he was succeeding.

"Yeah, sure. Just hang out? That's why I saw her sneaking out of the house this morning wearing one of your shirts. That seems to be a lot more than hanging out to me." Austin seemed to always have the perfect come back for anything Allen said.

Chapter 16
The Third Confrontation

Despite Allen's assertion that there was nothing going on between him and Tara that was very serious, they saw a lot of each other over the next few weeks. Allen talked to Austin, but it seemed to be a perfunctory conversations. They didn't seem to want to get close anymore. Lennox hadn't helped at all to bring them close together. Allen took care of the dog. He walked him, fed him and gave him water. He would leave notes for Austin if he was leaving for awhile, but when he came back, the kid hadn't done anything he asked him to do. He mentioned this to Tara, who was completely miffed by the fact that she was still yet to meet Austin. She hadn't spent the night since the second date, Allen had talked to her, and they both agreed that they needed to take some more time. They obviously couldn't do anything at Tara's house, so they were left to sneak around like a couple teenagers. There were times when they would rent a hotel room for the night, but only Tara ever stayed the entire night. Allen just couldn't leave Austin for a very long time included an overnight. He didn't know what the difference was if he left sometime in the morning and spent the entire day with Tara and returned near midnight, as opposed to leaving at 8 at night and staying and returning in the morning around seven or eight. It was just being there overnight. He assumed it was just the overnight aspect of the day. He was expected to be there as a parent.

Tara understood Allen's troubles with Austin, and was very supportive of their adventures as she called them. She never wanted to say they were sneaking around. "We are adults Allen, we don't sneak around. We just keep our love to ourselves and don't push it on others." She had that twinkle in her eyes as she said this. This twinkle drove Allen wild. He had to have her right away, so when he drove right past the restaurant they were planning to go to, she just have him a quizzical look with the raise of her eyebrows. She was fine with it and even led him into the room and took control.

To Allen, the sex was amazing, but more important to him than that was the feeling of just being needed by someone again. He hadn't lost that feeling with Cheyenne until he had read the emails. He had that feeling for a very short time and never actually got to confront her about it. He was scared of how he would react when and if someone ever had a romantic interest, but now that it happened, he had been fine. He had no fears about her cheating on him or anything.

The only fear that Allen had was that he would receive random phone calls on his cell phone from a blocked number. It happened at all hours of the day and night, and the person on the other end never said anything. Allen always assumed it was Tara's ex playing games, but as of yet, nothing had gotten serious in Allen's mind.

One day, while Allen and Tara were having lunch, Allen's phone rang. He had a bad feeling about this day for some reason. One reason was that he had an excruciating headache when he first woke up and almost cancelled his lunch date with Tara, but just a few minutes before they were to leave, he found himself waking up from a very refreshing nap and felt fine.

"Hello." He answered.

"Mr. Bennett?"

"Yes. Who is this?"

"This is Jason MacDonald; I work for Home Protection Security. We have an alert at your address. Can you verify your password, please?"

"Yeah, it is 'Strawberry'." Allen replied immediately.

"Thank you, sir. As I said, we have an alert at your address. It looks like one of the windows on the first floor has been opened. I have dispatched a police unit to your address, and they are currently en route. Are you at the residence, sir?"

"No. I'm out for lunch. Do you need me to return right away?"

"Yes sir, the police would need to speak to you."

"Ok. Let them know I am on my way." He hung up the phone and looked at Tara. "There's been a break-in at my house. That was the alarm, people. They said someone got in through a window and set it off. I have to go now." He stood up and left a twenty on the table. They had so far only ordered beverages and an appetizer, which hadn't even arrived yet and they left.

When Allen arrived at his house, there were three police cars, and Tara's parents were standing on the edge of his yard.

"They say anything to you yet?" Allen asked.

"Nope, just came flying in here about five minutes ago. I heard the alarm go off. Couldn't have been more than five minutes after you two left when it went off." Tara's dad replied.

"Excuse me, officer, this is my house. What's going on?"

"We are checking the interior now, sir. We have already checked the perimeter of the residence and found no one or evidence of someone having been around the residence. We want to make sure the perp is no longer inside." Just then, the officer's radio crackled to life

"Sergeant Wykowski? Are you there?" Said an unembodied voice on the radio.

"This is Wykowski, go ahead."

"Do you have the homeowner there now?" It asked.

"Yes. He just arrived."

"Ask him if he has a dog."

Before the officer could even turn and ask Allen he was answering.

"Yeah I do, his name is Lennox. He's friendly as could be, he doesn't need to worry."

"He says yes, he does. Name of Lennox. No need to worry. He's a friendly."

"I'm not worried. He's dead." The voice replied immediately without emotion.

Allen just stood there in shock. This meant someone had been in his house. He knew Austin hadn't been home. He said he was going to go to his friend's house. He had finally started to hang out with a friend. He said they met while he was walking through the woods. The kid had lost their dad recently and he took to walking through the woods. They had seen each other several times and never spoken. Austin said he hadn't been able to talk to her at first. Allen assumed the girl had to have been pretty. He thought a little girlfriend might be the best medicine for Austin. He encouraged it without seeming desperate. Maybe if he has a girlfriend he will accept that I have a girlfriend, was Allen's logic to himself.

"My dog is dead? How? What happened?"

Allen attempted to push past the officer in front of him and rush to the house but was immediately pulled back and slammed against the vehicle behind him.

"Sir, the premises have not been cleared yet. I can't let you go onto the property. Please wait until my officers have completed their sweep, and then you will be able to ascend to the property."

Allen was sobbing, "But my dog! Someone killed my fucking dog!"

"I know sir, and I'm sorry." This officer had a little more empathy in his voice, but it didn't seem to be much.

Just then, the officer's radio crackled. "Sir, we have cleared all areas of the home, and no sign of an intrusion or anything that seems to be missing. Send Mr. Bennett up to confirm, please." said the same emotionless voice.

"Okay sir, you can proceed." Officer Wykowski said, waving his hand at the house.

Allen went into the house, he wanted to see Lennox. He wanted to know what some sick fuck would do to his dog. Lennox had done nothing. He searched the house, because the police wanted to make sure nothing was missing. He looked around quickly. He didn't see anything major missing. He then asked about his dog. He was told that he was found on the back porch, and it appeared that he had been strangled to death. They had removed the body from the premises. Allen wasn't sure whether or not he was happy about this fact. He wanted to see Lennox and also wanted to bury him himself, but maybe this way was better. He'd already buried loved ones, and it wasn't easy. He thought maybe he'd just let him go.

Tara wanted to stay with him that night, but Allen didn't want to be touched or even looked at. He felt violated. He had never had anyone break into his house, and the fact that someone who may or may not have something against him never crossed his mind. He had come across crazed fans before, but nothing had ever gone this far. He asked Tara if she thought her ex might be capable of doing something like this, and she said she still thought he was more talk than action. He hoped she was right, because this was too close. He was worried about this sort of thing happening and it happened already. He didn't know what to think right now. He just wanted to be alone. That much he had known.

He asked Tara to leave and hoped it had been in a gentle way. She seemed to accept his excuse he just needed some alone time to process everything that happened.

He looked around more thoroughly in the house; he noticed a few things were out of place, mostly in his room. It seemed as though someone was looking for something specific. He couldn't see anything gone. The person would have only had a few minutes to get in, look around, and then leave. The police said they think the dog was killed first to keep him from barking.

Allen felt another headache that was settling in. He thought the doctor was right and that it was stressed induced because this situation certainly qualified as being stressful. He tried to get some sleep but couldn't fall asleep. Allen got up and walked around the house. He must have dozed off because he could hear movements in Austin's room. He opened the door and was immediately bombarded by Lennox bounding out the door and jumping up and down on him. He acted like he hadn't seen anyone all day.

"LENNOX! Oh my god, boy! I'm so fucking happy to see you! They told me you were dead! Oh god, I'm so happy!" Lennox was happy to see Allen, too; he was wagging his tail wildly and barking a little bit, which was rare for him. He wasn't much of a barker. After greeting Allen with enthusiasm, he tore off toward the door. Allen took him out, and he immediately went to the bathroom.

"Austin? Austin, did you have Lennox with you?" Allen asked as he came back upstairs, Lennox now wholly satisfied with his trip outside.

"Yeah, I thought Sara would want to meet him. I just got back a few minutes ago. I saw a bunch of flashing lights through the trees. What was going on?"

Allen didn't want to worry him. He obviously had been too

caught up in what he was doing to know anything was going on here. So he decided to lie. "Oh it was nothing, false alarm. I must have left the window open when I left, and it eventually triggered the alarm or something. Cops all came out and searched around. They didn't find anyone, and nothing was missing, so it had to be no big deal." Allen said.

"How was your little date?" Allen was genuinely curious.

"Oh, I would say it was better than yours. Sara loved Lennox. She gave him a big kiss. I got kind of jealous, and I don't even know why. But then she kissed me, and it tasted weird. Why do girls wear stuff on their lips?" Austin was asking a question, about girls. Allen was happy, this was turning out to be a good night.

"They think it makes them look prettier. What most of them don't realize is that we'd think they were pretty with or without that stuff."

"Dad, why do you think they do that? We are guys. We don't notice that stuff most of the time." Austin looked at his dad with complete innocence.

"Honestly son, half the time, I think they do it for themselves. They want to look pretty for themselves and maybe just as importantly pretty for other women just as much as for the men in they want to attract. Lastly, they do it for the men they are with."

"Do you think that Tara woman you're seeing is trying hard to look good so you'll think she's prettier than mom?" Austin asked.

"I don't know Austin. She will never be prettier than your mom. Your mom is the most beautiful woman I have or will ever see." Allen replied, he didn't know if he believed his own words, but it was important for Austin to believe them.

"Then why do you need this, Tara? You have mom! Just because she's dead doesn't mean you're not still together!" Austin's rage was upon him in a flash.

"Austin, first it was a death do us part agreement. She died, and I'm here. I need someone to be with, you know." Allen replied calmly, although his joy of earlier was quickly diminishing.

"You weren't with her much tonight, were you?"

"What's that supposed to mean?"

Allen was becoming angry again.

"Date got cut a little short, didn't it?"

"What'd you do?"

"Set the alarm off."

"Why the fuck did you do that? People could have gotten hurt. The cops could have wrecked getting here. That was very irresponsible." His voice was raising now.

"It is the only way to have you home. You spend all your time with that woman. How long did it take you to look for me once the cops left?"

"I didn't look because I knew you were not here. We left about the same time, and you said you wouldn't be back until around ten."

"I could have changed my mind. Or Sara could not have shown. You ever think about that? NO! You just thought about her, and that was it."

"Austin, you're being ridiculous. Of course, I thought about you. The police searched the entire house. They said no one was here. I knew you weren't home and they know you live here. There was no sign that anything happened. Nothing was even missing."

"Only thing missing these days is you. We were supposed to be getting close again, but the only thing you want to get close to is that woman's underwear." With that, Austin closed his door.

Allen just stood there. He didn't understand where he had gone so wrong. The kid was never here. He was off in the woods all the time. Allen and Tara didn't see each other every day and didn't even talk every day. Allen thought it was just jealousy on Austin's part because he was dating someone, he guessed you'd call it that. Austin certainly seemed to have figured it out. She was taking away time that Austin could have had, but at the same time, Austin didn't seem to want to spend time with him either. Allen went to his room to lie down. The headache was back in full force now, and he couldn't think straight, let alone figure out the working mind of a teenage boy.

Chapter 17

The News

Allen woke up, at first, very confused. There were reasons for his confusion. The sun was on the wrong side of the house for the morning, which was the first thing he noticed. If it wasn't evening turning into night, then it surely would be before much longer. He had slept the clock all the way around just about. He couldn't remember the last time bed slept twenty hours. But this led him to his second source of confusion, if he'd slept so long and obviously hard, why did he feel stiff, sore, and achy all over? He felt like he'd been out running a marathon. He looked around. He seemed to still be lying in the last position he remembered being in last night when he went to bed. Maybe laying in the same position for so long had caused some kind of rigor mortis to set in. He guessed that was very possible. The last thing that confused him was the dreams he had during the night. He lay there trying to remember any aspect of them but they seemed to be slipping through his fingers like water when you try to cup it. All he could remember now was that they were disturbing. And not only disturbing but violent. He was no stranger to violent dreams. In fact he had used many of his previous dreams as plots in his books. That didn't make them any less disturbing, though.

When he finally was able to work the stiffness out of his

muscles, he got himself out of bed and looked for his cell phone. He was happy that it was muscle stiffness and not joint stiffness. He didn't consider himself old yet, but joint pain might just change his mind. He looked for his cell phone some more, he was sure that someone had probably called and messaged him during the time he was asleep. He was thoroughly disappointed though when he looked at his phone, and there was only one text message, and it wasn't from Tara as he'd hoped. It was just a stupid advertisement. He sat back down on the bed. Goddamn, he was sore! The enormous headache he'd gone to bed with the precious night was gone; at least sleeping so much gave him that relief. He wasn't sure it wasn't all worth it then. He thought his head was going to just burst open like an overripe melon.

He finally got up and made his way down to the first floor of the house. He thought he heard music coming from Austin's room, which meant the kid was home for once. He didn't want to talk to him because he knew it'd end up in another fight. He figured he'd wait until tomorrow and see if the kid wanted to have a father/son day. Maybe go fishing. Haha. Fishing! That was a laugh. Allen had never gone in his life, and wouldn't know the first thing to do. But that's what fathers and sons do together, or so he heard. Besides, it was edging into the winter season. There'd be snow on the ground. Allen didn't much fancy the idea of ice fishing.

He got himself some cereal. That was about all he had

anyway. He thought that it was too late to order delivery because it was pushing nine. Nine! Allen was still shocked that he had slept so long, and when he woke up, he thought it was seven. Did he somehow lose another couple hours? He wasn't sure he had or hadn't. He couldn't focus on much more than the Leprechaun's cereal. He sat at the kitchen table and flipped on the TV. He couldn't remember the last time he sat down and actually watched anything on TV. He was never a big fan of the medium, as it were anyway, but he guessed it had been months since he had even turned one on.

The first channel to which he flipped was the local channel, and they were running a promo for their newscast that night. The pretty anchor said, "Tune in tonight at eleven for more details on the person found dead in Roseberry Park."

Allen was intrigued. Roseberry Park wasn't far from their old house; he and Austin had actually met there the day they moved into this house. He hoped it had not been one of his old neighbors or anything. Of course, Allen was always intrigued when people turned up dead. He was a murder mystery writer, so he knew murders were exciting to him. He was always looking for material. He always thought that comedians used politicians for their material; he used murder cases. Same difference really he thought. It wasn't like he was going out and committing the crimes.

He decided he would try to call Tara while he waited for the news to come on. He tried, and it just rang. Her voicemail never even picked up. He thought that might solve one mystery of the day as to why she didn't call or text; she seemed to be having phone issues. At least, that was what he hoped.

When the news came on, Allen actually had gone and retrieved his notebook. He was going to take notes on what happened. A slight sense of shame came over him, but he sat down like a student on the first day of school anyway. The news had his full attention.

The pretty anchor was there filling up the screen, she had a very serious look on her face as she looked directly into the camera. The area Allen lived in now and before wasn't much different. Really, they were considered to be part of one small city, murders didn't happen here very often, and when they did, they got a lot of attention. The anchor knew this, too, based on the seriousness of her eyes. Usually, there was some kind of preamble to the newscast, a welcome or something. Tonight, it was full bore into the story. The anchor didn't even introduce herself. "Tonight's top story. Murder in our city. Local police were called to a local park today at about one pm when kids who were playing there stumbled upon a man's body laying half buried in trash in one corner of the park. The kids began to scream, and when one of the parents arrived, they saw a hand sticking out from underneath a fast food bag. The parent immediately called the police. Now to Jody Disimone for more on this, Jody."

"Thanks Rachel, I arrived on the scene at about 1:30 this afternoon, and the police were already canvassing the area. As you can see behind me that they have strung yellow police tape up all around the park. I spoke with police officer Daniel Hale; here is what he had to say earlier." The story cuts to what had to be a previously recorded interview with the police officer.

"What can you tell us about the victim?" Rachel asked the officer.

"All we have right now is that the victim was a male, mid to late forties. He appears to have been strangled with some sort of wire. There doesn't appear to have been any kind of struggle. It seemed that he may have known the attacker. We haven't identified him at this time. There were no wallets or cell phones on him. He seemed to be carrying no identification of any kind. Robbery may have been the motive." The officer stated.

"Do you believe this was a random act of violence, or do you think the citizens of this city have to worry about having a potential serial killer on their hands?"

"At this point it's impossible to make any conclusions on one instance. At this point, we are treating this as an isolated case that appears to be a mugging gone too far."

"What else can you tell us about the victim?"

"At this point, we only believe that the cause of death was strangulation. He was found without a shirt on his body, and there appears to be scratches on his chest in back that we believe to be postmortem."

"Thank you officer."

"Back to you in the studio."

Allen snapped off the TV with the remote, vaguely disappointed. They hadn't described the victim at all except to say that he was a male around his age and he hadn't had a shirt on. He had already used that scenario. He decided to text Tara and at least tell her goodnight. He wasn't worried. He had looked out his window and saw the lights on in her upstairs bedroom and knew she was ok. She probably didn't want to seem overbearing or anything by coming over and telling him about the phone issues.

The next morning Allen decided it might be the last time he could get a good outdoor jog in. It was a lot warmer than it had been for a long time. He went to his closet and looked for his running shoes. They weren't there. He thought he remembered unpacking them but so much had happened since then that he might be remembering falsely. He went to the basement where they had placed some boxes of stuff he thought he wouldn't need but at the same time couldn't part with. As he searched through the stuff there, he heard his cell phone vibrating on the table above him. He was about to give up anyway because he wasn't going to find them. He rushed upstairs to grab his phone.

He didn't recognize the number, but it was a local, "Hello."

"Allen?" The caller had a note of panic in her voice. It was a familiar voice, an older woman. Sixties maybe. Allen shuffled through his memory and couldn't place a face with the voice.

"Yeah, this is Allen. Who is this?" Allen hated when people knew who he was, but he couldn't place who they were, especially when they sounded like they were about to lose their shit and start screaming.

"Allen, it's Annabelle Rittory, we used to live across the street from you." It clicked. The people across the street were always nice. Not nosy and wanting to be in his and Cheyenne's business. But pleasant enough to pass a few words with and carry on.

"Yes, Mrs. Rittory?" He asked.

"Have you seen the news?" She asked. She seemed barely able to hold it together.

"Not since last night, no. Why?"

"That body they found down in the park. You know who it was? Have you heard?" She was on the edge now.

"No, I haven't watched the news or read anything yet. Why?"

Allen replied

"It was Robert Goldsmith. Your old next-door neighbor!" She screamed this last bit out. She was sobbing now.

"What? It was Robert? How do you know? They said they hadn't released the name yet." Allen was shocked, but wasn't able to feel much else. He had never liked the man all that much, but never hated anyone enough in his life for them to die.

She had calmed herself a little bit now. "It's him. I went over to his house yesterday to see if he had seen all the commotion down at the park. I knew he had been out walking yesterday morning because I talked to him. It was about 5:30 am because I was on my way to the church to help set up for their rummage sale. I may have been the last person to see him alive, Allen! This sort of thing doesn't happen here! Why did this happen?" She was again tottering on the edge. Allen thought that she was going to slide down the wrong side soon.

"I don't know, Mrs. Rittory." She was sobbing hysterically now. Allen tried a few times to calm her down but did not succeed. He thought it would be best to just hang up. He did that and sat down. He couldn't believe it. Robert Goldsmith was dead. He'd never liked the guy all that much, but he didn't want him to be dead. Allen sat at the table and cried. All thoughts of a morning jog were pushed from his mind.

Allen came back to himself after a short interval of time. He thought he'd tell Austin about it. Austin had liked Robert a lot and vice versa it had seemed. He felt the makings of another stress headache but he didn't think this was going to be too bad this time. He knocked on Austin's door and there was no answer, so he opened it. The room was as spotless and neat as could be. That was one thing you could say about the kid was that he was neat as a pin.

"Austin, you in here?" Allen called to what looked to be an empty room.

"Yeah." He was coming out of his closet. It looked like he just returned from somewhere, but Allen hadn't heard the door or anything.

"You okay, dad? I heard you crying." Austin's face immediately became concerned.

"No son, I'm not okay. I just found out some bad news. You remember our old neighbor Robert Goldsmith?" Allen said after a few moments when he'd settled himself back down.

"Yeah of course. He was always nice to me." Austin said, his face now showing no emotion.

"Well, they found him murdered in the park yesterday." Allen was holding back tears again. He had come to hate real death, he felt that he could still write it. But to deal with it in real life was so much different.

"What? No way? Why would someone do that to Mr. Goldsmith? He was always so nice!" Austin screamed

"From what I heard, they think he was being mugged." Allen replied, walking toward Austin as the kid started to break down.

Allen went to his son and hugged him. Austin was crying pretty hard. He'd known Robert for most of his life. He had been like a surrogate uncle to him because Austin had no real uncles, as both his parents were only children. Austin cried for a very long time in Allen's arms. Allen relished the feel of it. Not the sadness that was now beating off his teenage son like a bad fever, but the comfort and ease to which he let him hold him.

After he got Austin calmed and settled into his bed for a nap, Allen decided he wanted to see if there was anymore information on the murder. He went into his study to get his laptop to read the paper because he didn't subscribe to an actual paper anymore. His laptop wasn't in there. This wasn't all that uncommon as of late. He would carry around, and if he got the urge to write a page or two, he had it with him. Although he hadn't written in a while. He finally found his laptop in his bedroom. He didn't remember bringing it back in here. Or maybe it was he didn't remember taking it back out of here. Either way, it was here.

He brought up the newspaper website and started to read.

There wasn't a lot more information, except they had decided the scratches that were on Robert's chest and stomach had actually been writing. It was FMM. Allen sat and stared at this for a very long time and then went back and read the article again. It identified the victim as Robert Goldsmith. 53 year old male. So it was definitely him. He had been strangled by a string or small rope of some kind. His shoes were not that of his size, as his feet were much smaller. There were two sets of tracks from what appeared to be athletic shoes around the body, but those could have been from the people who found him.

Allen sat horrified at what he just read, closed out the browser and immediately brought up his new book. He skimmed through it, trying to find the second murder victim. He looked at what he wrote. Some details of the victim in his story jumped off the page at him. "Fifty-something male. Strangled. Shirtless. Shoeless. 4MW carved onto the victim's back. The victim left in a park."

Allen sat staring at this. Surely this was just a coincidence.

Surely.

Chapter 18

The Dismissal

Over the next few days Allen tried to catch as much about the story on the news as possible. He was hesitant to go to his old neighbors and talk to them. He didn't know why he should feel this way, but for some reason, he felt responsible. He didn't think his writing had literally killed his old neighbor, but it felt like someone read about how he killed the first victim in his book and did his best to copycat it. There were a few differences, though. The victim in the book struggled. The writing on the bodies was different and also the victim in the book had his own shoes on, or at least shoes that fit. So far, the entire case was baffling to the police. When the news talked to them, they had no leads so far and were more than just a little confused by the footwear. They had never shown the shoes on TV nor mentioned the size. Allen had a suspicion this was being withheld because when they got a suspect, they would be able to match it up more easily. Allen did his best to keep it out of his mind, but the only real way he could do that was to occupy his time with Tara. She was starting to consume his life much the way Cheyenne had when they first started to date. He thought about her almost all the time. The only time he didn't think about her was the hour or so late most nights when he stayed up to work on the new book.

About a week after Robert was found dead, Allen and Tara

were on the couch. They had rented a movie, and even though it was on in the background they were too busy to pay any attention. Allen really felt like a teenager with Tara. He couldn't keep his hands or lips off of her, not to mention his penis out of her. She was a willing enough partner. She always seemed willing to go. For the first time in his life, Allen really felt like the man in a relationship. He would take charge in the bedroom and lead sex; he would even wake Tara up in the middle of the night sometimes, although she rarely stayed. Only a couple times since that first night. Allen asked her to stay on the night Austin had asked him if he could stay at a friend's house. It was more convenient because Austin had flat out said he had no desire to talk or meet with Tara at this time. He avoided her on purpose. He didn't seem to be angry when he said this to Allen; he just seemed to be resigned to the fact that he was never going to be a top priority in Allen's life as much as he, Allen, had promised that the situation would change between them.

Allen was just about to make his move, when of course, the phone rang. Allen considered letting it ring and calling the person back but Tara looked at him, "Answer it. I'm not going anywhere."

"You better not." He said as he stood up. Tara burst out laughing because Allen sported quite the pup tent in his pants and seemed to have some difficulty walking. He laughed too and was laughing when he answered the phone.

"Hello." He said.

"This is him."

"Yeah, I remember you."

"Took them long enough."

"Yeah."

"That's what you said that night."

"Did they ever find the owner?"

"I'm sorry to hear that."

"Send them my condolences?"

"Thanks."

"So what did they tell you?"

There was a long pause while Allen seemed to be listening intently. He would make the occasional statement of "Uh huh" or "I see" but he seemed to not even be aware he was doing so.

"No sir, I don't know any myself, and I don't hunt to be honest with you. No one in my family has ever been hunters. We have always been the type to buy our food. Plus, I just moved in a couple months ago, I don't really know anybody anyway around here yet."

After a couple more minutes of listening, Allen thanked the

person and hung up.

"Who was that dear?"

"That was the cop that was in charge when the house alarm went off. He said the ASPCA finally got back to them about the dog they found on the back porch that night. We had all looked and agreed that we thought the dog had been shot with a gun, but he said that it was an arrow. The weird thing about that, though, is they don't believe it was shot. They believe someone held him down and stabbed him with it. It was too precise, and he was too small a dog to be hit while moving with it. And apparently the people from on the other side of the woods there had been searching for a dog, and it was theirs. He said that they had him leashed outside on a runner so he could run and go to the bathroom and that they never heard anything, but when they went outside, the leash was cut, and the dog was gone. No sign of anyone in the yard either. They said he had gotten away before but always came back within an hour or two. He also asked if I knew anyone who hunts with a bow and arrow or if I had any known adversaries that might. I don't know anyone like that. This isn't exactly a hunting area. Plus, I don't know anyone besides your family anyway."

Tara looked like she wanted to say something, and opened her mouth to do so. Allen had turned the other way so he didn't see her hesitancy and wanting to speak. And before he could ask her anything, the phone rang again.

"I feel like the phone is a bad thing lately. It's almost always bad news."

Allen said as he went to answer it.

"Hello."

When Allen came back to Tara after the second call, which turned out to be nothing important at all, his mind was off of dogs and break-ins and back to her panties. He walked over to her and said, "So, where were we?"

She reached up and caressed him gently and said, "I was about right here." She leaned toward him, pulling his pants off.

The next morning, Tara had a job interview. Allen didn't like the idea of her working. Said he'd pay her bills and what not, but she refused. Said they weren't married, and even then, she would want to work because she went to college and got her degree for a reason. "Besides," she said, "it's not a full-time position. It's just tutoring a few days a week after school. Probably won't even be twenty hours a week. But if I show I am a good tutor maybe next year I can get a job at the school teaching."

Allen kind of liked the idea of dating a teacher, or at least someone with a background in education. If and when Austin was ready to meet her, he would have a teacher that could help him.

Allen sucked at school stuff, never was good at math. He was always just good at stories and writing.

After two weeks, the news had pretty much forgotten about Robert's murder. Allen, on the other hand, had not forgotten. He knew it would do no good to go talk to his old neighbors and friends, but he felt compelled to. He had not mentioned anything about the murder to Tara. Not even the fact that they had known each other. He asked Austin if he wanted to attend the funeral and Austin had declined as Allen knew he would. He felt that he had to ask though, it wouldn't have felt right otherwise. At the same time, though, Allen thought it would be weird if he had shown up himself at the funeral. It wasn't a big secret in the old neighborhood that he and Robert didn't get along, so he thought it might cast suspicions if he did show up. Not that he felt responsible. But somewhere inside of him, he did feel that way. It was unreasonable and even asinine to think it, but sometimes what we believe and what we think we know are not in conjunction.

Allen eventually went and talked to everyone in the area. Just to see what happened. He might be able to piece things together from the different stories all the old neighbors would tell, but as he talked to them all, he gleaned very little. Every one of them was repeatedly saying how sorry they were about the accident. How unfair it was and how terribly tragic. Allen accepted their condolences with grace. Although he wondered what they would think if he told them he was now seeing a woman who was nearly half his age merely months after his lovely wife was killed. He decided to hold onto that nugget of information.

When Allen got home from the visits to the old neighborhood, he was ready for a nap. He was never really a people person and didn't really enjoy conversations all that much. This was probably why he always seemed to have better conversations with himself. As he opened the door and walked in, Austin was sitting on the stairs.

"Hey dad, what's up?" Austin said, as thought he was waiting on him.

"Oh, not much, just got back from talking to some of our old neighbors. Seeing if they heard anything new about Mr. Goldsmith. No one does though. It's a shame. He and I never saw eye to eye on a lot of things, but I don't think he deserved this, that's for sure." Allen blinked a few times, a headache was settling in on him yet again.

"Yeah, it is a shame." Austin replied in an almost dead voice. He seemed to be completely devoid of emotion tonight. Allen thought the kid must be almost as tired as he was.

"Is there something you want to talk about Austin?" Asked Allen

"Yeah. I just wanted to tell you that I lied to you." Austin said, still in that dead voice.

"Lied? Lied to me about what?" Allen seemed to wake up. He had a feeling Austin hadn't been staying over at a friend's house lately. He wasn't ready for the answer he received.

"When I told you a couple weeks ago when the police were here. I told you I had taken Lennox and gone into the woods and set off the alarm. I had muzzled Lennox and put him in my room. The cops probably didn't see him because he hides under the bed when he gets scared. And he's small enough to fit, but it's not big enough for a person to hide under. Sara is allergic to dogs. She doesn't want to see him. Also, I didn't set the alarm off. I thought if I told you those things were me, then you wouldn't worry so much and be able to sleep. You say all the time how tired you are. I just thought that I could help you sleep." Austin looked between his knees during this telling.

Allen was dumbfounded by this proclamation. He couldn't really think straight. He could only think of one thing to ask, "They are saying that the dog they thought was ours that they found on the back porch was killed with an arrow. That someone had to have stabbed it with an arrow and that it came from a house that is through the woods. Did you see or hear anything or anyone that night in the woods?"

"No. I wasn't at my usual spot. I didn't lie about being out there; Sara and I went out and walked around. We weren't anywhere near where the house is where that dog came from, and then when we heard sirens, we came back to my usual spot, and then we saw when they left, and I came back here."

Allen wondered briefly how Austin knew what house the dog had come from and dismissed it. "Ok, thanks son. I'm going to go to bed."

Allen went to his room. He had a lot on his mind now. He felt like Austin had opened up a new can of worms by saying he didn't set the alarm off. At the same time, he was in a perverse way, touched by Austin's statement that he had lied. Hoping to ease his stress so he could sleep. He may have even partially said it in anger because he had been out with Tara that night. Also, Allen thought this would be a stretch, but maybe he had wanted to take credit for it because he hadn't thought of it and it did bring him back home immediately. There was a lot for Allen to think about. He wanted to write some more tonight but just didn't have the energy. For now, he dismissed everything as it was. The murder and the relation to his book were just a coincidence. The detailed knowledge that Austin has about the dog and where it came from, could be explained by the simple fact that he had walked all through the woods and had seen it before and knew where it lived, and Allen had described it to Austin as well. Allen didn't know and didn't much care. Right now, he was thinking too much and wanted to sleep, so that is what he did.

Chapter 19

The Absent Son

Allen woke up a few hours later. He didn't have any answers to the questions he asked himself when he went to sleep, but he did have an idea for his book. He got up and went to the dresser where he was currently keeping his laptop. He didn't dare work on the book in his office because it was next to Austin's room, and he would be able to hear Allen pounding away at the keys. Because when he got excited and really got going on a part he hit the keys exceptionally hard.

When he got that out of his system, he felt better. Sometimes, he felt the need to almost bleed himself of his creativity, or he wouldn't be able to settle down until he did. He didn't always have to write a few chapters or anything in a book. Sometimes, just telling himself a short story was enough, but he felt he needed to get it out sometimes.

The next morning, when he woke up, he barely remembered what he had written. He wrote it so fast that he barely thought about it before it was put on the page. He went to grab his laptop and noticed that it wasn't on the dresser in the same place this morning, but on the opposite side. When he wrote last night, he was in his bed, and he just placed the computer in the most convenient spot on the dresser, now it was on the side nearest to the door. The door remained shut, and there didn't seem to be anything else out of place. He also noticed that it was now plugged in, where he knew he didn't do that when he finished writing. He thought he must have gotten up in the night and went to the bathroom, saw the "feed me" light blinking, plugged it in real quick, and has since forgotten he even got up.

He dismissed it all and went downstairs to get breakfast. Austin, as usual, wasn't here, but Allen was glad for once. He wanted to sort through their conversation from last night a little more. He poured himself a bowl of cereal and looked out the window into the backyard to the pool they hadn't yet used. He thought it was going to be the key to bringing them together. He and Austin both loved water, and it was a huge pool with a diving board and a slide. He also thought he and Tara could make use of the attached Jacuzzi. Before Allen got much into this thought, he noticed that he hadn't gotten rid of the headache from the previous night. He was beginning to think that there was something seriously wrong with him. He was always prone to headaches and such, but they were never this intense or frequent. These days, he had almost one per day, and sometimes the medicine he took didn't touch them. It was as if they laughed at his medicine. It was mid-morning, so he thought maybe he'd just try to get some more sleep. He wasn't sure how long he had been writing the previous night, but he thought it had been a while.

He lay back down and waited for sleep to come, but it just wouldn't. He felt tired, just had too much to think about. He wished he could have worked on his book but he thought Austin would know what was up for sure if he did. He also wished that since he couldn't work on the book, Tara would at least text him. She wouldn't today, though. She had plans to meet up with some friends from college and was going to spend a few days hanging out with them after her job interview. She urged Allen during this time to get Austin to come out of his shell and at least meet her. Allen planned on doing that today.

He finally decided sleep wasn't happening again and went to knock on Austin's door. He knocked, and there was no answer. He knocked again and said his name. No answer again. He opened the door, and the room was as neat and dark as it usually was. Austin was a very neat kid now. Before, he never would have made his bed; these days, he always had it neat.

Allen thought that he must have walked to his rock in the woods. He decided to walk back there and talk to him. Make it so it was on "his territory". Maybe he'd feel more comfortable and open up. Allen had a good idea, and that may be the case today. He had a good feeling about this conversation.

He didn't realize it until he walked outside, but it had snowed during the night. It wasn't but a dusting. Barely enough to cover the grass, but Allen always loved snow, and in that moment, he missed the woman he loved more than anything else in the world. He missed her so much he ached with it. He was alarmed to realize that the woman he was thinking of was Tara and not Cheyenne. He was dismayed at this thought. He never thought of Tara as someone he loved that much. However, out here in the woods in the snow, she was his first thought. And that thought filled him with fear for some reason.

Allen's headache had not let up any, but at least it was still bearable at this point. He came into the clearing and saw a reddish lump on top of the rock.

"Austin?" He called out through the trees.

Austin turned and looked at his dad. He appeared to be unsurprised by his sudden appearance. It was a look of complete understanding.

"Hi dad, what brings you out here?" He seemed calm, almost to the point of tranquility. Allen suddenly wondered if his son was doing drugs. Or it might have just been this place. Allen felt almost tranquil here. This place was a place of great peace.

"I came to see you. Knocked on your door, and you weren't there, so I assumed you were out here." Allen answered.

"You know what they say about people who 'assume,' don't

you?" Austin laughed. The laugh didn't touch his eyes, though, Allen noticed.

"Ha. Ha. Using my lines against me, are you?" This was the first time since before Cheyenne's death, they seemed to have a little banter back and forth. Allen was enjoying it tremendously.

"Of course. I'm your son." Still no emotion.

"Yes. That you are. You even have my nose to prove it." Allen laughed, but it wasn't really contagious.

"Ugh! Not that beak!" Austin was making a motion to pull his nose off. All the while, he was finally laughing. In that moment, Allen thought to himself, "Now, that is what I miss more than anything else in the world. That laugh right there."

Allen didn't want to end the good humor so soon, but he would lose his nerve if he didn't talk to Austin about the whole reason he had trekked through a little bit of snow and the cold to do.

"May I sit?" The rock was plenty big enough and had no snow on it. Austin nodded, and Allen sat down. The rock still held some warmth from the previous day's sun. He now understood why Austin was able to come here even more when it was cold. He could lay back, and it'd almost feel like a spring day.

"I wanted to talk to you about something."

"Is it about the dog? I heard people calling for him from that direction. I saw him before and even petted him. I saw his collar, and it had his name on it." Well, that was the mystery that solved Allen's thought. He dismissed it, though, because he didn't care about the dog all that much. It made sense, though so he didn't give it much else thought.

"No, not about the dog. It's about Tara. She really wants to meet you. I know I kind of lied to you about things not being that serious between us, but in a way, I didn't because, at that time, things weren't that serious. However, since then, things have gotten a little more serious. She wants to go further in the relationship, but she wants you to be a part of it. She wants to meet you. Will you go out with us...?" Allen left the sentence hanging, hoping Austin would finish it for him.

"She's not my mom, and she never will be. We won't be a family together, and I won't act like we are. I know that's what you are going to say. That she wants us to be a family. My family is me, Mom, and you. We don't need anyone else around." The laughing boy was gone that fast, and in his place was this surly, confrontational teenage boy.

Allen let Austin have his say. "Is that why every time I want to bring her over, you are already gone?"

"Yep." Just the one word. Allen had hoped he could get more explanation from Austin, but he seemed reluctant.

"She knows she is not going to replace your mom Austin, she just wants to be friends. Have you even seen her?"

"Yeah, I've seen her sneaking through the house. I've seen her open my door and try to peek into my room. But I know what she wants, and I hide when she's there. I don't want her to know me. She will say whatever now, but later, she will be all about being my new mom. I don't need a new mom. Besides, if I start to love her as a mom, it won't matter, you'll just kill her like you did my real mom. Then where will I be? Just another fucked up kid with two dead moms and a clueless dad."

"Now Austin, that is unfair to say I killed your mom. She was killed in an accident. It wasn't my fault she decided to sneak around behind my back and see another man. She was the one that had an affair. She was the one who could have come to me and said she wasn't happy. I always told her if you ever decide that you need to cheat, just come to me, and I will let you go. I always thought she was too good for me, far too much for me to handle. I told her that, too. She didn't need to sneak around. She could have gone freely, and I wouldn't have put up much of a fight. But no! She decided to sneak around like a little slut in heat!" For the first time since her death, Allen had thought all these thoughts. They just came pouring out of him. It was like his cup of bad thoughts for his dead wife had overflowed, and the dam had broken, and whatever other cliché you could think of, he was tired of holding it back. He knew he shouldn't say these things to Austin, but right now, he couldn't help it. He was venting for the first time, and Austin just happened to be his sounding board.

"You pushed her away. You didn't care about us. You pushed us both away. And I know you will start writing again and will eventually push Tara away. That's why I won't meet her. That's why I'm always gone. Because you're just going to do the same thing, and I'll be the one left with nothing. You always have your made up people. I HAVE A FUCKING ROCK!" He screamed this last so loud Allen knew people had to hear it. He looked around, but the area seemed to be completely undisturbed. No birds or anything moving.

"Well, you're going to have to meet her eventually. She is here to stay. I'm in love with her." It was the first time he had said it out loud. He knew she should be the first to hear that proclamation, but here he was, making it to his son instead.

"I won't. You can't make me. You can't make me do anything. And I think you know that too. You are afraid of her meeting me. Admit it. That's why you have been seeing her for a few months, and it still hasn't happened. I know you only let her stay when I go to a friend's house to stay. Even though you don't even know I'm going to a friend's house. You never call and check on me." Said Austin. He seemed to be inside Allen's head.

"That is because I trust you and don't feel the need or necessity to check up on you." Allen came back quickly

"That's the excuse that you use. You just don't care that much about me anymore. I don't think you ever did." Austin was speaking venomously

"Is that what this is all about? You're trying to prove something? Trying to prove that I don't care. I don't know what I'm doing here, Austin. I thought you needed space. I was giving you space. I don't want to smother you with love. I know when my parents died when I was young, people were all over me. They wanted to know how I was doing every second of the day. I thought that you would want the same thing I did. I just wanted to have someone available to me. I didn't want people all over me all of the time."

"How would you know what I want? You've never asked me. You just always assumed what you wanted was what I wanted. I leave the house because even though we moved, you brought everything associated with Mom here, too. She's all over the house. I'm surprised you don't have her pictures everywhere. Bad enough that you have her things. You brought her desk. Her computer. Her clothes. Her chair. Her stupid collections. Why? You and I both know neither one of us wants them. I leave the house because I understand she's dead in a way you seem not to comprehend. You think you can keep her alive by having stuff around that was hers."

Allen thought that Austin was wrong in this. Hadn't he just thought on the walk here that he missed Tara more than he missed Cheyenne? So why was he keeping her stuff? He didn't know. He just couldn't get rid of it right away. And now he barely thought about her stuff. His focus had been more on Tara lately. He was with her, either out on dates or at home watching television. Maybe Austin was right, he needed to get rid of the stuff.

"If I get rid of her stuff, will you meet Tara? Maybe you can bring your friend Sara and we can double date. How would that sound?" Allen asked, he felt like he was clutching at straws now.

"You're not meeting Sara. She doesn't like dads. She doesn't trust them not to leave her. But I'll think about meeting her but you need to be more involved with me. I feel like you're breaking your promise that you made that we will be closer." Austin looked directly into his dad's eyes as he said that.

"Ok. I will try to do better. I won't say I promise because I seem to be bad at sticking to them lately. I'll just say I'll try to do better." Allen said, barely able to meet his son's gaze and breaking eye contact as soon as he felt it prudent.

"Fair enough," Austin said.

"Want to come back and order some pizza?" Allen always

felt like he needed an abrupt subject change. He felt better about the situation with Tara and Austin even though nothing had really been resolved. At least he had an idea why Austin was so hesitant to meet her; he was scared to lose someone else he cared about. Allen knew he would care about her, too, because Tara was such an easy person to love.

"No thanks. I brought a lunch out with me. I'm just going to hang out here. It's supposed to warm up during the day, and the snow will melt, and my rock will be warm." Austin said, stretching out as he lay back.

"Okay Austin. Change your mind, and I'll gladly order." Allen said, getting up. He glanced around, looking for the lunch, and saw nothing.

"Thanks Dad," Austin said, not looking at his dad.

Allen walked away. He looked for his footprints and found them easily. He looked around for Austin's and couldn't find them. He guessed Austin took a different path. There seemed to be a lot of paths to this particular area. It seemed a popular spot for many creatures.

Chapter 20
The Second Murder

Allen made his way back to the house. A part of him thought that hunger would bring Austin out of the woods sooner rather than later, but he thought that he would sit down and pound out a few hundred words on his new book. He had been neglecting a little as of late. He wanted to work on it and even had ideas that he put in his notes, but with everything happening lately, he hadn't worked as much as he liked. He sometimes found it difficult to think of negative things when he found himself so madly in love with Tara. He freely admitted this to himself now, even though he wasn't sure he was ready to admit it to her as of yet. He loved Cheyenne. She was sadly, he always thought, the first woman he had ever loved. With Tara, it was different. He didn't feel like he owed her anything, whereas with Cheyenne, he always felt inferior. He assumed that was why he had so much trouble being the man of the relationship because he felt that at any second she could and would just up and leave him. It turned out his fears weren't as baseless as he was beginning to think they were because she was cheating. Now, though, things are completely different with Tara. He's able to act more of the man in the relationship. He's able to make moves and let his desires be known. Before, he would assume his wife didn't find him attractive and then pleasure himself in the study using the

Internet. He wasn't sure when it all changed, but he thought that maybe he was the type of guy who got better looking with age, at least, he had noticed lately that more women were taking notice of him. He thought that he was in pretty good shape; he exercised regularly (until he lost his running shoes. Better get another pair he made a mental note to himself), and he still had all of his hair, and it hadn't a single strand of gray in it. He had gotten laser eye surgery, so he no longer wore big, bulky nerd glasses. So yeah, it was safe to say he felt much more confident in himself.

So he pulled out his laptop and decided to put down some words. Even if they weren't any good, he thought he'd at least get into a grove eventually. He found the grove after just a few minutes. He finally figured out where to go with his next murder. He thought he'd add a twist, and he was excited to be finally writing it down. He wrote for about an hour until he thought he heard the door downstairs open and close. He was ready to quit writing anyway because he felt a headache creeping back into his life. He wished these would go away, but they seemed to be a part of his life no matter what anymore.

He glanced through what he had written, ran a word count to see if it fit in with the amount of words he liked to average and saw that he had actually written what would work out to be about twenty-five pages. He didn't realize he had written so much, but he was glad to have finally broken through that dam. He never liked to think of it as writer's block exactly, because he had the ideas; he just was too busy to write down what his ideas were. He was reading a little of what he had written, he hoped that this particular murder would come as a surprise to the reader. He liked to keep them on their toes and hoped this would do just that.

At that moment, he heard the doorbell ring, he wasn't expecting any company, so he was at a loss for who it might be. He thought Tara was going to be out of town all day, so he didn't expect it to be her. He closed his laptop after saving the file and then encrypting it. He thought that maybe this was a little too paranoid for his taste, but he wanted to keep Austin from knowing that he was writing again.

He went to the door and answered, as he went, he checked on Austin's room to see if he was there, but the kid hadn't returned yet. So he must have been imagining things or something when he heard the door open and close.

He opened the door and was surprised to see his real estate agent, Audrey, at the door.

"Hi Mr. Bennett. Sorry to just randomly show up like this, but I've been calling for a few days now, and your phone seems to not be working or something. I have a buyer for your house, and they've made an offer. They told me I have to talk to you today, or they are going to pull the offer."

"Really? I've been using my phone. I haven't had any issues with it. Maybe it's entered wrong in your phone contact list?" He looked at her quizzically.

"I don't know, maybe. I just know I want to try to close this deal for you. I'm sure you're tired of paying the bills for two houses." She said, she looked flustered to Allen.

Allen, who hadn't even thought about it, just nodded. "Sure am," he said. Then added, "Come in, sit down. Can I get you something to drink?"

"No, thank you. I just need to get this done, to be honest." Allen remembered her as being flirty when he was looking for a house, but now she seemed to be a little stand off and didn't want to meet his eyes. He wondered if it was just his imagination or if she somehow felt in danger in his presence. He decided he was being a little weird about it and tried to relax.

"So the offer, what is it? Do you think it's fair?"

"Well, it's under what you are asking."

"I don't even remember what I'm asking, how's that for senility setting in at an early age?" Allen joked. Audrey just gave a wan smile. Allen decided to get this over with soon. His headache was back again, and once again, it was in full force. He was almost to the point that if they offered a hundred dollars for the house, he'd accept. At this point, he just wanted to get her and this awkward feeling out of his house.

"You were asking $795,000. They found a few things wrong with the house and said they are willing to fix the issues themselves but want the cost to be taken off the final price of the house. They are offering $675,000. They said the roof needs to be replaced, the basement needs to be resealed, and the driveway needs to be repaved. Finally, they said that the heating and air conditioning units need to be replaced soon. They are each fifteen years old. They priced all these things, and the cost for everything will be around 40 thousand. They will split the cost and raise their offer to six-ninety."

Allen interrupted. "That doesn't seem like splitting the cost. They only added fifteen thousand. Half of forty is twenty." He laughed. He was going to accept the offer. Let them fix whatever they thought needed fixing, and he could be done with the entire process. "It doesn't matter though. I accept their offer of 675 and will let them fix it up as they see fit." Audrey looked relieved.

"Were you worried about me not accepting it?" He asked.

"Yeah, you seemed pretty firm when we set the price. I think that's why we haven't had any offers to this point. I told people who toured it that you were firm. I had a couple offers that were much lower that I rejected out of hand myself because they were laughable. One person offered 300 thousand. I told him that's ridiculous and escorted him out." She forced out a laugh

"Well, I think this is fair, and we will go with it. Do I need to sign anything?" He asked, looking at her as she pulled out the paperwork.

"Yeah, here's their offer sheet with the straight-up sale, with no provisions about you paying to fix anything." She said.

Allen signed. He had actually forgotten all about selling his house. He honestly couldn't even remember meeting Audrey in order to set up everything. He obviously had, he was looking at the paperwork right now. Oh well, he thought. It's done and over with now, and he won't have to worry about it anymore.

He saw Audrey to the door and watched her drive away. He couldn't figure out why she seemed to be so tentative around him, but she was for some reason. Maybe he said something during the meeting he just couldn't seem to remember at this time. He hoped he hadn't said something that weirded her out, but he had a strong feeling he did do something.

He decided not to worry about it. He'd have one or two more meetings with Audrey, and then he'd be done with her, and he wouldn't have to worry about her anymore. He still thought she was super sexy, but he had Tara and wanted to focus on that.

Allen went to bed and waited to see if he heard Austin come

back into the house. Eventually, he heard the door open and close.

"Austin! Come up here please." He shouted.

He didn't hear anything as Austin suddenly appeared at the door of his room a few minutes later.

"Yeah Dad?" He looked in the door.

"I have something I want to tell you." Allen said.

"Okay. What's up?"

"Audrey, the woman who helped us find this house, just stopped by. She said she has a buyer for our old house."

"Oh." Austin looked a little crestfallen.

"Are you ok with that? I mean, I told her I accepted the offer. I can call her back and say we aren't ready to sell at this time." He studied his son's face.

"No. No, it's ok. I think we need to sell it. We need to move on." But Allen could see in his eyes were saying something else, as the tears welled up there.

"Okay. Well, I sign the papers and everything in a couple days. You want to come with me. Meet the new owners?" Allen pretended not to notice them

"Not really. It'd just be weird for me right now."

Allen wasn't feeling up to an argument with Austin right now because he just accepted it as being okay with him.

"I need a nap. You want to get a pizza when I wake up?"

"No. Not really hungry. Just going to lie down, too."

Allen slept hard and long. He didn't realize just how exhausted he was until he woke up the next morning, and it was only morning by a few more minutes. He was in a panic. He had arranged to meet Audrey at the old house at 9 am this morning. He found his phone and saw he had a total of zero missed calls. Of course, she said she had been having trouble getting ahold of him on his cell phone. He dialed her number from the card she had left the previous day. It went straight to voicemail. "Hey Audrey, it's Allen Bennett. Sorry, I missed our meeting. Hopefully we can get together later today and sign the papers for the house. I know you said they were cash buyers, so it'll be a nice smooth process. My number should have shown up correctly on your caller ID. Just give me a call back as soon as you get this."

Allen was still lying in bed as he made this call. He tried to move and was extremely stiff all over. He felt like he'd been lifting weights or something. He looked at his phone and was about to text Tara to see if she wanted to go with him to sign the papers. When he saw Audrey called and that's when he saw the date. It was two days later. He'd slept for almost 42 straight hours! He gasped loudly. "Austin?"

There was no response from Austin. Surely, he would have noticed his dad hadn't been out of bed. And speaking of which, why hadn't Tara called or texted? He looked through his texts and saw one from her the previous night. It was sent at 8:48 pm. He read it. In his sleep, apparently, "Going to stay at my grandparents an extra day. Gpa feeling sick, worried it is his heart. Be home tomorrow evening, most likely. XOXOXO."

He even responded with, "That's fine, babe. Hope he feels better. See you then. Love you lots." It was the first time he'd said he loved her, and it was a text. He felt pathetic at this point. More so because he said it for the first time in a text than because he did not even remember saying it. He also searched his mind to see if he remembered that she said she was going to stay with her grandparents when she went back home. He supposed she did, but he missed it somewhere in the conversation. He guessed she would have to stay somewhere if she didn't stay with her friends, a relative was the most logical choice.

He decided to open the laptop and read the paper. The headline was huge and caught his eye: "LOCAL WOMAN, REAL ESTATE AGENT FOUND DEAD." Allen was caught immediately. He read the article once, and then twice. He couldn't believe what he was reading. He had written this murder two days ago. It was a woman who was found stripped down to her underclothes. She had been strangled from the front. In his book, his second victim was a woman. The woman had been the best and most frequent customer of the wife of his main character. He was disgusted by this more than he was by the men. He was disgusted that his wife was fucking a woman. The idea had enraged him. And when he found out the woman was someone he knew, that made it even worse. He was no angel; he had cheated on his wife. She had never known about it. Although now he wondered if she had and this business had been her subtle revenge. The woman was the woman he'd cheated with off and on over the past few years. So it was easy for him to call her, meet and then kill her. He stripped her down and wanted to make it look like a rape. He had also used her lipstick to write to write 4MW on the stomach. And she was found in an abandoned lot that was for sale.

Allen read the article a third time. The victim was found in a lot that was for sale. Young woman, stripped to underwear. Wearing an abnormal amount of lipstick. It was also said to be an unusual color, but the lab had not been able to confirm the brand or color at this early time. The article said there were no lipstick cases found around the victim. Also written across the back of her underwear were the letters FMM. Allen couldn't believe it. It was his murder all over again. As he was ready to close the computer up, he saw the time of the article. It was time stamped for 8:09am that morning. He saw it was now after 1 pm. He had read the article over and over for more than an hour. He hit refresh, and the name was now in the article. All color drained from his face as he hit the floor. Across his screen, it now read, "LOCAL REAL ESTATE AGENT AUDREY WATERS FOUND DEAD IN VACANT LOT."

Chapter 21

The Murder Scenes

Allen just sat staring at the screen. He wasn't sure what he was looking at. He knew the words, he understood the message they conveyed, but all the same he didn't understand. How could Audrey be dead? He'd just talked to her a couple days ago. He felt a headache coming on; he wanted to push it away as quickly as possible. He needed to process this information. He was still staring at the words on the screen. His first instinct was to say it was a coincidence, but he knew that was highly unlikely because how many real estate agents would have the exact same name? He thought none. He took a deep breath and tried to clear his head. He was having trouble focusing. It was like he was having a feeling a déjà vu. He felt like he had lived this moment before. He didn't think it was true, but at the same time, he had a queer sensation rush over his body. He scanned the article again, looking for more information he may have missed, but there wasn't any. He felt like he already knew the scene. He knew how her body was positioned. He knew everything. Not because he was there, but because he had written it down.

Allen started to panic. Once was a weird coincidence, twice was just fucked up. He'd written two people's murders in his new book. And not only had a lot of details, but also he knew the two victims. He knew he hadn't committed the crimes, but he wondered if someone would connect the dots that led to him. He led a pretty basic lifestyle; he'd never done anything against the law in his life. He didn't have anything to hide, but at the same time, cops made him nervous. He guessed they made a lot of people nervous in that way. It was unsubstantiated, but that didn't make it any less true. People were afraid of many things they had no reason to be. He himself had no reason to be afraid of squirrels, but the sight of one in the yard or crossing the road sped his heart rate up quite a bit.

He didn't think they would connect him to anything, which they couldn't anyways. He tried to relax. He took another deep breath and released it slowly. This one brought the real world back into focus.

He knew it was no longer just a coincidence that these were happening in his book and in real life. He needed more information. He needed to see the places where the murders took place. Scope out the scenes and see how much the similarities match his book. At the same time, though, he thought it might look suspicious if he showed up there. He needed to think this through. He wished Tara was back from wherever she was. She would help him by getting his mind off things, but she hadn't contacted him in the last few days. He was beginning to worry a little about their relationship, but he thought they were still good. She had seemed a little different toward him before she left a few days ago. She was stiff and awkward when he hugged and kissed her. He had asked her about it, but she just said it had nothing to do with him and that she would tell him about it when she returned. She said she was going to be home yesterday, but the message he received said she was staying because her grandfather was sick, he felt stupid. He knew his being sick wasn't the reason she went back to the area where she grew up. It was something else for sure, but with all his headaches and poor sleep lately, he couldn't remember what the original reason was. He just knew she was going back to stay for a couple days. He wasn't sure why, but when she had said college friends, it felt like a lie because she was going back to her hometown. If her college friends had lived in her hometown, he doubted she would have labeled them "college friends." Some unease was creeping in on him, whether he liked it or not.

Allen decided to text her to see what she was up to and if she would be home. He kept it short and sweet and said he loved her again. He wanted a response from her immediately, but it didn't come. He waited a few minutes, and nothing. He hoped she was just busy and not at the hospital.

He looked in Austin's room, but it looked as undisturbed as ever, the kid was neat if he was nothing else. It was then that he looked outside and saw it. Laying just off the sidewalk, in plain view, really, was a cell phone. He opened the door and looked down at it from about fifteen feet away. It was a nice phone, but he couldn't tell what kind it was. He only knew iPhones by sight anymore.

Smartphone is all he thought. He walked up and looked down. He noticed his feet were bare. His toes were freezing. It was probably the coldest day of the season so far, and he was outside in his bare feet. He still didn't recognize it. He picked it up and turned it over in his hands. He'd never seen a phone like this one. He'd seen almost everyone he came into contact with use their phones, Austin, Tara, Audrey, everyone. He knew this wasn't any of theirs. He fumbled around with it, he was extremely nervous now. He didn't know what to think. He looked at it and finally figured out how to make it come on and then found the contacts list. There was only one contact, it was a very peculiar name for someone, and it simply read "Dead Man". He messed around with it some more and saw there were no text messages, no dialed calls, no missed calls and nothing that had shown that the phone had ever been used. He went back to the contacts list and figured out how to find the number. He dropped the phone. It was his number.

He ran back into the house. He didn't know what to think except that he was meant to find that phone out there. He wondered if someone was just fucking with him or not. He couldn't decide right off hand. He closed and locked the door and yelled for Austin again, knowing the kid wasn't home. He was suddenly worried about his son's safety. There seemed to be a lunatic on the loose and had targeted him for some reason. As if he hadn't been through enough lately, now he has to deal with a crazed stalker. His phone began to ring; he didn't want to answer it. Someone was watching him. They knew he had found the phone and they knew he was scared. Now, they were calling to give some kind of crazy demands. Allen hoped it was just money. He had money. He wouldn't give his son, though; he'd give his life first before that would happen. The phone was in the kitchen, he ran in to answer it. Knowing a stalker would never leave a voicemail.

He picked it up, "Hello?" He did not even look at who was calling, just answered. It was a female voice, and at first, it wouldn't register. He tried to place it, but he doubted he would recognize anyone's voice in his current state.

"Allen? Are you ok?" He was able to lock on the voice. Tara.

"Yeah, just been a weird morning. How are you?" He said, trying to get normalcy back into his voice.

"Been better. Grandpa died this morning. He knew it was his time and he just gave up. I'll be here another week. I didn't want to tell you in a text. That's why I called." She sounded as if she had a cold, but she didn't seem to be crying at the moment.

"I'm sorry to hear that. Give me the arrangements information and I will send flowers. Do you need me to come up there?" Allen hated funeral talk, and supposed he always would.

"No. No, it's ok. Mom and Dad came up yesterday evening.

We are here. It'll be fine. Thanks, though." She sounded genuinely pleased with the offer.

"What was the other reason you went up there?" Allen blurted it out before he realized what he would say. He wanted to know but also felt like it wasn't entirely his business. He had sensed that it was deeply personal, but for the moment, he couldn't help himself.

"Well, I don't really think this is the best time to talk about it to be honest." Defensive Allen noted, he'd never heard this particular tone of voice. It was defensive. It was like when a rabbit would put its ears up to maximize hearing. If it sensed danger, for some reason, Allen felt that Tara sensed danger from him. He wanted to let it go. A part of him needed to let it go, unfortunately the majority of him needed to know. He recalled how she was different when she left, stiff and awkward. He said, "I don't need details. Just a general sketch. You didn't mention family, so I know your grandpa getting sick was a shock to you."

"Allen, please. This isn't the time. I don't want to think about it anymore. It's over and done with."

Something clicked with Allen and he knew with all the intuition man had developed since the caveman days, he knew. "It's your ex, isn't it? You told me you were done. You never finished the divorce. You told me it was over." Allen was angry. He was disappointed. He didn't think this would have changed anything in their relationship, except they may have gone slower.

"Yes. How'd you know?" Now he could hear tears in her voice, but they weren't tears from her grandfather dying. He had just hurt her.

"Guessed. You should have just told me." To Allen, the cell phone in the yard made more sense now. The guy worked with phones for a living. He could easily have gotten one. He decided not to tell Tara.

"How did it go?" He tried for a casual tone, and felt he had achieved it admirably.

"It didn't. He never showed up." She said, that hurt still in her voice. But now, was it for him or for the ex? He wasn't sure.

"Any reason he wouldn't?" Allen was struggling to keep his tone light.

"Several. At the top of the list is he doesn't want a divorce. Another is he is kind of obsessed with me. You know that from receiving calls. He's basically harmless, though. All bark and no bite. He will be served with the papers. He will either sign them or not, and then it'll be over either way."

"Good." And then Allen added, "Look, I'm sorry for being so nosy."

"Don't worry about it, you're fine. I should have just told you." The hurt in her voice had subsided, and he believed her.

"Hey," Allen interrupted, "How long is the drive up there?" Allen hoped she would take this as he was back to thinking about the funeral again.

"About ninety minutes. Why?" She asked. She couldn't keep the suspicion out of her voice.

"Curious is all." Allen said while he tried to laugh a little.

"Ok. Well, hey I better go. Everyone is starting to show up at the house." She said with no hint of laughter.

"Ok. If you need anything, let me know."

"I will. And thanks. Bye"

"Bye, Tara."

Allen started to pull the phone away from his ear when he heard his name,

"Oh hey Allen, one more thing, I love you too."

"I love you too." He was tempted to play the teenager's game where they went back and forth saying I love you and I love you more, but he didn't feel it was a good time to do that. He thought that everything was going to be alright with them; he had hurt her, and she had hurt him, but they had gotten through it and told one another that they loved the other. When that happens, it can't be too bad, he thought.

She said, "You have no idea how nice it is to hear that from someone and know that the person behind the voice isn't crazy obsessed with you. I read not too long ago that being in love has similar brain properties as someone who has OCD. I think that makes sense. I remember when I was young, people used to say, 'This person is a perfectionist, or that person 'is extremely neat'. Nowadays, everyone has a diagnosis. I don't think it is right. I think a little obsession is good; a lot is obviously bad."

"I agree." He said," I think it's a fine line between the two, though. Between wanting to think about something several times a day and being unable to stop yourself and then acting on any kind of urges that come with those thoughts."

"I agree. Well, I better go. Bye." She said.

They hung up the phone. Allen's troubles from the morning seemed to be distant now. He was still disturbed by Audrey's death, and he still wanted to go by the place where he was found. He knew the information was in the article. He even thought the phone was not as big a deal as he first thought. He went upstairs and got dressed. He was going to go by and at least see where she was found. He decided that, at least. He had the return of the headache again. He wanted to lie down for a few minutes and did. Hoping it would go away. He nodded off. He looked at the clock and realized he'd slept for about an hour or so.

He left a note on the table for Austin, saying he was going to be out for a while, and then dug into his wallet and pulled out some cash. Told the kid if he wanted some delivery, he would pay for it tonight.

He then went and got into his car and drove away. He wasn't thinking about the cell phone in the yard because he went into the garage from the house and backed away quickly. His thoughts were with Audrey and her untimely demise. He had taken her nervousness around him the other day as being the cause, but he wondered if she had some kind of personal issues going on and was just unable to keep them off her face and out of her voice. He thought maybe he had crossed some invisible line before, but not now. He thought it was something in her personal life.

He drove by the place where his old neighbor was killed. He could have a ready-made excuse if anyone asked him why he was there. He would just say that he wanted to check on the old house. He drove slowly past the park. He looked at it in every detail and, for the first time realized that it was the park that he used in his book without even thinking about it. From the placement of the equipment to the bathrooms and even the trees. He was a little freaked out at this point. He didn't want to go past where Audrey was murdered.

This was different. He had a reason to be here. He had no reason to be there. He went anyway. And again, he was shocked to find that he'd already been here at some point. It was just as he described in the book. The neighboring structures, the broken glass, the height of the grass, everything was the same.

He stopped. The "POLICE LINE DO NOT CROSS" tape was strung all around the area. He didn't need a picture. He knew where her body was found. He could picture it in his mind's eye. He tried to convince himself it was the story teller in him that was making it up, that he was spooking himself. That was when he saw it. The cell phone. He knew without getting out of his vehicle. It was the same kind. He thought it was probably even the same one.

Chapter 22

The Deception

Allen pondered the phone as he drove. He was driving to Tara's grandparents' town. He decided this as he sat staring at the phone in the grass. At least, that's what he told himself. He had really decided as soon as he asked Tara how far away it was from the town. He didn't have an address. His plan was to just show up in town and then call her and say, "Surprise! I'm here!" He hoped she would take it for what it was meant to look like, him coming to offer support in a time of need. That's what he told himself he was doing. Just being a supportive partner. What another part of him, the monster inside of him. The one that growled if another man entered "his territory" and put his wind up, didn't give a shit about dead grandparents and crying family members. What that monster cared about was ensuring that Tara had returned to sign divorce papers and go through the hearing.

The fact that she had kept it from him all along made him feel betrayed. He didn't show it outwardly, but on the inside, he was a raging fire of jealousy, anger, and vengefulness. He stopped to think about that word for a minute. Vengefulness. What was he vengeful for? That she hadn't told him? Maybe. But what could he do about it now? Not a whole lot when it came down to it. She obviously had her reasons. It was his business. He felt that way, for sure that it was his business. When he's receiving calls and hang-ups on his phone, which still happened, not with the frequency as when they first started, and he's having random phones left in his yard with his number listed under "Dead Man" in the phone book. Yeah, he thought he had a right.

Sure, she said he was harmless. What was the phrase? "All bark and no bite." Well Allen thought that this dog was ready to show it could bite. He needed to know there was nothing to it anymore. He needed to know that Tara was solely his girl and not harboring any thoughts of rekindling that old relationship. He didn't want to go through that, he'd had enough problems with that when he was younger. He always told people that if a girl wants her ex back or whatever, all she has to do is go out with me once, and then they'll get back together. It had happened far more times in his life than he cared to remember. So yeah, his trip was more about protecting himself rather than being supportive. He could be both, though. He knew he could. It wouldn't be a problem. In her upset state, Tara might even divulge a little more information than she would normally, and that would be fine with him.

Allen checked his phone; made sure he had no texts or anything from Tara, and saw he didn't. Good. He wouldn't be expected to answer and it would be hard pressed not to tell her what he was doing. He knew she would be surprised, but he wasn't sure if it would be a good surprise. She hadn't explicitly said for him not to come. She had just said she would let him know if she needed anything.

Allen reached the town limits and saw a gas station. He was ravenous. He hadn't eaten since, well he couldn't really remember when, and thought that something to eat would be good while he called Tara.

He pulled in and went in, got a sandwich and a small bag of chips. He usually didn't go for gas station food, but this was a special situation. He got up to the counter and laid his items down. He waited for the clerk to ring his food up and looked the other way when she spoke.

"How are you doing today, Mr. Bennett?" She asked him timidly

Allen was brought back out of his daydream quickly and snapped his head back around.

"Excuse me?" He asked.

"I said how are you doing today Mr. Bennett?" She repeated, a little louder.

"Oh, oh," Allen was having that queer sensation that he'd lived this moment before. He couldn't explain it, but it was as though he'd had this conversation before, with this clerk and her flirtatious eyes. "Oh, I'm doing good. Just hungry, you know. Even writers have to eat sometimes, right?" He assumed the young woman had recognized him from his book jackets. He hated to have his picture taken personally, but his agent and publisher absolutely insisted on it because they wanted the public to know his face. The clerk looked at him questioningly and then gave the total. Allen paid, said, "Have a good night" under his breath, and headed for the door.

When he got back to the car, he noticed the clerk was still looking out the window at him. He couldn't shake the sensation that he'd talked to her before. Like they'd had a real conversation, something beyond the normal clerk and customer idle talk. She seemed noticeably perplexed when he said something about being a writer, as though she didn't recognize him from the books. Then again, his mind had been far away when she spoke, she may have said more and he missed it.

Allen didn't have time to wander his way through the mind of a pubescent girl. He seemed to have them more attracted to him now, but when he was their age, none of them would give him the time of day. He assumed they took in his nice clothes, nice watch, and expensive car and saw security in their lives long before they saw his ugly face, hairy arms and wrinkles.

He picked up the phone and dialed Tara's number. It rang and rang, and finally, the voicemail picked up. This was the one contingency that Allen hadn't really planned for. He didn't know what to say to her voicemail, so he just hung up and pondered his options. He probably could find her grandparents' address on the Internet, but that just seemed back handed and sneaky. He dialed again. This time, it connected after the second ring.

"Hello." A male voice. The monster inside Allen growled again. He told himself to calm down. It's probably a cousin. He sounded fairly young, early twenties or so. Allen realized he hadn't said anything back, "Is Tara around?" Then immediately mentally scolded himself. He knew he had instantly come across as rude. He never said a greeting back.

"No. She went down to the funeral home to help make arrangements. She should be back in an hour or two. She left her phone here because she didn't want to get interrupted or something. Can I take a message?" The young man said. There was no jealousy in his voice, which almost convinced Allen that it wasn't a love of any sort.

"Uh, yeah, tell her this is Allen, have her call me as soon as she can?" He knew he wasn't coming across very well, but was helpless to make it sound better. He was nervous, and discombobulated. He didn't know how much or how little Tara had said to her family about him.

"Oh Allen? The writer?" The young man asked, a note of excitement entering his voice now.

Allen was stuck on that. Not "boyfriend" but "writer". Maybe he was jumping to conclusions or something; he was just about to say something else when he noticed the man on the other end of the line was still talking. "Excuse me? I missed what you were saying there." He said, getting more angry with himself.

"Oh, I was just saying that it is really nice of you to help her get started on a book. She's been saying forever she wanted to write something. She always loved to tell stories and make things up, ever since we were kids." This convinced Allen he was a relative. Allen wiped his hand across his forehead, mocking, wiping off sweat. She had known him since they were kids. This guy had to be a cousin, then.

"Yeah, she was always making people laugh and entertaining everyone. She used to drive all the adults crazy because she wanted to know everything about everything." He was laughing as he talked, apparently remembering some funny story.

Allen was completely baffled as to what to think. Tara had never mentioned writing a book, and he didn't see this overly inquisitive side of her. She usually let him drive the conversation on almost all occasions. Also, she had a sense of humor but she wasn't overly witty or sarcastic either. Allen began to wonder if he knew this woman at all.

"Well just let her know I called and was making sure she was doing ok and everything." He wanted to not sound angry, but he didn't know if he could manage that because he was angry.

"Ok, I will." The laughter was completely gone from the kid's voice now.

"Ok. Thanks. Bye" Allen said and started to hang up.

"Oh wait, there's a truck coming in now. It might be Jimmy's." The kid almost screamed into the phone.

Before he could stop himself, Allen said, "Jimmy?"

"Oh. Her husband. You know all about him, I'm sure. Those two have always been like teenagers in love. Can't keep their hands off one another. Hurts the marriage, I'm sure, with her and her parents moving away like they did. Necessary though, she had some crazy stalker guy that she worked with after her. He wouldn't leave them alone for nothing. Her parents were moving anyway, so they just said move with us until this dies down, and then come home. Jimmy has a job he can't just up and leave. It's tough to just up and leave a business when it's just starting to catch fire. He had to stay behind and feed the flames. She moved away and was lucky enough to move next to a famous writer, which is what she wants to be. Well, listen to me, I'm just rambling like an idiot. Not every day I talk to someone famous on the phone. And it's not like I'm telling you anything you don't know." He was rambling but Allen was stuck on the third word of the ramble and missed most of what was to follow.

All Allen was able to do was say, "Yeah, true. It's ok. It happens to me sometimes." It was hard enough to choke out these words. Allen wasn't sure how much more of this conversation he could stomach. He knew Tara had to be getting close to the house by now.

Allen was floored. He had no idea what to think now. He just found out that not only was Tara supposedly using him to help her write a book, but she was married and not only married but apparently happily married. Well, it didn't add up to Allen. Something was amiss here. He needed to find out what it was, but he didn't think talking to Tara would solve that problem.

He missed something again, "I'm sorry, say that again. This damn phone gets the shittiest reception, I swear."

"I asked if you wanted to hold on a few minutes and talk to her or not?" The young man seemed to sense something was wrong because his tone had completely changed now.

"No, it's ok. I was just making sure she was ok and it sounds like she is in good hands." Then added quickly, "I gotta go." And hung up before Mr. Bad fucking news could say anything else.

Allen just sat in the parking lot of the gas station. He looked up and noticed the clerk was still looking out the window at him. He didn't care about her and was no longer curious about anything she said. His heart felt as though it was in his shoes. He didn't know what to feel. Betrayal, anger, disgust, rage, or anything. He mostly just felt heartbroken. He knew it was too good to be true. He knew all along she was far out of his league. He knew she would never stay forever, but to blatantly lie to him and deceive him. He thought it was bad when he thought she had just hidden the fact that she was still married all along and was just now telling him about her divorce. Now, he's finding out that she is only hiding out from a deranged stalker. She told him he was her ex-husband. Now he learns it is a coworker. He wondered what other lies she had told him. He had never had his foundation so fundamentally rocked in his entire life in this way. With Cheyenne, it seemed to be different somehow. He didn't know how it was different, but it seemed to be different to him. Maybe it was because Cheyenne had been first, and he accepted some, if not most of the blame for her infidelity. With Tara, he felt as though she should have known better because she knew he was coming back from being so hurt. Yet she went along and just hurt him again anyway for what gains, he did not quite understand yet. He doubted that he would understand. And the worst part of it, he thought, was that he had a shitty gas station sandwich in his stomach, which was threatening to rupture his gut, and a ninety-minute drive home to deal with, and all he would do is think all the way home.

All other things were driven from his mind as he drove him. He didn't care about dead real estate agents and asshole ex-neighbors. All he could do the entire drive was play that one snippet of the conversation over and over again in his head "'Jimmy?"

"Oh. Her husband. You know all about him, I'm sure. Those two have always been like teenagers in love. Can't keep their hands off one another.'"

Allen had to stop twice on the drive. Both times he vomited. The first time wasn't so bad. He had the brick of a sandwich in his stomach. The second was rough. He retched until he thought he was going to die from the pain. He couldn't take it anymore, and that's when it stopped. He didn't produce anything but some spittle the second time, but it felt as though he ruptured something inside of himsclf. Which would make sense, he thought. I feel torn in two anyways. He kept thinking to himself, "She's got a logical explanation for everything. Nothing is different. She is in love with you, not him. She even said so this morning."

Allen hung on to that thought as he pulled into his drive. He had forgotten to turn the lights on outside, but it seemed Austin was home because there were a couple lights on inside. He hoped he was home because he wanted someone to talk to, not about Tara. Tara was the only person that could answer the questions he had, and he felt it unfair to burden them on anyone else, especially a fourteen year old kid.

Allen was glad to be home. He had a headache. It was bad. Maybe not the worst he'd ever had, but it was pretty damn close. He knew it was stress. He needed to do something to get his mind off things. His chest ached with the pain of heartbreak and utter disappointment. He knew he needed to do something. He walked into the house and yelled for Austin and was disappointed to not hear any movement in the house. It was not overly disappointing, though. He went up to his room and flopped down on the bed. He needed to rest. Forget that he slept forty or so straight hours. He needed to rest. He felt like he had only slept a few hours.

"Dad?" Austin was knocking on the door. He was home, after all. "You ok?"

"Not really Austin. I've had a rough, rough day, and I don't know how to process it all right now." He was barely audible, because he had even bothered to lift his face off the pillow.

"I'm willing to listen if you need someone." His son said gently, but stayed standing in the doorway, closer to the shadows.

"Thanks. We will talk in the morning. You get some pizza or something delivered to eat?" He asked after considering the offer.

"No. I just ate some leftovers in the fridge. Your money is still on the table." Austin answered.

"Ok." Then added, "Hey, why don't we go out to a movie or something tomorrow?"

"Yeah. That sounds good. Let's do something together." Although the words were happy, there was no change in Austin's voice.

"I gotta get to sleep, son. I'm wiped out. I will see you in the morning. Goodnight." Allen glanced at the clock. It was barely eight. He'd left for Tara's grandparents around three. It was a three hour round trip normally. He must have been poking along coming home because he hadn't been home for more than ten minutes, and the phone call with Mr. Bad fucking news couldn't have been more than a few minutes. He didn't care. He was tired. He was going to sleep. Before that, though, he registered the fact that for the first time since Cheyenne died, Austin had agreed to do something with him outside of the house. He smiled as sleep overtook him, because, in the end, all things will just work out for the best no matter what.

Chapter 23

The Apology and Police

When Allen awoke the next morning, he wasn't quite sure why he was in such a good mood. Then he remembered that Austin had finally agreed to do something with him. He hadn't been alone with him outside the house since they moved in. This, he thought, was a giant step into the recovery of losing Cheyenne for the both of them. Allen knew he hadn't properly dealt with her death up to this point; it had been about four months. Four months! Already, damn. He looked at the clock and saw it was after 9. A good thirteen hours of sleep and he felt completely refreshed. He even momentarily forgot why he was so tired going into the night last night. Then, one glance at his phone, and he was reminded. Tara. She had lied to him. Had used him. For what reason, he didn't know. He thought one of the ten voicemails or twenty-two texts from her might bear some explanation.

"Do I even really care right now, though?" Allen asked the room out loud.

He then answered his own question, "No, I don't really care right now. I need to focus on Austin." So far in the past few months Allen had been remarkably disciplined when it came to looking at things that might hurt him. He never went back and read Cheyenne's emails with her boyfriend and never checked the phone for texts or anything after the police had delivered it shortly after the funeral. No, some things he kept telling himself were better left unknown. He thought he'd have to eventually go through the calls and texts to delete them. But for now, he was just going to ignore the phone altogether. He reached the top of it, pressed firmly down, and slid the power bar to the right, shutting it down. Good, no distractions now. He opened his bedside stand drawer and tossed the phone inside it. He didn't care if he ever got it back out.

It crossed his mind just to say that one was lost, and then he would never have to deal with it again. He would like to destroy it and possibly never listen or read the messages. Before he powered down, he did notice, though, that every call was from Tara. The last text message she sent was at 4:18 am. So she had been up all night, while he slept comfortably. "Good" Allen thought, the way it should be.

Allen left the room pondering this idea; he noticed that, for once, he didn't have a headache. He seemed to always have them anymore. He walked to Austin's room, and the kid was gone. He hoped he didn't forget that they were going to a movie. He looked around the house and didn't notice anything out of place or anything. He thought about walking into the woods to see if Austin was back there but decided against it. Austin would be back when he was ready, and the movie theater was open late.

Allen turned on the TV, he was hesitant to do this anymore with all the murders that had been occurring that were similar to his book. He was nervous about that; he would never admit this fact to anyone. But he was. He didn't know what to think about the coincidences that had been showing up in his fiction and in the news. He had not given it a lot of thought. He would have yesterday after seeing the two similar cell phones.

He jumped up off the couch, ran to the window, and looked outside. He couldn't see the spot where the cell phone had been, so he walked outside, not surprisingly it was gone. He wished he would have gotten the one that was at Audrey's murder scene. He could have at least seen if there was the only contact number in there like the one that was here in his yard. He thought about driving by the scene again and seeing if it was still there. Obviously, the police already searched the area. The phone would have been noticed straight away. He thought that if it was the same phone they would have to know he was not involved because the phone would have had to been placed there after the initial find of the body and the start of the investigation. The phone was outside the tape, though; maybe they had not searched that far of a radius yet. Allen was getting nervous, but he could not explain why. He knew he had not killed anyone, not Audrey or his old neighbor.

There was a knock on the door. It was as though Allen had had a premonition of this moment. A feeling of déjà vue was hitting him like a tidal wave. He knew he was going to go to the door, and there would be two police officers there. They would tell him he was needed downtown for a few questions. He would ask in regards to what, and they would say he would find out when he was taken downtown. Allen thought about making a run for it, he didn't know why, but this urge was almost overwhelming. He was innocent, though. He had nothing to hide. He did not need to fear the police, yet he did with every fiber of his being. He sat rooted to the couch. He couldn't see the shadow or reflection of the person or people that were standing outside the door, but he knew there were two. He felt like he'd already lived this scene a dozen times in his life, and it was etched inside his brain. Burnt into his memory even before it had happened in real time.

Allen walked to the door. He felt like he was floating on a fast current. Working away from his goal. It was a tremendous effort just to make it to the door. He tried the peephole but couldn't make himself look so he just opened the door. He knew how they would be standing too, even before he saw them, one slightly behind the other, hand on the butt of his gun in case Allen decided to be in trouble.

He had even started to say, "I'm no trouble." Before the door was even fully opened, he got all the words out, and then he realized that they made no sense because it was not two police officers standing in front of him, it was Tara. She looked exhausted, to the point of near collapse. Allen looked at her and couldn't say anything else, she did, however. "No trouble? You think you're no fucking trouble? Why the fuck did you call me? I told you I didn't need anything." Allen was shocked by these words. He had never heard her talk like this before. He didn't know what to think. She wasn't done, though. "You made a fine fucking mess for me. I got the shit beat of me last night because of you. Yes, Jimmy is my husband. I'm divorcing. No, the rest of my family doesn't fucking know. Now they are all asking questions about what's going on because you decided to try to be Prince Fucking Valiant and be my knight in shining armor or whatever other fucking stupid cliché you want to use. You have fucking ruined my life. Do you understand that? Now my family doesn't fucking trust me. You're a fucking dickhead. I thought you were fucking different. No. You're just like him. You can't give me an inch of space to take off the business I need to take care of. Now I have bruises all over my back from being whipped with a belt last night and a bunch of family members who love Jimmy like he's the second fucking coming a Christ who wonder if I'm fucking you and dumping him." She was screaming, tears streaming down her face, which was black with rage.

Allen just stood there. He didn't know what to do or how to respond. He had thought up many responses to this situation but had never even dreamed it would be this venomous. She hated him at this moment. He didn't understand why. He had never insinuated that they were anything more than mentors and students. Apparently, though, her family had read a lot between the lines or something. Or maybe the husband had confiscated her phone and read texts and listened to voicemails that were very incriminating. Allen felt bad for a moment. Then he realized this all could have been avoided. She was standing there panting, and staring daggers at him. If looks could kill, Allen would be dead as fuck.

"You should have told me." He responded with finally. "You should have let me in on your final plan. Imagine my shock when I call the woman I love and her phone is answered by someone else and I am told she is out with her husband, and they are 'like teenagers in love'. What am I supposed to think, Tara? I will tell you what I thought that you're a lying piece of shit that was using me. And where did this writing a book thing come from anyway? I never knew you had a desire to do that!"

Tara had calmed a little.

"I told you that my ex worked at a cell phone store. He checked my records. I used that as something to tell him so he wouldn't think anything was going on because he knew I've always wanted to write." She wasn't screaming, but there was still an edge to her voice.

"Yeah, tell him. Of course. He is the one who knows everything about you when I don't know anything because you barely talk about yourself. How do I know you're not setting me up for blackmail or something?" Allen wasn't angry, he wasn't even mad necessarily. He understood that people could be that rude and mean and just accepted that someone he proclaimed love to twenty-four hours ago was one of these people.

"Allen, I meant it when I said I love you yesterday. You make me happy. Doesn't it mean anything I drove all the way here just to talk to you? I tried calling you all night. You didn't answer. I sent you so many texts and you didn't answer. I had to talk to you. I had to make sure you understood that it is you that I love, not someone else. I used to love him not anymore. I can't go back to someone so bad when I've been with someone so good. I know it's only been a couple months, but I love you more than anything else in the world." There were more tears, but there were tears of pain, not anger.

This seemed to get through to Allen. He was pacified for the moment.

"You promise it's over?" He knew that wasn't the best way to start, but it had to be asked, and sooner was better than later.

"Yes." She pulled an envelope out of her purse and handed it to him. It contained a court date for a divorce hearing. It was the previous day's date.

"I'm sorry I caused so much trouble, my dear. Do you want

to come in?" He stood aside.

"I can't. I have to get back. The family is expecting me to be there. I had to tell them we were getting a divorce, and the story I told them about a stalker at work was a lie, that I was being stalked by my husband. My parents agreed to move only to save me from him." She explained.

"They still hate you?" Asked Allen incredulously.

"Oh yeah, they love him. Most think he's the best thing since sliced bread. He's just a natural charmer. I've found most of those smooth talkers in my life are almost always complete assholes." She sounded utterly exhausted.

They talked for a few more minutes, and Allen made Tara a strong cup of coffee because he was seriously worried about her sleeping on the drive back. He offered to get someone to drive her back, but she, of course, refused. Her family already hated Allen even though none had talked to him except for the cousin. They saw him as a home wrecker. Saw him as the reason for the split of their happy union. None seemed to realize that the marriage was over before Allen even came into the picture.

They kissed goodbye and Allen made sure she was more awake. He gave her a big hug and helped her into her vehicle.

As she drove away, something clicked in his head. She had

said he had used a belt on her back, but she had not winced or anything when they hugged. Maybe she had a higher pain tolerance than he expected. He didn't want to make a big deal out of it, at least. Perhaps she had exaggerated in order to drive the point home.

Allen was feeling really good about everything. He felt convinced that Tara was telling the truth. It was the divorce hearing paper, more than anything she said, that convinced him. He didn't know why, but that felt good. He knew he would probably never win her extended family over because of their initial impression of him, long term though he didn't give two shits about them. He cared about Tara and Tara only. Her parents seemed to like him, and that was good enough for him.

Allen went to go up the stairs when there was another knock on the door. He had no premonition about this knock, and why should he? The last one could not have been more wrong. He went to answer it, smiling. He thought, more like hoped, that it was Tara back saying she decided she was too tired to drive and would like to stay for a nap.

He had lived this scene, sort of, because there were two police officers standing there just as he had pictured them before. The only difference was that they were not in a position where he was ready to run. They were in a conversational position.

"Mr. Bennett?" The one standing closest to the door said.

"Yeah, that's me. What can I do for you, officers?" Allen asked. He was slightly nervous. He was always nervous around cops when they came to his house because it was almost always bad news. Death or arrest. That's the only reason cops come to your house.

"We just wanted to ask you a few questions about the break-in you had a few weeks ago." The officer said.

Allen was somewhat relieved. He had completely forgotten about that happening. "Oh, ok. Would you like to come in?"

"No thanks, sir. This will just take a moment. We wanted to know if you thoroughly searched your house for any items that may have been missing?" He asked

This question seemed odd to Allen, why would missing items be important. He had told them that nothing of value was missing; he didn't think anything else mattered that much.

"Uh, I don't recall anything missing. Though it'd be hard to say because we just moved here. I wouldn't want to report something missing that was just lost in the move." He responded, wondering if anything besides his running shoes was missing.

"I understand. But is there anything you know to have survived the move that is no longer here? Anything at all. Anything that might have been easy to get away with by the perp in question." He seemed to be driving to some point that Allen didn't see.

"I can't really think of anything at the moment." He did not want to say anything about the shoes because he had, in all honesty, never looked for them.

"Ok sir. Thank you for your time. We will be in touch if we need to ask anything else." He looked satisfied.

The officer turned and walked away. Allen was completely perplexed now. He had no idea what that was supposed to be about. He wondered if they somehow thought him a suspect and were just setting him up right now. Trying to trap him. He didn't think that was the case because he had nothing to hide. He was completely innocent. He had a strong compulsion to get in his car and drive by Audrey's murder scene again, but he knew he might have someone watching him now.

Someone who is looking for him to go back to the scene of the crime and look for any clues he might have left behind. He went up the stairs. He was getting another headache. He just needed to lie down and go to his room. On his way down the hall, he saw Austin sitting on his bed. He decided not to say anything to him. He was sitting in the dark but Allen thought he saw a smug look on his face for some reason. Allen didn't even know when the kid came home. He had not heard the door or anything. He couldn't think about that now. Right now, he needed more sleep. If he kept this up, he thought, "I'm going to sleep away the remaining years of my life."

Allen had gone from one end of the emotional spectrum and back twice today.

He awoke on a high because he and Austin actually made plans, which had come crashing down when Tara went berserk on him. She had made him feel great again because she said she loved him several times and provided what he felt was conclusive evidence about her divorce. Then he was brought back down again because now he feels he's a suspect in what was going on around the area with the murders. Even though neither officer had mentioned anything about the murders to Allen. Allen seized upon that thought. They had not mentioned it. He was just jumping to conclusions because he had been thinking about them off and on all day, and he knew that a similar, not necessarily the same, cell phone was at the scene of the latest murder. He thought maybe he was being too paranoid because of the coincidences between the murders and his book. He didn't have anything to worry about. With that thought, he blacked out for the next twelve hours.

He had completely forgotten about the movie with Austin.

Chapter 24

The Vacation

Allen woke the next day refreshed as could be. He couldn't remember all the paranoid thoughts he had been having the previous day. He did know he had slept soundly and didn't feel the traces of any headaches or anything. He felt himself, for the first time, he thought to himself, "I feel pre-Cheyenne death myself." He couldn't figure out what brought about this feeling. He just knew he felt that way. Then it hit him. It was being loved again. He knew Cheyenne had loved him and that always made him feel tremendous about himself, and for the first time since she had died, he was being loved again by another beautiful woman. Sure, she had more baggage today than he had known about this time yesterday, but you had to take the good with the bad sometimes.

Allen wanted to write some for his book. He'd had a couple ideas for it on his way home. It was weird he thought, that in such a stressful situation, he would be thinking about his book, but he had never been that way. When he got stressed, he escaped into his imagination. That was most likely how, upon returning home, he had seemed to lose track of time. He just went into his own mind and worked on the story, letting his medulla oblongata take over or whatever happened in those situations. He snuck out of his room, trying to be as quiet as possible. He checked Austin's room, it was neat as ever. It was pushing mid-morning, and Austin had seemed to become an early riser. Allen returned to his room just in time to hear his phone stop ringing. He went to check who the call was from, and it was from Tara. He was nervous all of a sudden. He didn't know why, but he was. He felt that she had a night to think about everything, and she was calling to change her mind. She wasn't going to choose him, or that he would discover that her showing up yesterday had all been a dream.

He waited to see if a voicemail would pop up, and when it did, his sweating hand was suddenly cold and clammy. He didn't know what he was so nervous about. He knew he wasn't dreaming when Tara had shown up, and she showed him the divorce papers, and everything was just fine. That was fine and dandy to try to tell himself that, but when you made a living using your imagination, things never worked that way. You were always telling yourself stories and making things out that they were not. He hoped this was the case in this situation. Then, it popped up "New voicemail from Tara" on the screen. He tapped the listen button, prepared himself for the worst, and hoped for the best. That's all you could do in these situations, really.

"Hey, babe." That alone was enough to tell him it was good. She sounded happy, tired, perhaps even into the land of exhaustion, but happy. "I just wanted to check in with you and say I love you again. I have to tell you it feels so good to say that to someone and mean it again. Even though I haven't loved my ex for a long time he insisted on my telling him that I do every time I saw him or talked to him on the phone. Anyways, I digress, I was wondering if it would be possible if we got away for a couple days. We could take Austin if he'd want to go, but seeing as how he hasn't even wanted to meet me yet I doubt he will. And you said before he could take care of himself. Maybe we can just get a hotel or go up to the lake and rent a cottage on the beach for a few days. I don't know about you, but I could definitely use a get away for a while. Let me know. I will pay for everything. Well, my dad will pay for everything. It was his idea and it has taken me by storm. Let me know. Love you, babe."

A mini vacation. Allen hadn't been on vacation in a couple years. Austin and Cheyenne took one last year, but he had gotten sick the day before they were supposed to leave, and he told them to go. He wondered now if she thought he'd faked it to stay home and write. He had written while they were away. And a lot at that, but that was not the reason. He really was sick. He felt better the next day after they left, but when he called, he played it up a little bit more than was strictly necessary. How he regretted that now. It was the last time he could have gotten away with his family, and he prolonged an illness that was serious at first but turned out to be just a twenty-four-hour bug. He sometimes wondered if his actions, or lack thereof, might be a better phrase, had somehow led to Cheyenne's death. Well he knew it had led her to another man's bed, but he wasn't thinking about it on that level. He was thinking about it on a karma level. Did he screw up so much with his wife that she was taken away from him as punishment? She was taken to God's paradise while he was left here to suffer and have so many unanswered questions. He didn't know for sure and would probably never know. At least not in this life, anyways.

Allen turned his mind from unanswerable questions to questions that could be answered easily. He loved the idea of getting away with Tara. He wondered if Austin would want to go. Perhaps it could be a way for them all to connect and start true lives as a family. He'd thought about that a lot lately. He thought he would eventually like to marry Tara, but not right away. He wouldn't even broach the subject with her. With him still being a relatively new widow and her just now finalizing a divorce. He doubted she wanted to even think about marriage at this point. Hell, they'd just now confessed love for each other for the first time in the past couple days. However, he could see himself with her long term. He did wonder what his family, and also Cheyenne's family, would say if he were to be married within a year or two of her death. He didn't really feel all that guilty about it because she was cheating on him. She would probably have left soon anyways, so it wouldn't matter. She was dead, though; that was different than just a divorce. If he had been divorced people were more likely to understand that he moved on. With her being dead, he wondered if they would be just as likely to understand about him moving on without him admitting to everyone about her infidelity. He hasn't told anyone, actually. Austin and he were the only two people alive who knew about it. Other than the boyfriend that was, Allen doubted he was going to say anything about it any time soon.

Allen pushed that all aside as he heard Austin down the hall. He needed to ask him a couple questions. He seriously doubted the kid would want to go with them, which seemed obvious from the fact that he refused to meet Tara up to this point. But he also wanted to make sure the kid was ok with him even going out with Tara for a few days. He knew Austin would be capable of handling being by himself for that long. Allen would leave enough money for food and stuff or at least buy groceries. He could even have the lady that cleans the house a couple days a week come and fix him some meals. For the most part, though, he thought everything would be fine, and he would get to get away with his girl that he loved and have some much needed fun for the both of them.

"Austin? That you?" As if it'd be anyone else.

"Yeah. I was just out walking. I was going to finish my homework for the day and lay down. I have a headache." Runs in the family, Allen thought.

"Okay, this won't take long. I just wanted to ask a couple questions." Allen was getting that nervous, anxious feeling in his stomach again. It was like Austin was going to be able to dictate the course of his life with the answers to the next couple questions.

"Okay. What's up Dad?" He smiled. He looked so much like Cheyenne. When he smiled, Allen suddenly felt something else in the pit of his stomach. Pain. The pain you feel when you miss someone so bad and all of a sudden you remember just how bad you've missed them, and it crept up on you that you had not quite forgotten them, but at the same time, they weren't at the forefront of your mind anymore. For a moment, Allen forgot all about Tara, the vacation, and the fun he hoped to have. In that moment all he wanted was his wife back. He wanted to hold her and tell her he'd be a better husband, that he would take more time off from writing, and that they could be a happy family again. But that was just for a moment. Then that moment passed, and reality reasserted itself, and Allen remembered why he was talking to his son.

"Dad? You ok?" He sounded concerned.

"Yeah. Yeah. I'm fine. Just had a moment there." He wanted to tell Austin what had gone through his mind. What he was thinking and feeling. He wanted to share those things with his son. He wanted to see if Austin had, in some ways, felt the same way. Missed his mom as much as Allen missed his wife. He couldn't do that, however. Because then he wouldn't be able to ask Austin what he had called him into the room to ask him. If he unloaded his heart now, it would all echo back tinny and fake in a moment when he talked about going on a mini vacation with another woman. Allen knew Austin knew the word hypocrite, he would probably think Allen was one, and right now, to be honest, he felt like one.

Instead, he said, "Tara has had a rough week. Her grandfather passed away the other day, and she wanted to know if you and I wanted to get away with her for a few days. We didn't work out any details yet, but I just wanted to see if you wanted to come. So you can finally meet her. She is very special to me, Austin. I want you to see that." He paused, waiting for a response, but none came. He went on, "It has been six months since your mom died, and I have been seeing Tara for almost four. It's time you stop being so hurt and let her into your life."

Allen paused again and looked at his son. He wondered what he was ruining, because his face was blank. Completely void of emotion.

He responded in a completely flat and emotionless tone, "I'm not going."

"Austin, come on now. Be reasonable. You have to meet her sometime. There's a chance, I hope a very good one, that she will be your stepmom someday." He pleaded with him

"Fuck you!" He screamed.

"Watch your language around me, Austin. You need to have respect for me and the decisions that I make that affect MY life. I've let you run free for the past few months because I knew you needed time to heal. This is happening. You need to accept it and get on with your life." He kept calm, only raising his voice on the word my.

"You just want me to forget Mom like you have. You think just because I talk to a girl that I'm happy. You think that because you found a new fuck buddy and are happy that I should be too. Well, I'm not fucking happy. Don't you get that? I haven't been happy. The wrong fucking parent died to me. You were the one that abandoned us long before Mom cheated. You were the one that chose your books over your family. You should have died, and then she and I would be happy. We would have forgotten about you so fast. You're the worst parent ever!" Austin stopped to catch his breath. He was crying, whether from pain, effort, or anger, Allen didn't know. Most likely a combination of all three.

"I loved your mother, and I love you. She's dead. We are not. We need to move on with our lives at some point. I've offered to help you. To take you to counseling, but all you want to do is go lay on that damn rock in the woods." Allen's voice was rising a little; he was getting angry, and he couldn't avoid it.

"You know why I always go back there?" He didn't give Allen a chance to answer and just continued on, "Because no one bothers me. It's my place. It's not a place where you will go because you hate being outside. You hate being away from your technology. I bet you haven't even noticed that I've slept out there. It didn't matter the temperature. My hatred for you and your house that you made me move into kept me warm. I fucking hate you. You and your fuck buddy can go where the fuck ever you want, I'm not fucking going. And no, I will not watch my fucking language around you anymore. I fucking hate you."

With that, he slammed Allen's bedroom door and ran to his room. Allen couldn't hear his footfalls, waited to see if he heard the door, and when he didn't, he assumed he went to his room. Allen just sat in stunned silence on his bed. He knew Austin had been upset with him. He'd been talking less and less. He was probably a little upset about Allen not mentioning going to the movies together. It may have been a miscommunication. They were both waiting for the other to bring it up, and when neither did, they both thought the other had changed their mind. He knew his relationship with Tara had been a hard one for him to swallow. That's why he didn't force the two of them to meet. But he didn't know that Austin had held it in such contempt. And the language! He knew Austin swore but never thought he'd hear anything like that out of his son's mouth.

Allen really didn't know what to think or so now. He knew he wasn't going to make someone happy, and in that, he wasn't going to be happy either way. He had to decide who he was going to disappoint and hurt. Of course, he had not told Tara he would go at all, but she probably assumed that he would be all for the idea. Not because of the money or anything but just a chance to get away. He felt like he was fucked, and not in a way that felt good, either. He laid back on the bed, thinking.

Allen was just about to call Tara and tell her that it wasn't a good idea for him to go away when he saw his door slowly opening.

"Dad?" He sounded mournful.

"Yeah Austin." He tried to sound polite and thought he would have got a passing grade. What he really wanted to say was, "What the fuck do you want, you ungrateful little fucker."

"I'm sorry about the things I said. I don't want to go with you and her, but I don't mind if you go. I will be fine for a couple days." He sounded downright miserable now.

Allen was flabbergasted. What had brought about such a one hundred and eighty degree turn around in his son in just a few minutes? He then realized it hadn't been just a few minutes. He had fallen asleep for a few hours.

"Are you sure? I would prefer if you went with us you know." He asked.

"Yeah, I know. I just don't think I'm ready for a new mom yet, but I understand you want to move on. It's ok." He sounded sincere.

"I don't want any parties or anything, and you can invite Sara over, but only during the day. I will leave a couple hundred in cash so you can get food and stuff. And I can have Margery come cook for you." Allen wanted to get past the argument as quickly as possible.

"No. I have money. And it's only a couple days. I can get a couple pizzas and make them last while you're gone. I doubt Sara will come. She will be too busy. I will just read, do my homework, and stay up late." There was a rye smile on his face.

"You sure?" Allen asked.

"Positive. Go have fun. You deserve it." Again, with such sincerity, Allen began to wonder if that wasn't a different kid in here cussing and screaming earlier.

"Ok Austin." Was all he could reply with.

"No problem Dad." He actually smiled.

In the end, the kid had completely dictated how his decision was made. Allen felt dirty for some reason, like he was still supposed to not go. Even though he had gotten permission from Austin. He hated feeling like this. He hated the feeling that he had just been manipulated. He knew if he went, and who was he kidding "if" he was going, that someday and probably soon Austin would throw it up in his face, and his only defense would be "bu...but...but you told me I could go!" Like he was a groveling child.

He picked up his phone and called Tara.

"Hey baby." Was how she answered, and he wondered how he could have thought about not spending a few days with this beautiful woman, most of which he hoped to be semi or completely naked during.

"Just tell me a time and place to meet to leave, and I will have my bags packed." He was so happy he completely forgot the dirty feeling Austin caused, and was just thinking dirty now.

"Ohhhhhhh yeah!!" She screamed into the phone.

"Please tell me Austin is coming too?" She asked when she calmed a little after celebrating.

"No hon, he's not quite ready for that yet. But I think that's coming soon. I promise." He said.

"I sure hope so. I will be at your house tomorrow at 8 am to pick you up. We just got back from the funeral, so it is all taken care of, and I'm ready to relax." She sounded so relieved. Allen wondered how he could have said no to her.

"Tomorrow? Are you saying you already made reservations somewhere?" He asked. His excitement was palpable.

"I may have. I may not have. That is for me to know and you

to find out." She was laughing hysterically.

Allen loved the playfulness in her voice. He felt like, with every word, he was falling in love with her again and again.

"Well, where we going?" He asked finally after listening to her breath for a few seconds. It was such a comfortable silence.

"The lake. And no, I don't have reservations. My grandparents own a cabin up there, well I guess I do now. My grandfather willed it to me even though we haven't gotten that far yet. But everyone always knew it was going to be mine. Not because I am the favorite, though, but because it is my favorite. I love going there and just relaxing. I can't wait to take you there!" That excitement in her voice.

"I'm so excited I can hardly contain myself. I just wish we could leave now." He really felt that way, he couldn't believe it.

"Tomorrow dear. Tomorrow. You can wait that long. I just wish Austin would go, too." She sounded a little disheartened at the end.

"Me too hon, me too." Allen wished she'd stop bringing it up. He didn't understand why hearing once wasn't enough. He felt a little annoyed with her persistence on the subject.

Chapter 25

The Proposal

Allen woke in the middle of the night, and fought his way through the fogginess of his dreams, which were confused and haunting. He tried to assert reality upon himself and still couldn't. He fumbled for the lamp and realized that the clock on the bedside table was off. He looked around for signs of power and saw none. He didn't know what was happening because he didn't hear about any potential storms. Not that he was all that attentive to the news, he was thinking about getting away with Tara most of all. He was a little disappointed that Austin wasn't going to go, but a part of him, and he would never admit to this, it was a large part of him that was happy that he wasn't going to go because he planned on having an X-rated getaway. He and Tara enjoyed sex, but it was usually quick, and rarely did they have the chance to lie around and relax afterwards because they would be worried about Austin finding them again or just not being that comfortable in a hotel room or going in for seconds. Allen wasn't exactly young anymore, but his little Bennett could be talked into a second go round without much effort.

He looked out the window and saw no snow or anything that could have equaled a power outage. He went to the window, looked up and down the street, and saw the few neighbor's houses he could see were also without power. He thought that could only equal one of two things, a transformer blew or a car took out a utility pole. He hoped it was a transformer. Even though he made a good living by writing about death and tragedy, he hated death with a passion. He never understood how he was so much more accepting of it in his writing than in life, or why his writing almost exclusively focused around murders or mysterious deaths. He thought maybe some part of his brain was attempting to alleviate some of his fears by familiarity. Like in "Venom Murders," where the main character used snake and spider venom to kill people as part of a great science experiment, he was forced to research snakes and spiders, and even though he greatly feared both of these things, he was able to lessen his fear somewhat as he wrote more and learned more about them.

Allen decided that since he was up and awake and the power just came back on, he rarely woke this time of night, and on the occasions that he did he was equally rarely able to return right back to sleep. He always equated this to his active imagination. As soon as he was awake it kicked on and wouldn't rest until it was done. He hated it most of the time because he liked to be in his study and working on some new material when he wrote, but this new book was coming along in a very different manner than any he had ever written. He wasn't sure if it affected the quality at this point or not, but he knew he'd never written anything like this. He kind of enjoyed the sneaking around writing. He thought it helped him get into the mindset of his main character because he had to sneak around and find out his wife's customers.

He wrote for a couple hours and started to feel sleepy again, but by then, he knew Tara would be arriving soon. She said they would leave around 8 am. He hoped to be up and ready to go as soon as she got to his house. He failed in this because she was pulling into his driveway a little after seven. He was not surprised. He felt she wanted to get away just as much as he wanted to. He didn't know if they had the same sexual agenda or not, but he would soon find out. He thought that she might because she had never once turned him down and, on several occasions, had initiated it herself. She was pretty much the perfect woman for him, he thought to himself.

As they drove away, Tara was driving. Allen had offered, but she had talked him down. "It's my idea. I should drive." Allen was ok with this once they got rolling because he was feeling his short ration of sleep from the night before right away, which he felt was also giving him a bit of a headache. He was also dwelling on the conversation with Austin from that morning.

"You sure you're ok with me going? I mean, we will be back the day after tomorrow. I will have my phone if you need anything." He told his son.

"Yeah Dad, for the hundredth time. Go. Have fun!" Austin sounded exasperated now. Allen had asked him at least three times since he realized that Austin was awake just to make sure. He thought that maybe a part of him wanted Austin to be mad, to give him an excuse to stay home. He knew he'd have fun with Tara and all they would do even if they did nothing. But at the same time, he felt a strong sense of apprehension. He didn't know where the feeling was coming from or why he would have it. He thought possibly because of this being his first getaway with Tara, but he wasn't sure. He had stayed overnight with her. Maybe it wasn't a romantic getaway, but they had done everything around each other and were comfortable. He didn't know. He just felt like something bad was going to happen on this trip. He thought about his neighbors Robert and Audrey and how they were murdered. He thought about the similarities between them and his book. He didn't know what to make of that yet. All he knew was that it scared him a little. Hell, maybe it was a lot. He tried to push it out of his mind as he reached out for Tara's hand. There was no hesitancy in her as she grabbed his and drove on.

Allen was lost by the breathtaking view as they pulled up to the lakeside cabin several hours later. Allen wasn't sure how long they were driving because he had fallen asleep while holding onto Tara's hand and knew they had stopped at least once. She had awoken him to see if he needed anything. He vaguely recalled answering no but then was right back to sleep so fast the entire conversation may not have even happened at all. He was taken aback by the calmness of the water. It looked like a clear window. He knew even in his grandest efforts as a writer, he would be unable to duplicate the beauty of this scene with mere words. He doubted at this point that even a picture would be able to do justice. The sloping hill to the beach. The open area of clear white sand. The area was pristine. The cabin was a single level and looked to be all windows. Allen was in love immediately. You could look in any direction and see everything around you, not that there was anything to see except water, sand, and trees. No neighbors to speak of, and that suited Allen perfectly, considering his hopes and his plans for this excursion.

Allen was wide awake now as they sat in the living room area. There were no televisions in the house.

"My grandfather wanted this to be a place to get away from everything. He didn't want a TV or anything like that here. He said all the time 'I go there for a vacation. If I have all that shit with me, how can I relax? I might as well stay at home'. And I tend to think he's right. Although I'm happy my cell phone works, I'm glad there is nothing else here. No cable, Internet, or landline phone. Nothing to distract us from us, babe." She had been walking around in the bedroom that was just off the living room. Allen had assumed she was unpacking, as it turned out she was, in a way. "And right now, I need your undivided attention." She said as she stepped out into the living room with a pink lace negligee that didn't leave much to the imagination, which is the way Allen liked it to be.

"And you shall have it, baby." Allen's excitement was already showing through his jeans.

Afterward, Allen went to the small kitchen to make them lunch. He figured out they had driven about five hours, so it was a late lunch after the sex. It was just as he had pictured it to be. He could be completely relaxed. The day had warmed considerably for early spring, and Tara was sitting on the screened in porch with nothing on but a smile. He said he'd make something, and she agreed saying she hadn't hardly eaten the last few days. He made a salad and some sandwiches, and everything was fine until he heard somewhere in the house someone's voice. He couldn't tell what they were saying but he could hear them just the same.

"Tara?!" Allen shouted as he ran to get the clothes Tara had unceremoniously removed from his body.

"What is it? What's going on?"

"Who's here?" Allen asked angrily. He didn't know where his anger had come from, but it was there, and it was evident.

"I don't know. I don't hear anyone." She said back, she looked scared at his immediate anger.

"There is someone back in the back of the cabin. I know I heard them." He replied, his anger still rising.

"There's no one back there. Do you think I would walk around naked if someone was back there? Why are you getting so angry so fast? I don't get it?" she stepped back from him.

"I'm not angry!" Allen said heatedly. He did know where it came from, though. Maybe it was that overactive imagination again, but in his mind's eye, he had, on the spot, concocted a scenario where Tara and her (ex) husband had planned out his murder. He sometimes hated how his imagination would run away with things, but that's just how he was, he'd made a lot of money with it, so he wasn't hoping it would go away any time soon.

Tara walked back to the back room and looked around. There was no one there. "No one here. I think you're just going crazy or something." And laughed.

"I'm not fucking crazy." Allen tried to joke back, but there was still an edge to his voice. Then added, "I'm sorry that came out wrong. I meant it. I sound more goofing around."

"It's ok. I know you'd never be that overtly mean to me." She smiled seductively at him, and he felt some stirring in his loins. "Eat first?" He asked her.

"Yeah. But let's go fast this time." She pleaded with him.

Allen dozed after the second time and was deep asleep when he felt Tara shuffling beside him. He thought she was trying to get him to put his arm around her because she was messing with his hand. He moved to spoon with her, and she let out a huff of disappointment that brought him to the surface immediately.

"What? You ok?" He was concerned.

"Yeah." She had a huge smile on her face. "Way better than ok, actually."

Allen looked at her and couldn't help but smile himself. "Good. Good baby. I love you."

"And I love you. Stay right there." She said as she got out of bed.

She got up and ran into another room. Allen could hear her rustling through one of her bags. She reappeared in the doorway, looking at him.

"Close your eyes." Her smile seemed to be radiating.

"Why?" Allen asked, but his tone said he was very curious.

"Just do it silly." She seemed to be reverting to a giddy teenage girl.

"Ok ok. I will." Allen closed his eyes.

"Now, pick a hand. Right or left?"

"Uhh, let's see. Left."

"Ok. Hold out your hand." Allen couldn't see her face at this point but could just hear the happiness in her voice. He held out his hand tentatively.

She placed something small in his hand. It didn't feel like anything Allen had ever held in his hand in his life. "What is it?" He asked.

"Open your eyes up and see for yourself." She was actually bouncing with happiness at this point.

Allen looked down and saw a stem of plastic about six inches long that had a giant plus sign in the middle. At first, he didn't know what to think. This was so unexpected, so outré that he was flabbergasted and speechless. Then he caught some of Tara's giddiness and hugged her and kissed her. He didn't have the stamina for a third go at that point just yet, but they kissed away as their smiles burned into each other's lips.

"Is this really real? You're pregnant?" Allen was beaming. He was extremely happy.

"Yes. Yes, WE are pregnant, dear. And before you can even let your mind run to this idea, I will nip it in the bud. It is yours and no one else's. I did not have sex with my ex for the past six months, and we have only been together for four. So WE ARE HAVING A BABY!" Tara screamed the last part. Had they had neighbors, they surely would have heard.

"I love you, Tara!" Allen shouted back to her.

She fell into his arms and started to kiss him again, and with passion, now it seemed that he was ready for another round as he responded immediately, and Tara took control.

Afterward, he dozed again, this time with her asleep at his side and hand in hand.

When he awoke what seemed like hours later, and it had to be because darkness had come to their part of the word, Tara was again playing with his hand.

"What are you doing, babe?" he asked groggily.

"Oh, just checking something." She said, laughing.

"Oh yeah? What's that?" He asked, waking up a little more.

"Well, hold on again." She sat up and seemed to gather herself.

"I love you," Allen started to speak but she put her finger to his lips and continued, "I loved you even before I met you. I know how dumb that sounds. It's like something from some stupid romance novel, which I know you don't write about. I had always had this idea of the perfect man in my life. I had a list of attributes that he would possess. I didn't care all that much about looks or money or even age. It was what was inside that I cared most about. You fit that so perfectly. I know I didn't behave well the first day we met. I knew my dad liked your books and read them. I hadn't read them. He said he knew a little about you, and some part of me wanted to just be a groupie or something for once and I just wanted to do something crazy and dangerous at that point because of the relief of getting away from my now ex. My dad saw the way I looked at you that first time. He didn't care about your age or anything. He knew I wasn't happy before and that maybe you would do that for me. I have been in love before. A couple times, I thought it was the greatest thing ever, but then it soured. I never felt like I do with you. I'm willing to give up my everything for you and be with you forever. And I want you to be with me forever. So what I was checking was to see if this ring would fit on your finger so I could ask you to marry me." The tears had started about halfway through her speech. Now, they came in full force. Allen had an idea what was coming and was still unprepared for it as the words came out of her mouth, and she slid the ring on his finger. He seemed unable to speak.

She was sobbing hard now, "Please don't break my heart. We are going to be a family. Let's do it right."

Allen came out of his daze. He wondered if he was still dreaming. He sometimes had extremely vivid dreams. He would use these in his books if he could. Now, this seemed like he was dreaming. But the feel of the small gold ring on his finger told him he wasn't. It was real, and so was this. He lit up at the idea. "When did you have in mind?" Was all the answer he needed to give her.

Chapter 26

The Computer Hacker

Allen couldn't believe the whirlwind that had been the last few days. He was awake in the morning the day they planned to return home and was all smiles. He was in love, he was going to marry his love, and he was going to be a father again. He never knew he wanted kids ever until Cheyenne had announced she was pregnant with Austin. She had told him she had some problems when she was younger and that she would most likely never conceive a child. So they had taken no special precautions, and one day, Cheyenne confided in Allen that it had been nearly three months since her last monthly cycle. She made an appointment with the doctor for the next day. They both couldn't sleep that night. She hadn't shown any signs of being pregnant. No morning sickness or anything like that. She just woke up one day and realized her Aunt Flow had been missing for a few months. When they got the news, they were both ecstatic. Allen had never really thought about kids. He would be happy either way because he knew he'd be around to see everything. All the milestones. First steps, first words. As well as the not so glamorous aspects of raising a child, namely potty training. And Allen had been there for it all. Had helped out with everything. He would even venture to go so far as to say he had done more than most fathers would have done. He didn't know when he had stopped being such an attentive dad, but it had happened. Gradually, as Austin got older, he got more demands on his writing. When he was a relatively new author, there was not much demand because there were no publishers or editors or worse yet, fans were clamoring for more of his words in print.

So Allen reflected on how different he was from before they had arrived here and how different his life was. Three days ago he was certain that Tara was lying to him and using him, for what his mind was never quite able to figure out, but that she had lied to him for sure. He hated his life. He had people dying around him, and he seemed to think they were going to link it all to him, although there was no evidence to do so. He had just written about similar killings. That doesn't make you a murderer. In the same way, just wishing someone would die doesn't make you a murderer. Now, though, he had everything in his life pointing up. He felt like he'd been through a sort of hell. Trying to deal with everything that Cheyenne had put him through and dealing with that. He knew there were worse things in the world but he felt like being betrayed was by far the worst.

He didn't know how Austin was going to take this. He and Tara had already said they wanted to keep it a secret as long as they could. Since she was just more than a month along, they had enough time to figure things out. She had said she wanted to be married before the baby arrived, and he agreed. She said she didn't care if she was "big as a whale" when she walked down the aisle, it was just important to her that the baby not be born a bastard. He would have married her that day, secretly if necessary, and said as much. "I'm not quite that ready, babe." Was her response to that suggestion.

Allen felt her stirring beside him and knew she would be waking up soon. He was going to miss this place, but knew they'd be returning here soon because they had agreed to marry here. And since sit was barely spring, they had several months to make sure that happened.

It was a very different Allen, who was a passenger on the ride home. He had been quiet and introspective on the trip up. On the trip back, he was talkative, inquisitive, and beaming from ear to ear. He rattled off ideas for names and honeymoon locations. He seemed to have caught a happy fever and hoped it would never leave him. He never thought that it would as long as he could get Austin to come around.

"I want to talk to Austin when you do about the baby and the marriage. I think we should do it together. I have to meet him. If he refuses to meet me still, then I don't know how we can do this. He has to understand we are all linked now. We are a family." She said flatly.

"I know. I was just thinking about that. I will talk to him tonight, and it will happen soon." Allen said with confidence.

"It has to honey. I can't have a stepson I've never talked to or even seen other than pictures. I understand he's hurting, but maybe I can help him out of his depression like I seem to have helped you." She said seriously.

"Well, I don't want you to help the same way, babe." Allen turned and looked at her and gave her a wink.

"You know, I've always wanted to try something." She was in the passenger seat and reached over and rubbed his leg.

"Hon! I'm driving!" Allen squealed as he jerked the wheel a little.

"I know. Watch the road." She said as she unzipped his pants.

That night, Allen was lying in bed. He was alone. Tara had wanted to wait for Austin to come home but Allen had talked her down and asked her to go home because he was getting another killer headache that was only going to be remedied by sleep. He lay down for a long time, and no sleep came. He couldn't figure out what it was, but he just didn't want Tara in the house while he was having one of his headaches. The doctor said there was no real reason for them anymore. He didn't think it was stress anymore. He went to him a few times and received no real answers or prescriptions. The doctor just said over-the-counter items would probably work best.

Allen finally was just about to fall asleep when he heard

Austin approach. He hadn't heard him enter the house but sensed his presence in the doorway.

"Dad?" Austin called softly.

"Yeah, Austin?" Allen said louder, letting him know he was awake.

"How was the trip?" He asked.

It was good. Very relaxing. I wish you would have gone. It's beautiful there." Allen said.

"Maybe next time." Said Austin

"I doubt it." Allen replied.

"Why do you say that, Dad?" Austin asked.

Allen took a deep breath and tried to find the words he wanted to say. He wanted to say something scathing, but at the same time, he didn't want to hurt his son's feelings. He wanted him to know how much he hurt his feelings by being so standoffish about meeting Tara. He had been lenient, but he was running out of patience. He wanted to say all these things in the nicest way possible.

Instead he said, "It seems you never are going to want to meet her. She's been in my life for four months and hasn't met my son."

"I know. I'm just not ready for a new mom." Austin said this very knowingly.

"Who said she had to replace your mom? Look Austin," Allen sat up in bed and felt a wave of pain rush through his head, "No one is ever going to replace your mom. We all know your mom was a wonderful person and mother. She made a mistake at the end. I willingly take my share of the blame for that, but you have to understand that she made the decision. All she had to do was come in and shut off the computer, and tell me we needed to talk. She didn't need to fall into the arms of another man. That's what she chose to do. I was hurt, and I needed comfort. I found it. It's time you find some, too. Tara wants to meet you so bad and she won't let our relationship develop until she meets you." As soon as Allen said this last part, he regretted it. Austin had a glint in his eye, it was just there momentarily, but Allen felt that he knew Austin knew he could sabotage everything.

"You're meeting her. This week. You're meeting her. There's no two ways about it. We are all having dinner." Even though he had told Tara they could be together when Austin found out, he decided he should tell him alone at this moment, "We are getting married. I don't know when, but we are. And you're going to have a little brother or sister. So it's time you accept her as family. Not a mother but family at the very least."

"Married? Pregnant? I thought you didn't want anything like that. You basically said you were just hanging out with her. I know what grown-ups do. I knew you were--fucking-," he infused this word with such venom that Allen felt like he'd been struck by a snake," I knew that was going on. But not only did you use her to replace mom now you have her with a kid to replace me. How long before you ship me off to a boarding school or Grandma and Grandpa's? Just get rid of the entire family?" Austin's voice was rising. And for a few words he was eleven years old again and was approaching puberty. His voice was shrill. It was full of angst and fury.

"Not going to happen, Austin. That's why I'm forcing you to meet her as soon as possible." Allen replied coldly.

"Not going to happen either." And he ran down the hall. Allen tried to get up and give chase, but he just swooned as a wave of disorientation engulfed him, and he collapsed back onto the bed and just lay there. It felt like he was drunk, as the room spun and spun, he seemed to have very little control over his body.

Allen woke up some unknown time later. He couldn't pinpoint the amount of time that passed. Everything looked the same. He thought maybe a few minutes, but it could have been an entire day. He looked around and his phone was gone. He couldn't remember the last place he had it. He looked everywhere and couldn't remember bringing it in from the car when he had Tara drop him off. He tried to remember her number but couldn't do it. He would just call her from his landline phone. He knew he could look up her number if he could find his laptop. That was also missing.

Finally, still sleepy and looking for anything he could find, Allen went downstairs and looked. His laptop was on the counter in the kitchen. He now remembered that he had last used it when he was looking up information about Audrey's murder.

He opened it an immediately noticed that his book was opened and that he was looking at something he didn't remember writing. It described in detail about another murder. One he hadn't planned to have his main character commit. He read on and on and realized that he didn't write this. There were the grammatical markings of his son's speech in the wording. He knew Austin had been in his book. He suddenly became overwhelmed with fear.

"What if he was reading the books and then committing the crimes?" Allen asked himself out loud. He wanted to find Austin but knew he wasn't home. He had looked into his room when he was on his way downstairs. His room was neat as a pin, as usual.

Allen didn't understand how he could have figured out the file lock password because he had used Tara's birthday. They had not even celebrated her birthday because it was still two months away. So Austin wouldn't have been able to know. Maybe he was better with computers than Allen ever thought he could be. Maybe he was a hacker or something. He knew there were some people who could do anything with a computer, break through any kind of encryption or secure document no matter how well you attempted to protect it.

Allen was furious, with himself for being so careless and leaving his computer out for Austin to snoop in. Also, at Austin because, he had been snooping in his private business. Yes, he had promised not to write anymore, but someone doesn't understand the brain if they think you can just turn it off whenever you want to. It continues to make up stories and be creative because that's what it's used to doing.

Allen read through what he figured to be Austin's contribution to the story. He wondered where he was going with it. Was it a veiled threat? Or did he really think that this was a good idea for the way the story should go? Allen sort of liked it as a story, but didn't know if he would like it so much if it was some sort of threat.

He needed to come clean with Austin. Tell him he wasn't sacrificing time that could have been spent with him to write, because Austin never wanted to spend time together. He was always in the woods or in his room with the door shut. Allen didn't think he could be blamed. He needed to find something to occupy his time, so he wrote. This is what he did best. He also met a girl, who wasn't planned but sometimes the best things that happen to us in life are the things that are spontaneous.

Chapter 27

The Dream

Allen was walking down the road in just his underwear. He couldn't figure out where he was. He looked around and none of his surroundings made any sense to him. He tried to get a fix on his location by landmarks and failed. He wondered why he was wearing just his underwear. It was cold out, raining, and yet he felt like he had been here before. It was not a sense of déjà vu, but something similar for which he didn't have the words. This was frustrating, as a person who made a living on words, he hated not being able to describe something. Yet here he was, standing on this stretch of country road, unable to describe why he felt like he knew where he was, yet knowing he had never been here. Nor did he really have reason to believe that he would ever be in this place, especially in the dark, in his underwear, in this type of weather. He spun around and tried to get a fix on the sky, but it was cloudy. Not that he could have figured out where he was by the stars anyway, he was surely no ship captain.

Suddenly, there was a sound behind him, off in the distance. He couldn't pinpoint the distance, but it seemed to be a mile or more. He saw the headlights coming. He froze. He was standing in the middle of the road in his underwear still, no shoes and knew what it was to be a deer. The headlights were on him and he was sick with fear. He couldn't move. The car was traveling very fast for this road and the conditions, he thought. They would not see him. He was going to be crushed. He was going to die in his underwear. He had time before the car struck him to think to himself, "At least I hope they are clean." And then the car passed by.

He had a queer sensation of being inside the car. He felt the warmth of the heater, the smell of perfume that was pleasant and yet oh so familiar and the faint smell of something that was underneath, something that was not pleasant at all. It gave Allen a sense of betrayal and broken hearts. He didn't understand how the car didn't crush him to death. How he wasn't lying in the road of this abandoned stretch, except for the car which he at the moment passed through.

The thought left him as the car started to go out of control. He had tried to look at the driver and was unable to see her face; he had only seen her hair color. He was now behind the car, the brake lights flashed in his face, and he shielded his eyes and tried to turn away as the brakes locked up and the tires squealed.

Smoke rose from all four tires, and he saw the make of the car, and suddenly, he knew where and what he was doing. He was being punished. He was going to watch his wife die. This was her car. It wasn't bad enough that he had to take the phone call from the police officer, but now he had to witness it. He had to be a ghost of himself in which he couldn't do anything except be here and watch and look and hate himself for everything that happened from this moment forward.

In this moment, Allen hated himself, Tara, and even Austin. He hated everyone who survived while his beautiful wife had to die. He forgave her in that moment. He didn't care that the smell underneath was the smell of sex, and it wasn't produced from an intimate moment with him. He didn't care about it. He just cared about his wife, and he wanted her back. He would forgive everything just to have her next to him. He would give anything not to witness this moment.

The car went out of control and skidded off the road and toward a tree. Allen now recognized the tree. He didn't recognize it before because when Cheyenne hit it going around fifty miles per hour, it was with such force that it snapped and fell on top of the car, but not before pushing the engine as far back as the center console of her BMW. Allen tried to run toward her, knowing he could not stop it. He wanted to tell her that he loved her. Now, his legs worked. The car hit the tree he didn't recognize before, but now did, and there was an ungodly sound of metal crunching, glass breaking, and, worst of all, the sounds of his wife screaming. He ran toward those screams. He knew what he was about to see, he knew that because of what he was about to see, there would be a closed casket funeral a few days from this moment in time, but he had to see it nonetheless. He ran as fast as he could. He felt like he was running in quicksand. His feet felt heavy. They didn't want to work. He was never going to get there. His wife was still screaming. She was yelling for help. There was no help on the way, only her ghost of a husband that was in his underwear still. He could smell the gasoline, he knew it wasn't dangerous, but that didn't matter. It tautened up his guts and made them feel watery.

He again wished that he had on clean underwear, knowing how ridiculous it sounded even in his own mind. He was next to the car, the screaming had stopped. He feared that his wife had died already. The coroner had told him she had lived for several minutes after the accident. He said more, but Allen had "checked out" of the conversation at that point. He had always vowed to take care of her, and protect her from any kind of pain, and here she was in pain for several minutes, and he didn't do anything about it.

Even then, however, a small part of him, maybe a big part, who knows how the dreaming mind really works, was happy that she was in pain. He pushed it away, though, and came up to the driver's side door. He had no trouble seeing into the car and smelled blood and shit along with her perfume now. He knew he was too late. He wasn't going to get to see her. He had wanted to see that last breath and he failed her again. He banged his hand on the roof of the car and screamed, "FUCK YOU GOD!" With this exclamation, Cheyenne rolled her head toward him, what was once a beautiful face was ruined.

The people from BMW had no explanation for why the airbag had failed to deploy. They had said it was a faulty system in that particular car. Cheyenne's once perfect and beautiful face was a ruin. It was reconstructed in such a way that it looked as though it was a caricature done by something that vaguely knew what a human face was supposed to look like. Her eyes, once beautiful and bright and full of life, were now dark and shrouded in blood. She was speaking. Allen leaned in close to listen.

"Would she have survived had the airbag deployed?" Allen asked the coroner. It was the only question he needed to have an answer to from someone that wasn't his wife. All other questions would have been needed to be answered by her, but he knew he would never get answers to those questions at this time because she was dead. He would never know where she was coming from up that road or why she felt she needed to be up that road in the first place. The look on the face of the coroner was all the answer he would need. No, she was going to die no matter what. He wouldn't blame the car people. He didn't care about money, no use in suing. Nothing was bringing her back.

"Why you in ro bayhe?" she said.

"I don't know Cheyenne. I was sleeping, and I woke up here. I'm going to call for help." He reached into his pockets, and then realized he had no pockets. He yelled. He knew it would do no good. His wife was going to die.

"You scare me. Whe you pans?" She was full of questions for a dying woman, Allen thought.

"I don't know." And before he could stop himself, he blurted out the questions that had been eating at him since the accident, this accident, actually. Because even now, he knew he was dreaming, but this felt like much more than a dream. It felt like it was redemption. "Why were you up this road? Why did you feel like you had to cheat? I was working my ass off us, if you wanted out, you just had to tell me. You didn't have to fucking sneak around and cheat on me. Because of this, our son hates me, and I've lost him too!"

Allen knew his several minutes had to be just about up, he noticed that her breathing was getting more and more shallow. Her eyes were becoming unfocused. He was going to get to watch her die. He knew this was punishment and not any kind of redemption. It felt like it was anyway. He was trying to move, but felt rooted to the spot. He wondered if he'd have to relive the phone call as well. That was hell, this was worse.

"I luh yew." Her voice was barely above a horse whisper, but he understood perfectly. "cheeeehhhhh aaillllll." This was his wife's last word, and she couldn't finish. He couldn't figure out what she was trying to say either. It sounded like cheese. He had no idea why she would want cheese. It didn't seem like it could be a word that answered any of the questions that he had just blurted out.

"I love you too. Please don't go. Come back to me. Or at least take me with you. I can't live without you anymore." He was shouting, but it did no good because his wife had gone beyond where shouts could reach her. She died with her head lolling toward him; her eyes on his, except the life had been taken from them.

Allen shot up out of bed. He was screaming. He thought that if it were possible to wake the dead, then he would have with that scream. He was still screaming when his voice gave out, and he just choked on his own fear. He was panting heavily and sweating. He had lost his orientation. He again had no idea where he was. He wondered if this was still part of the dream. Was the phone about to ring? Was he going to have to watch himself relive the phone call, or was he just going to have to do it as himself? He stared at the phone beside the bed, willing it not to ring. He didn't think his mind could take going through that again. To have just watched her die and then have to go through being told about it. All the details the cop insisted on giving him. All the details he missed because he just focused on a couple of sentences.

"Sir, there has been an accident. Your wife was involved in a single motor vehicle crash. She struck a tree and it appears that the airbag on her vehicle malfunctioned. I regret to inform you of this sir, but your wife did not t survive the crash."

Allen would not be able to do that. He tried to get up. He wanted to get away from this room as fast as he could before the phone could ring, and he would have no choice but to answer it. He got out of bed and walked hurriedly toward the door. He walked straight into a wall and fell down. He sat on the floor. Rubbing his head. It was hurting pretty bad, he wondered if it was true. If you could feel pain, then that meant you weren't dreaming. He hoped it was true, but that didn't explain why there was a wall where there should have been a door. He closed his eyes and willed himself back to the present, and it seemed to work because he realized that he was trying to exit from the room that he had shared with Cheyenne, but he had moved, and the door was on the other side of the room. He was back in the present.

Allen walked into the master bathroom, ran some cold water, and splashed it onto his face, trying to reassert himself to reality. The dream had disturbed him greatly. There was no denying that. He had been dreaming about Cheyenne the night that she died. People probably would find it hard to believe that he had been asleep, considering what he had just found out, but that's what he did. When he was upset, he went to sleep. He escaped into his dreaming mind. Some people self-medicate with alcohol or drugs, some eat, but he slept.

He went back to his bed and sat down. His blankets were everywhere. He figured he had been running in his sleep. Maybe that was why it felt like it was quicksand, because the blankets were tangled around my legs, he thought to himself.

Allen wanted to try to go back to sleep, but knew any effort was going to be futile. He just lay in bed and stared at the ceiling. Had he realized the time right away, he would have known that he wasn't going to get a call from the police. It was almost 5 am. The sun would be coming up soon and he could start his day. He didn't know what he was going to do today. He supposed he would have to talk more to Austin about the impending marriage and little sibling, but he didn't look forward to that. He hated to fight with him because he felt that every fight was just one step farther apart for them. He knew he could do better for Austin, but just didn't know how.

Since he had no answers for the situation with Austin, he turned his mind to the dream. It had been disturbing, to say the least. He had never seen where the car came to a stop, only pictures. He had never been on that stretch of road in his life. He never wanted to go. He thought it would be much too painful. He knew though, if he had traveled out there today, it would look exactly as it did in his dream. This thought disturbed him even more. He felt like he was being punished by God, or whatever, because he had fallen in love with another woman.

He gave going back to sleep up as a bad idea and dressed and pulled out his laptop. He wanted to review more of his book. He figured that since Austin knew about it, he didn't need to hide it and write in the dead hours of the night anymore. He read through what Austin wrote. He was still unsure where he was going with it; it made sense in the story, and he liked it. He hoped it was just make believe, and not something else. But since he wrote this, Allen wasn't sure what he planned with it. He hoped he liked the book and wanted to add something.

Allen wondered if maybe Austin had something to do with the murders. He seriously doubted it. This was a kid that, a few months before his mom died, cried when he saw an opossum get run over on the road. He was extremely sensitive. He had to have gotten that from his mother. He had never been cruel throughout his childhood, and was never into burning ants with a magnifying glass or anything like that. He seemed to have a deep appreciation for all living things. Allen remembered when a bird had flown into their house when Austin was about six or seven years old. It had broken its neck, but Austin heard it and ran outside and brought it to the house. and wanted his mom and dad to take it to the vet because he said everything deserved to be cared for. He cried and threw a fit when Cheyenne told him that the bird was probably not going to make it, and they didn't even know where a vet was. The kid was smart, though, because he knew. He had seen them around. He told his parents exactly where to find it. In the end, they tried, but the bird was long dead before they even got to the vet.

Allen decided to not write anymore, and got on the local news website to read about the murders. He wondered if they had made any connection. Since he had been away with Tara and everything that happened with her family, he hadn't been paying much attention. He found the stories, and since they were still unsolved, they made top stories. There seemed to be some connection between the two, which was easy to make. But at the same time, the chief of police was quoted as saying, "There seems to be a pattern here to a group of murders that occurred in California last year. We are diligently researching these to see if there is a detectable pattern. Before you ask, yes, that culprit was apprehended."

He read all the related articles, and it seemed that they were following several leads but had no real suspects. The police had a profile of the killer; they figured he had to be a "he" first of all. Also, according to the police, there appeared to be no connection to the victims. They were random. The person committing the crimes had to be at least 6 feet tall and was most likely ambidextrous. Allen knew Austin was most definitely not that tall, he seemed to have gotten his mother's height, and was barely five foot five. Allen breathed a sigh of relief; even though he knew Austin wasn't capable, he couldn't pretend that he wasn't worried that it might have been him. That he was breaking into his computer and acting out what Allen had written.

Chapter 28

The Anniversary Gift

Allen was still pondering the profile of the killer the next day. As a murder mystery writer, he was always trying to get into the mind of a killer. He loved to read the stories, and some sick and demented part of him wanted the people to get away with the crimes. He wanted to eventually write a series of books about a serial killer, but he didn't have the wherewithal to pull that off. Besides, people liked to have heroes in the series, not anti-heroes, just look at Harry Potter, for example, or even The Hunger Games trilogy. He thought it would be counterproductive to his career to write a bunch of books about a guy who actually got away with murder over and over and how he evaded capture. He thought he might actually have someone act out his books for real in something like this, or have someone go crazy like Annie Wilkes in Misery and kidnap him or something. Of course, these sorts of thoughts were more delusional than possible. Then again, you never know how people will take something they read. They might not have the capabilities to separate fiction from reality.

Allen did his best to put these thoughts to bed; he couldn't think his son was a murderer any more than he thought that Tara was. His phone was ringing; he heard it so infrequently these days that he was surprised to hear it. He was even more surprised when he saw that it was Cheyenne's cousin, Shane. He couldn't possibly think what he would want.

"Hello?" He answered.

"Hey buddy, what's up? Haven't heard from you forever. I tried your old number, and it was disconnected, hadn't changed your number in my phone, but luckily, we never texted all that much so I still had the number from where you texted me. How you been you old fucker?" Shane sounded drunk, which wasn't unusual for him, but it was 10 am. Allen thought it might be something serious to have him three sheets to the wind this early.

"I'm doing okay, you know, just getting through every day, taking them one at a time. How about you? You sound shitfaced already, Shane." Allen said back.

"Ah fuck, I miss her, man. Miss her bad. I know I shouldn't love anyone more than my own wife, but fuck I miss Chey bad. She was always the best."

"Yeah, I know." Allen had hesitated to answer, knew he almost blurted out that maybe she wasn't so much the best. That she had a dark secret. Maybe Shane would have taken her side, maybe he would have understood it if Allen had been able to convey the entire story. Hell, even Allen almost understood her side. He couldn't tell Shane though, couldn't burst the bubble he had nearly wrapped around Cheyenne.

"What's wrong, man? You sound off. You aren't so quick to agree with me. I thought for sure I could call you up, and you'd understand what I was talking about."

"I…I do agree. She was the best. She was far too good for me. I know that for sure."

"No way, man!" Shane exclaimed. "She loved the shit out of you. She had a lot of guys in her life, but I never seen her with anyone like she was with you. She said to me many times, 'He's the best thing to ever happen to me, and nothing will ever change that'. She loved the shit out of you man. She wouldn't do anything to hurt you. I know that for sure. You can take that shit to the mother fucking bank."

"Yeah, I know Shane, but why are you drunk this early on a workday? I know it's not your usual vacation time. And you never call off."

"Workday? Damn dude, are you out of touch or something? It's Sunday! I have been drinking since yesterday morning. First thing I did was pop a top on a cold one. The wife hates it, but she doesn't say much. She knows it is my way of coping. I think she also thinks had I not been related to Chey, or had cousin marriages been legal here, I'd be married to her but she's wrong. I love her too, man. Just miss the hell out of Chey. I'm sure you understand."

"Yeah Shane, I understand. Understand fully."

"Also, I was thinking about something, and with everything that happened, I didn't know how you liked it. For all I know, you had it burnt because it caused too much pain." Shane seemed to struggle to get this out; he seemed to be making sure he didn't go too far.

"What are you talking about?" Allen replied

"Well, you should know it was delivered on what should have been your anniversary."

"I wasn't home that day. I was out for most of the day." Allen said suspiciously.

"Oh, well never mind, man. I didn't want to say anything, but the wife wanted to know how it turned out. Let's just try to forget I said anything. Pretend it was the booze talking or something." Shane said, truly embarrassed by his words. "Uh, I'm going to get off here, I'll talk to you later, Allen. If you need anything you let me know." And with that, Shane hung up.

Allen was truly perplexed by this; he had no idea what Shane could have been talking about. He tried to push it out of his mind, but it wouldn't go. He had never known him to be a nosy type; he wouldn't have called and asked how Allen liked something, which was for sure. Allen knew his wife had put him up to it. Also, Allen knew that Cheyenne and his wife Kelly were best friends most of their lives, so she was shaken by everything that happened as well.

Maybe that was just the two of thems-way of checking to see how he was doing. Allen knew he was being very distant with the entire family, well, Cheyenne's family anyway. He had no family to be distant with. His parents were both only children, and so was he. No aunts or uncles or cousins for him to talk to. He didn't mind it that much, but he thought sometimes he would have liked to have someone that was blood to talk to about everything. He just felt like he couldn't trust anyone in Cheyenne's family because he knew they'd take her side. Like he said before though, she had a good case because he wasn't being a great husband. He needed an intermediary, and her family wasn't a good place to find one. Austin certainly wasn't a good place to find one either, because he very clearly blamed Allen for his mom's death.

So, all in all, Allen was completely alone; he had no one but himself to turn to. He didn't even have Tara to turn to because he had never told her that he learned about Cheyenne's infidelity the night that she had the accident. Some part of him told him that she may have even suspected foul play on his part, that he had, indeed, enacted a scene from a book and decided to kill his wife rather than deal with her betrayal. Also, he thought there might be some evidence of that, because he was never overly emotional about her death, and he also was very quick to jump back in the saddle and start dating her. That was one reason he didn't really want to talk to Cheyenne's family because even though it was little their business about his personal life, he knew they'd be scornful about him getting back into dating so soon after her death. "Sometimes," Allen reasoned with himself, "You never know what and when something good is going to happen, and you have to take advantage of it or you'll miss it forever."

Speaking of which, Allen wanted to talk to Tara. He tried to call her, but there was no answer. He hadn't any missed calls from her either, which was unusual. He knew that she almost always called him when she was home. She didn't do much when she was back home taking care of business, which he understands more now. As they had talked she had told him the entire story about the bad relationship she was in with her ex-husband. She told him about the stalking; he would follow her everywhere, hidden out of sight. Or he'd have friends tail her and report to him where she was and who with. He used to look up her phone records. She said she even tried to get a phone he didn't know about, but she had made the mistake of using her own social security number to get it. He was able to look it up by that somehow. She said he was a wiz with electronics. He could have been a great thief because he could disable any burglar alarm within a few seconds, regardless of the company or anything else.

Allen asked her at this point if maybe it was him who had broken into the house and killed his neighbor's dog. She said she didn't think so. This didn't convince Allen, as she looked away. It was more of a hopeful way of speaking than having any real conviction to it. She also said that he would show up at her school where she taught, and wait outside until she would come out and talk to him. He would interrupt her classes by barging in on them without warning. He had gotten to the point where the principal was going to fire her if she didn't control her husband.

The principal, she said, was "Old School" in that he didn't want to hear about home problems and that when you did try to explain anything to him, he would take the husband's side no matter what. She said it didn't matter if you tried to tell him that he was beating her. He'd somehow twist it back to her fault. She said she never said he beat her, because he didn't; he was more of a harassment type of abuse. Emotional control and all that sort of thing for control over her. And when she would present clear evidence, notes he'd left her, he would take his old stand and say, "leave personal stuff at home and make sure he knows he is not allowed on the property without a pass or you will pay with your job." She said it was completely unfair, but that's how it went at that school. Even her friends, the women, that is, who were close enough to almost be called friends, wouldn't want to see her outside of school because he would randomly show up and just "happen to be in the neighborhood and wanted to say hi" which she knew was bullshit, but what could you do? She asked me. Allen didn't have a clue. He just listened.

It was the first time she had talked about her relationship and why she had to run like she did. Her parents believed her, they were willing to help and they did. They uprooted their entire lives to move hours away from their home and make sure their daughter was safe. She said that even though her ex never came right out and said it, he implied many times that he could kill her any time he wanted and get away with it. She believed him too, because even though he was a clerk at a cell phone store, he was extremely smart, and he had resources, because his parents were very wealthy. He also did a lot of side work with computers and made a lot of money doing that. He made more from his freelance stuff than anything else, so he could quit the job at the store any time and just freelance all the time. He had said he'd do it too, just to make sure she wasn't "fucking around on him". She knew he would find her, but she didn't care because she just needed enough time to file all the paperwork in order to get the divorce started. She thought that once it had gone through, he would settle down.

She thought it had worked, he hounded her school looking for any kind of forwarding address, but they wouldn't give any information. He didn't ask her family because, to them, he was perfect, and if he showed up acting all crazy, then they would lose that perception of him, and that'd be bad for his self-image. She said she knew he could control it then, because if he could keep from going to her family and asking about her, then he knew what he was doing and thought that being away from her and realizing she wasn't fucking around this time then he would come to his senses and let her go. She said she wanted to leave from the very first few months they were together, because he showed how truly insane he was. She said he used to play a game; he would make her stay home while he went out. If she had completed some mundane, but time consuming, project before he returned home with a woman, then she could leave. She never did, and he always returned with a woman. He didn't have sex with them. He'd walk in the door and then tell them to leave. She felt hopeless, because then he'd demand sex from her, and she never felt aroused by him after they were married because she would look into his eyes and see insanity dwelling deep inside them. It scared her, and she knew she would have to get out because even though she bought all his excuses about accidentally spying on her, which is the way she later thought of it, she knew that he would eventually start to get violent. The look was there in his eyes.

He dialed Tara's number, but it went straight to voicemail. He wanted to leave a message, but for some reason, it said her voicemail wasn't set up. He thought that was very strange. He tried again and got the same message. He couldn't hear anything in the house, which was good. He wanted to be alone right now. He didn't want another fight with Austin. He was tired of those, and he would have to reconcile with the boy eventually, but for now, he wanted to leave bad enough alone, because it surely wasn't getting any better any time soon.

At this moment, he realized that he himself had a voicemail; he tapped on the icon and looked at the number. It said "BLOCKED". He had no idea who that could be, but he would listen anyway. At that moment, he had a very sickening feeling creeping over his body. He broke out in a cold sweat. He felt like he was about to receive bad news, again. He knew he wouldn't be able to handle any more bad news. He tapped to listen to the message anyway.

"Hello Mr. Bennett, I have tried long and hard to reach you. My name is Katrina Daniels. It was almost impossible to get ahold of you, I have tried to call your wife Cheyenne Bennett's phone for many, many months now, and it was never on. I left many voicemails, and even emailed her several times. I work for Roger Studios, we were working on a portrait of her and her son, and she said it was to be an anniversary gift for the man who had everything else. She never gave me any other contact information other than her cell phone and email address. I have spent months trying to find out your number. She didn't even leave an address for delivery, she paid with cash and said she would have her cousin pick it up, he never showed up either. I had finished it about eight months ago. However, just recently, I learned that your wife had met with an accident that she did not survive. First of all, I want to send my condolences, even though they are very late. Also, I was wondering if you'd like the portrait she had us complete for her. If you'd like to get the address, just call me back. If not, I understand."

The voicemail cut off there, she didn't leave her number and it had showed up as blocked on the caller ID. Allen was discomfited though, he had the name of the studio and knew that he could find it if he wanted to. Allen was left in shock, though; Roger had been the name on the email subject line, "For my baby" that he had seen. Did this mean that Roger was, in fact, the person she was emailing and that she wasn't cheating on him? He had spent months hating her. Austin had spent months hating him for driving her to another man's arms. His head was spinning. He couldn't think what to do. He wanted to get her computer and find out for sure. If he had just gone the extra mile of being a snoop, all of this would have been settled many months ago, but he had let his imagination run away with him.

He had listened to his mind rather than finding out the truth. His imagination was never his friend in real life, he had made a good living with it so far, but it had many times made him miserable as it created fantastical scenarios where he always ended up with the utmost burden or pain imaginable. Had it done it to him again? Had he been so hurt by the possibility that he had given in easily to his mind and listened without question? He thought it might be so. Without realizing it, he was standing at the door of what would be his wife's study, had she been alive still and had she ever lived in this house. Sitting right in the middle of the desk, with a clear layer of dust on top of it was her laptop. It was plugged in. This was odd because he thought he remembered it going dead on him before and not being able to find the plug. Maybe Austin had found it; maybe he already knew the truth. Maybe a lot of things. But for Allen, right now, he could find out the truth, and nothing was going to stop him. It would only take one email to confirm everything or completely wreck his world. He was either going to give his wife a full pardon, or he was going to hate her memory even more. Right now, was the time. He had it booted and clicked on the link to her email. It signed him in easily. He never knew the truth was only a minute or two away like this; he had hidden from the truth.

He was nervous. His palms were sweating; he was sweating all over, in fact. He was shaking. He could barely use the mouse pad; the pointer kept jumping all over the screen. He saw that she had, in fact, received many emails in the past eight months or so, but she rarely used this email for signing up for anything online, so the spam was kept to a minimum. He saw many emails with the subject line, "for my baby". He hesitated, he almost couldn't do it. Sometimes, finding the courage to learn the absolute truth, whether it is for good or ill, is impossible to do.

In that moment, Allen didn't have that courage. Even though he knew it could have alleviated so many things that he had feared to be true. He lifted his hand off the mouse; he wasn't going to be able to do it. He knew it. He just could not violate his wife's trust anymore than he already had, even though she had completely obliterated his, he loved her, and he felt if it wasn't what he hoped to be in these emails, his love for her would die completely and he thought he couldn't live like that. Then he remembered the dream that he had. She had been trying to tell him something. It was something he couldn't make out at the time, it was just "chhh illll." Maybe she was telling him to check the email. She had reached out from her grave and sent that dream. She had wanted him to know the truth. With that, he found the resolve and clicked.

Hello, Mrs. Bennett, my name is Katrina Daniels, I specialize in family portraits, and Mr. Roger forwarded your information to me. I would be happy to try to complete this type of project for you. I think a painting of you and your son would be a great anniversary present, especially for someone who, as you say, has everything. I think it will take about three or four sessions where you come in and sit and pose in different settings and changes of clothes, I will take photographs and work from that. We are lucky we don't live hundreds of years ago when a person had to sit still for hours to have one done aren't we? Anyway, time is short so please email me back as soon as possible to get things started. These things usually take about three months to complete, so we will be up against the clock, but I think we will be able to accomplish our goal.

Yours,
Katrina Daniels
Roger Studios.

Allen just sat there, flabbergasted. He had spent the last eight months of his life believing that his wife was cheating on him. She wasn't cheating on him at all. She was sneaking away to have a painting done for him because he already had everything he could ever want. Allen put his head in his hands and began to cry. He cried as though he had never cried before and wasn't sure if the ability would leave him soon, right after this. The sobs rocked his body, he hitched his breath, he choked, and he wished he would just die himself. He didn't feel he deserved to live. He thought that he deserved death for how he acted. How much hatred he held in his heart. He felt that it was consuming him now. He was overwhelmed with it, and he wanted to die. He didn't care about Austin at this point, his only hope was for death, and he would get it soon, he felt.

Chapter 29

The Guilt

Allen couldn't stop crying. He had managed to stumble back to his room. He had no recollection of getting there, but he was on his bed. The bed he had once shared with Cheyenne, one he thought she had betrayed, but he knew now she hadn't. He wanted to scream and rage, but the only person he could do that was himself, and he didn't have any way to do that, so he just cried. He hurt. He hurt. And he hurt badly. His heart was aching, and now his body was starting to ache as well. His head was starting to pound, and he was having blurred visions. Through his pain, he thought to himself, "oh great, now another headache."

"Dad?" Austin said from the door.

Allen was incapable of looking at his son. He just kept his face buried in the pillow, letting the waves of pain wash over him, squeezing out more and more tears until he was sure that the room was going to fill and he would drown upon his own tears. After some time, Allen had no sense of time at this point, he managed to look up and saw his son was gone. It seemed that he had given up on him, just as Allen had given up on himself. He wondered if it were possible to die of a broken heart, and he thought the resounding answer to what he always thought of as a rhetorical question was

"YES."

He slept, he did not dream, and for that, he was thankful when he awoke. He had no idea how long he slept; he only knew that he couldn't spend time at all. He wasn't sure even what time he had fallen asleep. He had completely lost himself as well as time. He was in a state where he felt like he was floating on a cloud of hell. There was no way off the cloud, and he just had to endure where it took him and see what it showed him. He didn't know what to do. He felt like his entire relationship with Tara was a lie because he had entered it mostly on the pretense that Cheyenne had cheated on him, so she had betrayed the marriage before him. It was okay that he started to date someone else.

She wasn't cheating, though, and now he was going to be a father to a child with a woman he felt would not understand what he was going through at this moment. He felt he loved her, which was true. Had said it to her, she had received her love. Had even received her ring and her proposal. Now, he was lost. He had lost his compass. A part of him hated himself for even finding the truth. He thought that maybe sometimes, if it happened long enough in the past, then the truth deserved to remain dead and buried. Sometimes, the truth and lies alike will haunt the living, and long after, the dead who spoke those truths and lies are dead and buried. It seems it is just as easy to be haunted by one as the other. Allen wondered now if he would have been better off without the truth. He had been getting over everything. He thought he could go to Austin and say he found out the truth, and he shouldn't be angry with him anymore. If anything, he thought that this was the only real benefit of finding out the truth. Other than that, it seemed to make everything much more complicated.

"Dad?" Austin was standing at the door again.

"Yeah, Austin?" Allen was wondering what to tell his son. Right now, he felt like it was too much to speak.

"You ok?"

"Yeah," Allen lied, "I think so anyway. Just had a lot on my mind, and it all had to come out at some point, you know."

"You sure? I saw you were in mom's office, and her computer was smashed against the wall."

"Was it?" Allen had no recollection of doing this, even straining his mind as hard as he could he couldn't remember it, of course, he knew he couldn't remember making it back to his room as well. He must have done it right after reading the email and having all the feelings of self-loathing.

"Yeah, the screen is busted, and it won't turn on at all." Austin looked at his dad with concern and something else that Allen could not quite place. Then it hit him all at once, fear. For some reason, he was afraid of his dad, even though Allen had never once in his life raised a hand to him. They had believed in time-outs rather than spankings, and it seemed to work because Austin had turned out to be a good kid. He was never in trouble when he went to school. He had actually asked them to be homeschooled because he thought that the private school he attended was getting into some unsavory characters.

"I was in there earlier; maybe I tripped over the plug or something and didn't realize it. I've had a bad headache all day. I might have just not realized I did it." Allen was trying to invent something, which was his specialty, and felt like he was failing at it because Austin looked unconvinced.

"There is a hole in the wall, too, where it was thrown against the wall, and it was up high enough to where it could have been done by tripping over the cord." Austin fixed him with a stare that dared him to get out of this one. Allen couldn't and gave up completely.

"Okay, I was in there earlier and read her email. I got pissed off and must have thrown it again the wall. I don't really remember. But I have a bad headache, would you leave me alone for a while, Austin, and take your accusatory stare with you. I don't feel like dealing with it right now."

"Yeah, you never feel like dealing with me right now. She's been dead for eight months, and all you've done is lie in bed and fuck the neighbor. That's ok though, dad. Things will change soon,

I'm sure."

"What is that supposed to mean, Austin?" Allen asked, his anger rising to the top now.

"Nothing, you told me to leave." Austin snapped back, "I'm going. You've never wanted me around anyways."

"That's crap, and you know it. You're the one always sneaking off, hiding when people are here. I always make excuses for you, especially when Tara comes over. You're never here."

"Well, you won't have to worry about that anymore." Austin screamed and left the room.

Allen tried to get up and follow him. Again, he was unable. He was crippled by the headache and swooned. He fell hard again on the nightstand, and the pain was immediate and intense as he bounced first off the stand, then again the wall, and then to the floor. Three different places, his head hit, and he felt lumps rising on each spot. He succumbed to the darkness that threatened him, vaguely wishing it was a permanent darkness.

It wasn't, though; he seemed to regain himself almost immediately. The best part was that the initial headache seemed to have disappeared in the few minutes he was knocked out, but he was having severe pain in the three places he had hit his head. He gingerly felt his head and felt a lump in each place. The one where the front of his head had hit the nightstand felt to be the largest, but he felt no blood, so he thought he was good on that score.

He stumbled into the bathroom and took a few pain pills. He thought they might work for this because they surely didn't help with the other headaches he had been suffering from. He popped about four in his mouth, drew a glass of water from the tap, and swallowed them. He still had no idea what he needed to do. He knew now he didn't want to die anymore. He had never been the suicidal type, although he wrote about death all the time in his stories, he had never really been intrigued by suicide. His parents had died when he was young, but the depression from that hadn't really manifested itself into suicidal ideations. So when he suddenly had a death wish a short while ago, he was scared by that as well. The feeling had passed, though.

The feeling of guilt had not passed, though. Allen felt extremely guilty that he had spent such a long time hating his wife for cheating on him when she never did. He had no idea how to assuage that feeling. He knew what most people would say, had he the courage to tell anyone, that time would heal it just as it had healed the pain he felt from believing she had actually cheated on him.

He thought that would be bullshit, though, because he thought it was usually much easier to forgive others transgression against us than it is to forgive ourselves for misjudging another person or a situation. People, by nature, he thought, just hated to be wrong, and when we were wrong, it stuck with us much longer than being betrayed by another person. He thought this may be the case because, deep down, we only trust ourselves and not any other people. And to admit we were wrong to ourselves, or worse, be proven wrong by someone else, made it so we didn't trust ourselves as much anymore.

Allen tried to go downstairs, but something told him to get his phone. He wasn't one of these people who carried it around all the time; he thought that sort of behavior was only decent in teenagers. But he grabbed his phone from his room, and he thought maybe Tara had called while he was asleep or something, and his love connection with her was sending out a signal. He was wrong; he had no missed calls whatsoever. He was shocked to see that it was now Monday, though.

He had slept another entire day away, but he didn't feel like he had slept that long. An hour or two at most. He needed to find out why he was sleeping so much, and he didn't think it was depression. He wondered if the headaches had something to do with it. He wasn't a doctor, so he couldn't say. He knew some people who had severe migraines would sometimes sleep a lot, but they usually seemed to realize that they were sleeping so much, he on the other hand, he didn't have a clue until he saw a calendar or something that he had slept a day or sometimes two entire days away.

As he walked by Austin's room, he checked in there as usual. It was neat as a pin. It was as though the kid never did anything in his room. He never left a light on or anything. Allen supposed that might be because he hated to have his dad looking in his room. Allen had tried the light switch, and it didn't work. He didn't know if Austin had taken the bulb out or if it had blown out, and he couldn't find a replacement. He wasn't sure. He didn't care. He had lamps, he probably just preferred them.

Allen made his way downstairs and looked around the living room. He realized he spent hardly any time here. He was always in his room or out of the house. He seemed to hate the "family room" because he felt like he had no family to share it with. As he walked across the living room, he noticed a flashing light through the window. He walked over and saw it was a cop car at Tara's house. Fear immediately enveloped him. His first thought was that her premonition that her ex-husband was going to someday become violent had come true.

He wanted to rush across the street, but couldn't he was rooted to the spot in the living room. He wasn't able to move, talk, or anything. He could barely think. Then, the added portion of his book hit him, and he collapsed to his knees. He couldn't remember it word for word, but he knew the results of it. He finally found his feet and made his way to the garage. He opened the door and fumbled for the light. He knew what he'd see even before he flipped the switch. He took a deep breath and closed his eyes. He prayed that he wouldn't see what he knew he'd see. He knew he would see Tara hanging from the rafters of the garage.

He knew this because what Austin had added was, "After all the clients were dead, there was only one person left to kill. That was the betraying slut. The one that had caused him to become a serial killer. The one he had given his heart over to and the one who had decided to crush it like it meant nothing. He wanted her to suffer, just as he had over the past months knowing all the pain he had, he tried to dump it into the people who had fucked his wife and paid her. That made it so much worse for him; they couldn't have just fucked her but had paid her too. She was a prostitute. She deserved to die to atone for her crimes. He was the judge, jury, and executioner. He had bought a length and used the skills he had learned in the armed forces, made a noose, and strung it up to the rafters in the garage. When she came home, he would hang the bitch and then himself beside her with the list of people he had killed in his pocket."

Allen flipped on the light, saw the illumination through his eyelids, and prayed again that he wouldn't see Tara hanging there. He opened them, and he collapsed again to his knees.

He saw her hanging there, swinging slowly in the draft that had to be coming from the vent in the rafters. His beautiful body is limp and most assuredly dead. Her face was swollen and black. Her tongue lolled to one side of her mouth. He saw all this and closed his eyes and wished it away. He slowly opened them again and looked at Tara, the life she had gone, as well as the baby she carried inside gone. He closed his eyes a third time. Again praying to undo the visions he saw before him, and opened them again. Tara still hung in his garage. His eyes stared into the vast emptiness that is beyond this world.

Allen lost it and started to scream again. He felt as though he had somehow lost the two women he loved again, and both on the same day. He knew who did it, too. He knew Austin had killed her. He had written it. He probably did the other murders, too. Allen was sick. He vomited repeatedly until all that was left was dry heaving, and when that happened, he wished he had something else because it was more painful than the vomiting. He screamed and screamed. He wondered on some level if the cops across the street would hear him. He couldn't believe they could. They were several hundred feet away, and the garage had decent insulation, and the door was around the back of the house. The driveway came up and circled behind and beside the pool.

Allen stumbled again to his feet, he felt on some obscure level of his mind that his new gait was going to be stumbling, and he started to yell for Austin. He screamed and screamed for him through the house. His headache was back, but he ignored it for the nonce, he needed to know why Austin had killed Tara. She didn't deserve it. He screamed and screamed.

Austin wasn't in the house. Allen then ran through the back, and he felt like his legs knew where they were going even though he had only been to the rock twice. He went there without any issues at a fast run. He saw Austin lying on the rock. He couldn't go after him and attack him. He wanted to, but that wasn't his nature.

"Why did you do it, Austin?" He fell to his knees as he shouted. "Why?"

"I didn't do it." Austin replied with absolute calmness.

"She is hanging in our fucking garage! You had to have done it!" Allen was losing control.

"Doesn't mean I put her there." Again, Austin was as calm as could be.

"I should call the cops, how could you do this to me? I love her, you little fucker! I now have to choose between my son and justice for the woman I love! She was pregnant, and you killed the baby too. You killed two people today. Why would you do this? I don't understand."

"Doesn't matter to me that she was pregnant. I wouldn't

have called anything she had a brother or sister. I didn't kill her, though."

Allen was stammering now, his words inaudible. He kept trying to gain his feet and would fall back to the ground. He just kept repeating the same phrase over and over again.

Finally, he said, "I can't turn you in. I have to help you. Help me hide her." Allen turned and ran back toward the house. He let himself in and started to look around the garage for picks and shovels, and he wasn't much of a yard person, so he had no tools. He couldn't risk putting her in the car and driving away. What if they were searching for vehicles? He was her current boyfriend, and they would see him leaving. If he didn't stop and ask what was going on, he would be pinned as a suspect right away.

He had to hide her in the woods. Maybe he could cover her with a bunch of leaves for now and go back and move her when the heat died down. He thought that might be the best option. He tried to pull Tara down from the rafters but couldn't because Tara wasn't there. In his haste to find something to hide her body with, he didn't even realize he would have needed to walk through her hanging body to get to the back of the garage where there were a few gardening tools kept. He was in a panic now, and he thought that Austin had to have gotten here before he did and moved her. But no, he took a direct path to the house.

There was no way he could have beaten him. The cops then? Maybe they heard him screaming earlier and came to investigate and saw her body hanging there and took it down. That didn't make sense to Allen either; it would have been considered a crime scene. They would have wanted to keep it as pristine as possible. Allen was in full panic mode now. He had no idea where Tara's body could be. He tried to find the rope. If someone had taken her body, they would have had to cut her down and surely left the piece of rope behind. He searched frantically and couldn't find any evidence. He looked everywhere. He even looked under the car. She couldn't fit there, but he was running out of options. Allen was running here and there, looking in places that couldn't fit a squirrel, let alone a human body. She was gone. Someone had taken her, and his son was going to go to prison because he was the one that killed her.

Chapter 30
The Arrest

There was a knock on the door, even though he was in the garage, Allen could hear it. It was the authoritative kind of knock that only a policeman can have. They must have gone to a special training in order to learn that. Allen froze in mid-search. He didn't know what to do, but he knew, without really knowing, that it was the police who were at the door. He was going to be asked about Tara, and what would he tell them? Her body was no longer in his garage where it had been, what? Twenty minutes ago? An hour? Who knew for sure? Allen seemed to have lost his concept of time. He hesitated because he didn't know what to do; he thought he was doomed either way. He could answer the door and give up his son, or he could not answer the door and make himself look guilty.

He knew he couldn't run for it because he would be caught within minutes. The knock came again, this time, Allen could hear someone saying something as well. Although he was far enough away that he couldn't make out what they were saying. The person didn't sound angry, but it was a voice that expected an answer. Allen resigned himself to the fact that someone was going to get in trouble today; he went toward the living room and heard the knock again. They were being very persistent.

He opened the door, and his worst fear was standing there.

There were two police officers. They looked serious. He knew he wouldn't be able to talk his way out of anything with them.

"Hello, sir." The one on the right said, "I am Officer King, this is Officer Stevens. May we ask you a few questions?"

Allen tried to remain calm and said, "No problem." In what he hoped was the absolute calmest voice he could muster and, he felt he had pulled it off, at least for now.

"Thank you, this won't take long." King said, "Have you been home all day?"

"Yeah, I was asleep for most of it, though. Why, what is going on over there?" He didn't want to ask too many questions but couldn't help himself.

"We aren't sure just yet. Did you hear any disturbances? Any screaming or anything during the early morning or late night?"

Allen had no idea where this line of questioning was going but answered honestly, "No, nothing like that."

Officer Stevens pulled out a picture, "Have you seen this person around here?"

Allen looked at the picture; it was of a young man, maybe mid-twenties. Allen honestly had never seen the person before.

"No, I've never seen this person before. Who is he?" He asked.

Officer King looked unhappy Allen that Allen was asking so many questions. As the authority in this situation, his face said that he should be asking all the questions.

"It is the young lady across the street, that is her ex-husband. We think he may have been in the area because his vehicle was spotted not too far from here. The young lady went missing sometime during the night. The father of the young lady said he heard her talking on the phone and then heard the front door open and close. He then heard raised voices, and he said the male voice 'sounded' familiar, but he couldn't quite place it. You didn't hear anything like that this morning?"

"No sir," Allen said, "I don't know if Tara's dad said anything to you, but we are dating. So this is very concerning to me."

"I understand, sir. Is there anyone living with you?"

"Yeah, my son lives here. But he's not home right now." Allen added, which was probably a little too fast because the two officers exchanged a look between one another.

"We will need to talk to him too. Does he have a phone? Can you call him to come back right now?" Officer King asked.

"He does, but I don't think he has it with him. He's just in the backwoods. He usually doesn't take anything back there. It is his thinking place. I can walk you back there if you want." Allen prayed that this wouldn't be a major mistake and that they would stumble upon Tara's body.

"Yeah, that would be fine." Stevens said after a non-verbal exchange with King, "Lead the way."

"Right this way." Said Allen and led them through the living room and out the back door. He was still dressed for being outside from earlier.

As Allen walked, he had an overwhelming sense of foreboding. He felt like something was going to go drastically wrong. He couldn't change his mind, though, without raising the officers' suspicions. He just kept walking. He didn't try to talk. They came up on the clearing, and to Allen's immense relief, Austin was nowhere to be found. He let out an audible sigh and then quickly tried to pass it off as he was out of breath.

"Sir, why is there disturbed ground all around this area?" Asked Officer King.

"I. I have no idea sir. I don't come back here too often. Austin is the one that is always back here."

"It looks like it was big enough to hold a body." He leaned down and brushed aside a clump of grass. It revealed a hand. "Can you explain this, sir?"

Allen looked dumbfounded. He just stared at the hand. It was a man's hand. He had no idea who it could belong to or how it had gotten here. He had walked this area a few times and never noticed the shallow grave. As he looked around, he noticed several of them; some were large enough for a human. Some were only large enough for perhaps a large dog, and he hoped they contained dogs. He prayed they did not contain children. He couldn't place a number right off the hand of the areas that looked like they had recently been dug, he thought maybe 5, possibly as many as 10. His mind was just not able to wrap around it.

"Sir, do you know anything about this?" Asked Officer Stevens while drawing his sidearm from its holster.

Allen just stood there, then almost inaudibly said, "My son."

"Pardon me sir?" Asked Stevens, now pointing his gun at the ground just in front of Allen's feet.

"It has to be my son. This is his place. No one else ever comes back here, as far as I know." Allen couldn't believe what he was saying; he was giving his son up to the police. His only hope was that there would be some logical explanation for everything, and as soon as he saw Austin, he would be able to explain everything. Officer King was on his radio but had walked away from the area. It seemed as though he did not want Allen to hear what he was saying.

"Sir, I need you to turn around and place your hands behind your head. You're going to feel metal and hear a click."

Allen turned and asked, "Am I being arrested?" He sounded incredulous.

"For the moment, let's just say we want to keep you here where we can find you with no issues."

"Pendleton says there is a spade and shovel both in his garage, and it looks like they were recently used. Perhaps in the last day or so." King said as he strode back toward the clearing.

Panic was rising up in Allen now. He didn't know what was happening. He was looking at one officer to the other. "You can't think I did this, can you? I'm telling you, my son comes back here. Not me." Allen's voice was rising with the panic. He was looking at the two officers while they searched the immediate area for more clues. Neither one of them had uncovered more than the hand from the one shallow grave so far, neither of them, it seemed, wanted to see more.

They were now about thirty feet away. They had both holstered their guns. They didn't seem to think that Allen was a real threat. He used this to his advantage and ran for it. He had made it to the cover of the trees before the officers had even registered, and he had gone. He didn't know where he was running or even why he was running. He just knew he was scared. He needed to find Austin and try to get away as fast as possible.

He knew that he wouldn't be able to go back to his house, it sounded as though the cops were already searching the place. He had no options; he didn't even have his cell phone on him. His panic, which had been at its worst, was now back, and though he thought it wasn't possible, it was worse as well. He needed to find Austin. He fell, sprawling. Not sure where he was, he looked around. He must have hit his head because it was agony almost immediately as he hit the ground.

"Dad!" Austin said in a loud whisper. Allen looked around for him but couldn't find him. He heard someone running behind him. He wondered how far behind they were. He couldn't see them yet, which told him they were a good distance. There was a screen of pine trees behind him and them, at any rate.

"DAD!" Austin said again, in a louder whisper. Allen couldn't see him. He looked everywhere for him. "DAD!" It was coming from above him. He looked up and saw Austin's face. It was calm.

Registered none of his father's panic. "Up here! Quick!" Allen looked; it was a cleverly disguised hunter's stand in the tree. If you were not looking for it, Allen thought you could very easily have missed it.

"You will need to help me." Allen whispered back to his son.

"Sorry, Dad, you'll have to do it on your own. You can do it." Austin said back, with what felt like a small laugh to Allen. Austin seemed to be enjoying himself.

"I'm cuffed!" Allen whispered back angrily.

"Slide your arms under your legs. You can do it. Hurry up dad. I can hear them."

Allen rolled onto his side and tried to slide his arms around his legs but couldn't do it. He, too, could hear them running. They had spread out. There was a fork, and they had split up to search for him. Allen tried again, and this time, it worked as his arms slid around his ankles. He reached up. It was a touch to climb, but not impossible. He pulled himself into the stand with an effort. Austin was standing over his father now with a smile on his face. Allen was face down, inhaling the smell of the lumber used to make the floor of the stand. It was hidden from the ground, but Allen could see very well from where he was laying.

There were no sides to it, just a board floor. It was camouflaged by the branches from below, but you used strategically trimmed branches to climb. Allen wondered who had built it and why it had been built because this was private property here and hunting was forbidden at all times. It seemed as though it had been built recently as well because he saw that the boards did not completely turn the weathered gray color you would expect them to be. He came back from his thoughts, attempting to stem his heavy breathing as one of the officers raced by below. It seemed as though Austin had saved him.

He sat up, still trying to catch his breath. Looked at his son with extreme weariness. He wanted to thank him, but then he remembered why he had been treated in the first place. So instead of thanking him, he blurted out, "What the fuck have you done, Austin?" In a hoarse whisper.

"I wanted you to keep your promises. For every promise you broke, I took out someone that you knew or cared about. I blame you for my mother's death. I want you punished. You have been left here with me, and you still don't care about me. I was nothing but smoke and vapor to you. Something to pass through to get to the next day. You never loved me. Now I have ruined your life the way you have ruined mine."

"Austin, your mom wasn't cheating on me. I don't know what you are talking about. She was out having an anniversary gift made for me. That was where she was on the night she died. She wasn't at some guy's house. I'm sorry that I led you to believe that. I'm sorry if she led you to believe that. But it is true. I read the emails. That's what I had her computer for. I confirmed something she had come and said to me in a dream. She told me to check her emails. I checked. She never cheated on me. She never betrayed us."

"It is not about whether or not she cheated on you. That is not the point. The point is that you made promises that our lives together were going to improve. They didn't, though, because I spent months waiting for you to come to me. I was in pain. I was hurting. You never noticed, though, because you were too busy falling in love with a whore and making my replacement with her. I did things to get your attention, and you just failed to notice. It was like I wasn't even around anymore. "

"I knew you were in pain. I was in pain, too. I'm sorry I didn't do all I should have done. You should have come to me and talked to me about everything. You didn't need to drop hints. You should have just come to me and said, 'dad, I need help getting through this'. And I would have been there for you, Austin. Now, though, I'm not sure what I can do for you. You've taken people's lives Austin. How can I get you out of this?"

"Tell them you did it. They will think it was you anyway. I wanted you to be punished, remember? I hate you, dad. The way you've always hated me. They way you've always hated a part of yourself that made me. They will soon figure out that Mr. Roberts was wearing your running shoes when he was murdered by a knife that matches the set of knives we have in the kitchen. They will know when they finally catch you and arrest you that your fingerprints match a certain cell phone that was found at the scene of the crime where the real estate whore was found."

"Again, she was killed with a knife that is sitting in our kitchen right now. She didn't want to meet you in a vacant lot like that, oh no. But she did. She just needed you to sign some stuff, and it seemed to be convenient. I enjoyed watching her die dad. You were right, though, she was sexy. I almost wished I could have lost my virginity to her before she died. I would have done it after she died, but that would have left too much evidence that pointed to me. I needed it all to point to you. Unfortunately, she didn't have her cell phone with her, she had left it in the car, and someone had stolen it before the police could get there. They tracked her last calls, but there wasn't enough to let them come after you. I left the other cell phone there. Hoping that they would find it, but they were too incompetent. I had to call and tell them that I had been out for a ride on my bike and saw a cell phone inside the police lines. They are easy to manipulate, small-town cops."

"The other people back there are just drifters and homeless people that no one would notice. I practiced on them. It was easy because I just offered them the food you gave me, you would think I was eating it, but really, all along, I was giving it to those hopeless saps. Then I killed them and buried them. All with the knife from the kitchen. I'm sure they won't have any trouble matching the knife, the prints, and the bodies." Allen was looking at Austin as though he had never seen him before. He had become almost transparent to Allen's eyes. He was something that wasn't even human to him anymore. He was this sick and demented person who could not have been his sweet and innocent son. The same son who hated to see stray animals die.

"...dogs were fun too." Austin had been talking all along, but Allen had missed it.

"What?" He asked.

"I said, 'the dogs were fun too'." Austin continued. "I enjoyed killing the dogs too. Especially that mutt you tried to buy my love with. He was especially fun because I got to watch him waste away to nothing because you had forgotten about him because you were so caught up in that whore's vagina. You hadn't even noticed he was missed once you returned from your little fuck fest. I killed him last. It was satisfying. He deserved to die, though, because you weren't worthy of something that offered unconditional love like that because you don't deserve love at all. You just take love, never really give love. My mother knew it. She was trying to make you realize you had a family, too, that's why she wanted that stupid portrait done of us, but it wouldn't have worked. You only care about yourself. You're going to be punished." Austin laughed.

"Mr. Bennett, I know you're up there. Show me your hands. I understand why you ran, you were scared. Please come quietly and let us sort this thing out." It was Officer King.

"My son, I told you." Said Allen as he looked over the edge

of the stand. He saw the cop standing there with his gun pointing directly at Allen's head. Allen suddenly felt something against his back, and he tumbled feet overhead out of the tree. He connected with several branches as he fell. He hit his head, his shoulder, his back, and his arms lodged between a fork of a branch, and he swung down, and he felt his left arm snap as the branches gave way, and he tumbled to the earth.

"Don't move!" Officer King shouted. With one hand on his gun, he keyed the mic of his radio and said, "I got him. Situation under control."

"I can't move." Allen said he was in pain from head to toe. Amazingly, though, the headache was almost completely gone. His focus was on the broken arm he had sustained. "It was my son. He is up there, too. He called out to me. I climbed up there. And, and I…I think he just pushed me back down, too." At that moment, about twenty more police officers rushed into the area, all with their guns drawn.

"Up the tree. And be careful." King said to the young athletic officer next to him.

The cop was up the tree in a matter of seconds and standing on the platform. Allen was on the ground face down. His broken arm was pinned underneath him.

"No one up here, sir. Nothing but a couple of spots of blood."

Allen attempts to roll over and look up to see if the cop is lying. His broken and battered body wouldn't cooperate, though. He just grunted and stayed in the same position.

"Don't move!" One of the cops shouted. Allen wanted to tell him he couldn't, that he was just trying. But nothing would come out of his mouth. He was in shock. He didn't know how Austin had gotten away from them so quickly. As far as Allen knew, there was only one way out of a tree, and that was down. Allen was confused, in pain, and heartbroken. He wondered about his son, but he also wondered about Tara. He didn't get a chance to ask Austin about her. He wanted to know what he had done with her body so he could tell the police. He didn't want Tara to be buried in a shallow grave. She deserved a grand funeral. She was beautiful in life and deserved a beautiful sendoff. He wondered if they would let him pay for her funeral, even though they seemed to be detaining him right now for something he didn't do.

He knew Austin had tried to plant evidence, making it look like he had committed the crimes, but he was sure that he would be able to provide quality alibis for the crimes. Unfortunately, though, he thought most of his alibis would have to be corroborated by Tara, and if she was dead, that would take care of a lot of his hope. It seemed as though Austin had screwed him good.

"Up you go." Someone said as they were grabbing his arms and pulling him to his feet. Allen screamed in agony. The cops seemed to not notice or care that Allen was in pain. They were dragging him back down the path that he had run up when he was trying to get away from the cops. He thought that would be the most they could get him for was trying to flee. Of course, that made him look guilty. Then again, Allen thought he had led them to the crime scene, if he was really guilty, why would he have done that? Things weren't making sense to him. He wanted to know about Tara. He wanted to know how Austin escaped when there were so many cops around. He didn't want to ask about Austin, and he assumed the kid would be captured soon. The more pressing matter was with Tara.

"Did you find Tara?" He asked Officer Stevens. He had a hold of Allen's broken arm, and though he seemed to notice it was deformed in some way, he was not very gentle. Allen wasn't feeling as much pain as he had before; he guessed that his adrenaline was still rushing through his body.

"Yeah. We did. Right where you left her, you sick bastard." He replied.

Allen had no idea what he was talking about; Allen had last seen Tara dangling from the end of a rope in his garage. He had been in the garage since he saw her and knew she had been taken down.

He had no idea where she was at now. He wanted to ask the officer more, but before he could, the officer continued on his own.

"What were you planning to do with her, Austin?" He asked Allen. "Why did you have her bound and gagged in what looks to be your son's room.

"Gagged?" Allen asked wearily. "You mean she's alive?"

"Yeah, but barely. She has been missing for three days. Her family didn't report her missing because it was assumed she had gone to a cabin she went to sometimes to get away. She hadn't returned any phone calls or texts. They became worried and drove up there. She wasn't anywhere to be found. Her dad stated that you were the last person he saw her with. That is why we came knocking on your door. We know about the crazy ex-husband. His insanity runs deeper than what we or you would have ever thought. She said he stalked her, and she was right. We found his car, and he had detailed notes on all her movements, along with photographs, cell phone records, and copies of text messages she had sent. I know you wonder why I am telling you all of this, and I'll tell you. It's because the hand I first found back in that clearing belonged to him. If you would just confess to us and say you killed him in defense of Tara, we would understand. The guy was obviously crazy."

"I didn't touch him. I told you it was my son. He has been trying to frame me for murders because he is mad at me and thinks that I am to blame for his mother's death."

"Mr. Bennett, his body is on your property. There are other bodies as well. None of them have any kind of identification on them; none of our officers seem to recognize them. We assume you lured them from somewhere outlying and brought them here and killed them."

"No, I did not!" Allen screamed. "It was my son. He is framing me for this."

Allen was being led into his backyard and around his house. Tara was standing with some police officers and looked up at Allen. She looked at him like she had never seen him before.

"Tara!" He shouted. "Tell them! Tell them that it was Austin. Austin took you and tied you up."

They stopped Allen as Tara looked like she wanted to say something or maybe the police were waiting for her to make a positive identification of him.

"You're right, it was Austin." She replied, looking at him. She broke down and tears and started to swoon. The cop nearest her caught her and helped her to the nearest chair, and she sat down. She never took her eyes off him. There was loathing in those eyes; Allen didn't understand where it came from. He also didn't understand why he was still being led away toward the cop car. She had told them it wasn't him. She had told him it was Austin.

Allen was put in the car. He started to scream, and the pain in his body was making its first full appearance. Also, his head was starting to hurt again. He couldn't think. He wanted to sleep. He looked toward the woods and saw a shadow. "Austin!" He screamed to his son. Austin walked away, though, back through the woods and disappeared.

Allen was taken to the station and then to the hospital. The entire time he was there, he just kept repeating the phrase, "It was my son." No one seemed to want to hear it, though, because he was the one being arrested. He was the one that was being roughed up by the cops. He was in pain. He knew there were more bones broken than just his arm. He figured there were two, maybe three ribs broken as well. The cops seemed to be in no hurry to get him to the hospital. They said they wanted to wait for Allen's lawyer first.

When Allen's lawyer arrived, he looked weary. He was an old man. He did most of the stuff for Cheyenne's estate. Allen doubted that he had ever had to deal with something like this before. He sat across from Allen.

"Mr. Bennett," he started, he had never called Allen anything but Allen before. Allen knew he thought he was guilty. "I don't have to tell you that I haven't been called for anything like this before. You might want to try to get someone a little more qualified."

"I don't need anyone more qualified because I didn't do anything. Right now, I need two things, and the first is to get to a hospital because I am severely hurt, and none of these fucking cops gives a shit. I've been telling them I have a broken arm, which they keep yanking and pulling on, along with two, maybe three broken ribs. The second thing I need is for you to find my son and talk to him. He may tell you everything, or he may not. At least find him and tell him to come see me. They will let him off. He's a minor. He can be free in a few years. If he lets me take the blame for his crimes, then I'll go to jail for the rest of my life." Allen finished and fixed his lawyer with a cold stare.

"Your, your son?" He asked.

"Yes, my son, you dumbass! Jesus Christ how did you ever get to be a lawyer if you are so dumb?" Allen screamed.

"Okay okay." He stood up to leave. "I'll get them to treat your injuries. Stay tight for anything else." He said.

"Thank you." Allen whispered back.

The next thing Allen knew; he was being taken away again. This time, his lawyer witnessed the escort. His appearance seemed to take some of the toughness out of the cops. Allen noticed that as he was walking by him, he had a piece of legal paper with some names and numbers on it. Allen assumed that they were the names and badge numbers of the officers in the room. That way, if it was shown that Allen had sustained more injuries than from a tree fall, someone would have to pay.

He was put back in a squad car and taken to the nearest hospital. He was overwhelmed with joy when they brought him some pain medicine. It was given intravenously, and he felt the effects almost immediately, and he slipped into darkness.

He awakes some time later. His arm was set in a cast, and he had heavy bandages around his midsection. So it seemed he had been right about the broken ribs after all. He was having trouble breathing. He didn't recognize his surroundings. It was a very sparse room. The only thing in the room besides his bed was a chair. On that chair sat a police officer. The officer watched him intently.

"What's going on?" Allen asked the officer. The officer didn't respond. He just looked the opposite way. "Hello?" Allen asked at the man. He sat there without saying anything. He was now staring at the floor.

"Will you at least tell me where I am? This doesn't seem to be a prison. It looks like a hospital, but certainly not a medical floor." The officer continued to look at the floor. Allen gave up, and that was when he realized that he had nylon straps on his legs. He was strapped to the bed like a crazy person.

"Why the fuck am I strapped to the fucking bed?" He demanded of the officer in the room, but again, he just sat and stared at the floor. "You're fucking useless. Asshole," Allen spat at the man.

Allen heard voices outside the room; he heard his son's name. He tried to listen more intently, but they were talking too softly for him to hear. The officer stood up and took a step toward a door that Allen couldn't see and heard him say something along the lines of him being awake.

"Good. Good," Allen heard someone outside the door say. Then someone walked in and looked at him.

"Good afternoon, Mr. Bennett. I am Doctor Taylor. I have been assigned to your care for now by the state." The doctor said. "Forgive me if I don't shake your hands; that would require unstrapping you, and I don't think we can do that just yet. You were quite violent when you arrived here. You've hurt several of the nurses and assistants. No one seriously, though."

"How can I have hurt someone if I don't remember it?" Allen asked the doctor.

"Well, there seems to be a lot you don't remember right now. We are going to work on that, though. We need to get you well. The first thing we need you to do is tell me your full name."

"My name? You know my name. You just said it." Allen replied.

"I said your last name. I need your full name. Your first, middle, and last names."

"Fine," Allen barked, "Allen Shane Bennett."

"Are you sure that is your name?" The doctor asked.

"Of course, I am sure. I think I would know my own name." Allen snarled back. He liked this doctor not all.

"Are you certain that your name isn't Austin James Bennett?" He asked Allen.

"No. My name is Allen Shane Bennett. Austin James Bennett is the name of my son. Are you sure you shouldn't be the one strapped to this bed? You're fucking retarded."

"So your name isn't Austin James Bennett?"

"Nope. Told you my name. How many times do you need me to tell you this?"

Allen looked at the wall. This doctor seemed to be stupid. He wondered how so many stupid people got jobs that smart people were supposed to have. First of all, there was his lawyer, who looked at him like he had gone crazy when he said to find his son.

"When was the last time you saw your son, Mr. Bennett?" The doctor asked him.

"Why? Is he ok?" Allen sat up as much as he could and looked at the doctor.

"Please help me help you, Mr. Bennett. When was the last time you saw your son?"

"I don't know for sure. How long have I been here? Anyway, I saw him on the edge of the woods just as I was being taken away by the cops. I tried to get the cop's attention, but of course, they didn't listen. They weren't listening to anything I was saying." Said Allen.

"So earlier today, then?" the doctor asked him.

"I guess so if it's the same day. When you've fallen out of a tree and have been hurt as bad as I have, it is hard to keep track of time."

"Did anyone else see him?" He asked Allen.

"No, that's what I am trying to tell you. I was trying to get them to go after him, but they were too intent on bringing in an innocent person."

"You certainly didn't act innocent. You ran from the police." The cop had finally said something.

"I panicked, okay? I knew my son had to have done those things you told me about after you caught me. I was scared and wanted to find him before you did because I was afraid you would hurt him." Replied Allen.

"Back to this now, Mr. Bennett. So, the last time you saw your son was earlier today. Did you talk to him today?" he asked Allen.

"Yes, as I ran from the police, he got my attention when I fell, and I climbed up in a tree stand with him. We spoke for a few minutes. He confessed to having done all of the crimes I was charged with earlier in an attempt to frame me because he blames me for his mom's death." Allen was speaking calmly now.

He felt like someone was finally listening to what he was saying. "He said you can find the knife that killed Audrey and Mr. Roberts in our kitchen. He also said that Mr. Roberts was wearing my running shoes. The cell phone that was found the day after Audrey was killed was planted by him after I had found it in our front yard and had picked it up and handled it."

"When was the last time you saw your wife, Cheyenne?" He asked Allen.

"Huh? Why would you ask that?" Allen's calmness left him in a hurry; he was becoming more agitated again.

"Please answer the questions Mr. Bennett; these are to help us all in the end." The doctor replied calmly.

"The night she was killed in a car wreck. I had thought she had been having an affair with me with someone named Roger because I saw some emails, but I never read them. She wrecked coming back from getting a portrait done. It was going to be an anniversary gift." He said, "I hated her for so long after that until I learned the truth recently."

"Was your son with her when she wrecked?" The doctor asked him. Allen was getting tired of questions about this.

"No, of course not, he probably would have been hurt or killed himself. He was safe and sound in his bedroom. I remember hugging him after I told him when the police called." Allen replied.

"So your son is alive, and his name is Austin James Bennett? And your name is Allen Shane Bennett?" he asked Allen.

"Yes. That is correct, sir. You need to find Austin and ask him about everything. He's only fourteen; he won't be able to lie for very long. I think a good cop could crack him." Allen stated.

"Mr. Bennett, I spoke with a young and lovely woman by the name of Tara Steele earlier. She told me a peculiar thing about your son and your relationship. She said that you had been dating for quite a while, but she had never met your son. She said she thought he was too upset to meet a potential new mom, but as time went on, she became suspicious. She said she became very suspicious after you checked into a hotel with the name Austin Bennett. She said you always told her to call you Allen, which was what you used as your pen name. It is not your legal name; we have had that checked out. She said that when she questioned you about this a few days ago, you became enraged and attacked her and then tied her to your son's bed, which was how the police found her. She is going to be perfectly fine of course; she just wants to know what was going on. I told Ms. Steele that you seem to be a very sick individual and that the death of your wife seems to have unbalanced you into thinking your son is alive when he died in the accident with your wife."

"No. You are full of shit mother fucker! Austin is alive; I have been talking to him for months!" Allen screamed, now fighting against the nylon straps.

"How come no one but you have seen him? Tara never saw him. Neither of her parents ever did. The police say the room where Tara was found was covered in dust and looked as though no one had been in the since you moved in. Here, look at this, Mr. Bennett." He held up a piece of paper that looked like it had been printed off the internet newspaper site. "Read the headline and the caption sentence, please." He said kindly.

Allen read aloud. "Local Author Mourns" Allen read the headline, then continued, "Austin Bennett, better known by his pen name of Allen Bennett, is seen as he grieves for his wife and son who were killed in an automobile accident earlier this week."

Allen just stared at the paper. "No, this is some kind of sick joke. No no no. My son is alive." He started to repeat this over and over again. The doctor called for a sedative. As the nurse injected him and sent him into a drug-induced darkness, the doctor leaned over him and said, "No, Mr. Bennett, I am afraid your wife and son died together."

About The Author

Robbie Blackburn is a passionate poet and writer who delves into the complexities of the human experience through his evocative and introspective work. With a background in psychology and over two decades of experience in healthcare, Robbie has dedicated his life to understanding and helping others. His writing reflects this compassion and insight, blending raw emotion with profound observations about life, love, loss, and healing.

Robbie's poetry captures moments of vulnerability and resilience, inviting readers to explore their own emotions and find solace in shared humanity. *The Darkness Within* is a testament to his ability to channel pain and hope into words that resonate deeply with readers.

When he isn't writing, Robbie enjoys spending time with his wife, Amanda, and their beloved cats. He finds inspiration in Civil War history, classic audiobooks, and the everyday beauty of life's fleeting moments.

Robbie Blackburn is also the founder of Scoboki Publishing, a platform dedicated to sharing stories that illuminate the human spirit.

Let me know if you'd like to adjust the tone or add any specific details!

Robbie Blackburn

9 781966 640700